ANYA KELNER

Awake

Rise of the Red Claws (Book 1)

First edition

This book was professionally typeset on Reedsy.
Find out more at reedsy.com

Contents

Rise of the Red Claws series

Part 1: Awake
Part 2: Hunt
Part 3: Legacy

Note for readers: Rise of the Red Claws is a three-part vampire romance and suspense story with no cheating. Book one ends with an unresolved plot element, which is completely resolved in book two. All three books have been released.

The demon plague

These were her final moments of life. Of that she was certain.

The evil had come sweeping into the village just before dawn.

Impossibly fast, impossibly strong, the demonic horde had lain waste to most of the two hundred souls that had once dwelled peacefully in the settlement.

Young, old, infants, even babies, no one was spared.

Now here she sat hunched on the cold earth, trembling behind the ruins of the small wooden house she shared with her mother and father. Her parents' defiled bodies lay discarded on the unforgiving ground in front of her. Throats slashed. Blood drained. Limbs twisted at obscene angles.

She swallowed hard and squeezed her eyes shut, ignoring the burn of salty tears that stung her eyes.

A high-pitched scream pierced the night air. Another villager being claimed by the ungodly creatures. One more victim of the wave of horror that had swept the remote Amish settlement she called home.

She had to get away.

Now.

She rose on wobbly legs and willed herself to get moving, sending up a silent prayer as she scrambled forward, her bare feet unsteady. If she could only make it to the forest beyond the burning homes, she would have a chance.

She darted towards the tree line, opting for speed over stealth. Her feet caught on something on the ground. She almost tripped but was able to right herself at the very last moment.

She looked down and her heart leapt in her chest.

A body.

Caleb Ebersole, the village baker, she realized as the surrounding flames illuminated his face. His cold, dead eyes stared up at her. Dark blood had congealed around the gaping tear in his neck.

Averting her gaze from the horror, she ploughed on into the cold night, racing for the dense oak trees that were only feet away now.

More terrible screams rang out over the crackle of burning as the remaining villagers were mercilessly dispatched. Thick, acrid smoke clung in the air. It burned her nostrils.

She made it to the trees and barreled into the thick brush beyond. Branches slapped against her face. Nettles stung her feet and ankles. But she didn't slow down. Not for a second. She ran as if her life depended on it, which it most certainly did.

After a few minutes scrambling across the damp forest floor, she lost her footing and slipped on an uneven patch of ground. Her ankle twisted and she crashed to the earth in a heap. Pain immediately swelled in her foot like a tidal wave, but she dared not cry out, lest she alerted the demons.

She swallowed down her agony, biting her tongue to distract her senses from the spasms of pain rising from her damaged ankle. She tried her best to remain perfectly still, closing her eyes tight shut and regulating her breathing.

After a minute or so, she allowed herself the luxury of weeping silently. For herself. For her family. For her village. For her life as she knew it. It was all gone. Along with her books.

It was an almost absurd thought. That amid the carnage which had claimed her parents and so many other innocent lives tonight she was thinking of her collection of books and journals. Yet she mourned them like family. They were precious to her. Her life's work in fact, though she had only seen eighteen summers. They contained her detailed notes on the wildlife and fauna found in this part of Pennsylvania as well as her family's history and ancestry.

Her thoughts were interrupted by a noise. The sound of twigs snapping under foot. She spun her head around, her heart hammering in her chest.

A shadow was moving towards her.

She tried to heave herself onto her feet, but her damaged ankle wanted no part of it. The jolt of pain sent her crashing back to the moist ground. All she could do was scramble away using her hands. But she was going nowhere fast.

The shadow closed in on her, resolving itself into the shape of a man. But this was no man.

He had dark hair and a narrow, almost feline, face. His skin was pale. Deathly pale. His eyes were coal dark windows onto a cruel soul. The eyes were predatory. Cunning. Evil. Streaks of blood covered his wide mouth. The stark red stood out against the bleached white of his skin.

She wanted to look away but found herself transfixed by his eyes. She realized she couldn't move.

He knelt before her then took a long moment to take her

in. He swept his gaze across her form, drinking in her face and body with those cold, calculating eyes. His gaze went to her neck before darting back to her face. He seemed to have come to a decision.

"Child," he said, in an almost sympathetic voice. "You are in pain."

These weren't the words she was expecting.

She said nothing, just held his intense stare. He looked at her like a predator toying with its prey.

"I can take your hurt away," he continued, moving his face closer to hers.

He reached up and placed a palm against her cheek. His hand was icy cold to the touch. She flinched but didn't attempt to remove his hand. He was so deathly pale. Like a ghost, she thought.

"All your suffering I can end," he added, his eyes boring into hers. "All your weaknesses. All the mortal shortcomings that plague your fragile, fleeting and meaningless existence I can undo. You shall be reborn into darkness."

A new figure emerged from the thick brush behind him and approached the two of them. The newcomer had a shock of unruly red hair and bright green eyes. Yet his skin was the same deathly white. He knelt beside the dark-haired one and stared at her. She could detect a primal hunger in his emerald irises. His mouth was slick with wet blood.

"Saving the best until last, I see, Zachariah," he said. "She looks oh so young...and oh so sweet."

"You will not touch her, Klaus," snapped the dark-haired monster. His tone was final.

The one called Klaus looked abashed, as if he had been slapped in the face. A small spot of pink rose to the surface of his otherwise alabaster cheeks.

"As you wish, Zachariah," he replied, lowering his head in submission.

"Tell me child, what's your name?" asked the one called Zachariah, turning back to her.

There was no point in avoiding the truth. It was too late for hiding. Perhaps now it would finally be over. She could see her parents again in the afterlife.

"El… Elliyahh," she replied.

"Elliyahh," he repeated, "Elliyahh", mulling the name, turning it over in his mind. "A pretty name, for such a pretty girl."

He bared his teeth. They were razor sharp and stained with the blood of innocents.

She stared at him wide-eyed. Surely this was it. The end. But ever the seeker of knowledge, she wanted to know one thing before her existence was snuffed out.

"What are you?" she whispered in a trembling voice.

Zachariah smiled, revealing more of his blood-smeared mouth.

"I am Zachariah. Simply Zachariah," he said. "As for what I am…" He paused for a moment to consider. "I am the protector of my beloved Family. The Red Claws. A Family I would like you to join, Elliyahh. I find you quite… captivating…and we are in need of fresh blood."

He placed his other palm on her cheek, so he was now cradling her head in his hands. She felt frozen in his grip. He leaned in closer to her. She could smell blood and decay emanating from him. She was repulsed. Yet she could not move a muscle.

"I give you the gift," he said in a whisper. "The greatest gift of all…eternity."

With that he pounced on her, and Elliyahh's world went black.

Prologue

ONE HUNDRED YEARS LATER - THE PRESENT DAY

If anyone had been paying attention to the seedy little tavern on the corner of Beach Street and Harrison Avenue in Boston, Massachusetts, they might have noticed something interesting on the evening of the 31st of October. They would have observed people avoiding the tavern the entire day and then, in the space of a single hour, no fewer than nine people dressed in robes with hoods entering the bar.

These were not the kind of people who blended easily with the rest of the Bostonians on the street. Though the city was full of Halloween revelers in elaborate outfits tonight, there was something just a little off about these particular individuals. Something you could sense but couldn't quite put your finger on.

An observer might also have noticed that they appeared to come from nowhere, seemingly materializing from the shadows just a few feet from the tavern door. Such an observer would have been even more confused if they happened to enter the tavern. All they would have seen was an empty bar behind which a wizened old man with a half-moon scar on his cheek was wiping down the counter with a greasy rag.

But the truth was, nobody paid any attention to this particular bar any longer. It had been part of the scenery on Beach Street for more than two decades. In that time, plenty of travelers had wandered in with the hopes of a good song on the jukebox and a nice, cold beer for an honest price. They had discovered a non-working jukebox, drinks that cost twice as much as any other establishment in the vicinity and watered-down beer that tasted more like dog pee than a decent brew. Plus, the bathroom had been in a state of disrepair (CLOSED DUE TO FAULTY PIPE) for most of the two decades.

If anyone had given a second thought to this little bar in Boston, they might have wondered how it stayed in business all of these years. Most days, not a single customer wandered in. But a few days a year, a handful visited so discreetly that no one around even noticed. Another strange thing that someone (if there had been someone to pay attention) would have noticed was that a good many of these visitors appeared to be quite pale in complexion and mostly traveled at night.

This run-down bar served as one of the secret meeting venues for the ruling body of vampires and was known only to a select few. This was both to stay hidden from Hunters and to prevent an over-ambitious Family from deciding to storm the place and murder the entire ruling body in one fell swoop. Meetings took place four times a year, always on a different day and sometimes the location was swapped at the last minute to one of the other clandestine places, of which there were more than a dozen.

On this particular Halloween, while kids were trick-or-treating across their neighborhoods and threatening the good citizens of Boston with "gunk and slime if we don't get our treats in time", one last individual made his way down the cracked sidewalk of Beach Street. The sun had gone down completely and darkness had enveloped the run down street, so there was no need to wrap himself tight or cover his face.

He was the Warden of the South. He had been turned at 52 years of age, though he barely looked 40 at the time. Now his preternaturally youthful looks would remain fixed for eternity — unless he was very unlucky. Though his body would remain 52 years old forever, he had been in service for almost 200 years.

There was no password. No secret handshake. He could smell the dead flesh on the bartender and the bartender could smell it on him. He gave a curt nod to the old man then crossed the room to the hidden door that only those who came for the meetings knew about. It swung open silently of its own accord as he approached. Old Magick. As soon as he reached the staircase on the other side, the door closed again, just as silently. He descended the ancient wooden stairs to the cavernous candle-lit basement.

He was the last to arrive at the gathering. There were four wardens in the United States — the North, South, East and West.

The Council of Elders was seated on the right-hand side of a raised platform, in a semicircle around a roaring fire in the middle of the room. The four wardens were supposed to be in chairs in a semicircle on the other side of the platform, which hosted a podium. However, since he had just arrived, only three seats were occupied. He took his place with his brothers and waited for the Council of Elders to start the meeting.

The Warden of the South had renamed himself Loris Valkari when he had begun his ascent to power. He could no longer remember what his original birth name had been. He didn't care. He was Loris Valkari to all that mattered. Right now, he was a warden, but he had seniority and would be the next to be appointed to the Council of Elders when someone, let's say, vacated their position. That could be a very long time since vampires experienced no natural death. Still, he eyed the six-member Council with interest, imagining one of them "ceasing to be" as was the parlance, pondering the power he would wield once they succumbed to eternal nothingness.

The Speaker of the Council rose and went up to the podium. He was named Dragos Vacarescu and had a scarred face and withered left arm. Dragos looked to be in his fifties but, truth be told, he was well over 500 years old. He had been one of the original brood turned when the Omni-Father Vlad Tepes (crassly known in popular culture as Vlad the Impaler) had discovered the secrets to eternal life after experimenting with hundreds of less-than-willing subjects in medieval Wallachia. He had created a highly infectious blood disease that heightened the mind, body and senses and induced a third state between life and death.

"Frați de Sânge," said the Speaker, raising his one good hand and using the old Romanian. "Blood brothers and sisters. We are gathered here under dire circumstances," he continued.

He paused and cast his eyes out over the assembled group, which instantly became deathly silent.

"Our numbers in this region have grown so small that we are in danger of being eradicated by the *nocturnae hostium*."

Several in the gathered group hissed. A few spat on the floor. He was referring to the *Enemies of the Night* — Vampire Hunters.

"The Hunters are becoming an ever-increasing problem," the Speaker said. "They are now using drones to track our movements and hunt down nests. They are equipped with computer algorithms that can predict our migration patterns and send out real-time alerts whenever a feeding cluster is detected. They use the latest technology as well as a deep understanding of Old Magick. Meanwhile, our kin stubbornly embrace the past. We use candles rather than electricity. We rely on padlocks instead of alarm systems. We depend upon our own senses instead of surveillance cameras. It is this lack of forward thinking that is causing our race to dwindle, and nowhere is this more apparent than in the southern region."

Loris rose quickly to his feet.

"I am the Warden of the South, Honored Speaker," he said. "It is true that we have been slow to keep up with modern technology. But what would you have us do? Associating with humans puts us at risk. Also, our governing body is small and our list of demands long. The diaspora is spread out and mistrust between Families hinders working together for the common good. Even more troubling, the growth of technology seems to speed up with each passing year. How can we keep up?"

"Perhaps the time has come for the South to show its teeth and stand up to the human infestation," said Gehrig Tal, the Warden of the West. He rose to his feet and spoke in his gravelly voice.

"We do not make our brethren follow paltry rules like limiting the number of kills in an area or restricting where they may settle. Nonetheless, the Hunters are no more a threat to us now than they have been in centuries past."

"As usual," Loris countered. "My honored brother from the west fails to acknowledge the advantages that his rural region has to offer. With the exception of California, populated communities are few and far between, and the brethren of the west can feed without worrying that their kills will be entered into a central database. States like Montana, Idaho, Wyoming, Oregon and Utah offer fertile ground. It is easy to preen like a peacock when you have all of the advantages."

Gehrig swept his cloak about him and growled at Loris, who stared him down, growling himself, deep in the back of his throat.

"Enough!" said the Speaker, sharply, banging his fist on the podium. "It is this very enmity that is holding our race back."

He paused before scanning the assembled vampires once more.

"Besides," he continued in a more measured tone. "This is only a secondary matter at this Quarterly Conclave. Have you forgotten the significance of the year, Loris Valkari?"

At first Loris was blank. He had come expecting talk of increased Hunter activity. After all, he had seen the reports on the three nests that had been burnt to cinders recently. But what was the significance of the year?

Then in a flash he remembered, and a strange sense of discomfort came over him. It wasn't fear exactly. Vampires didn't really feel fear. It was dulled — the same as the other emotions. You could call it apprehension, disquiet or foreboding, perhaps. The subject matter had been something he hadn't contemplated for a decade — and for good reason. He didn't particularly want to consider it even now, but his hand was forced.

Loris bowed his head to the Speaker respectfully.

"Of course not, Honored Speaker. You refer to the rising of the Red Claw Family."

There was an exchange of glances among the other wardens

that told Loris he had not been the only one to, either intentionally or unintentionally, not register the significance of the year. But thinking back, it all fell into place. The Red Claw Family had been forced into hibernation exactly one hundred years ago.

Loris looked up and studied the weary face of Dragos Vacarescu who, along with himself, had experienced the chaos and carnage first hand all those years ago. Standing behind the podium, the Speaker looked drawn, which was rare for ancient vampires, who had seen so much of the vagaries of life that little phased them. Yet the Speaker was visibly perturbed on the subject of the Red Claws. Loris wasn't surprised. Dragos was part of the Council of Elders that was forced to take unprecedented action a century ago.

The Red Claws resided in Loris's territory and he was technically responsible for them, though he hadn't spared a thought for the slumbering brood in at least ten years. But they would soon be awoken — and they would be hungry. A tremor ran down his spine, which was most unusual for him.

"Has the Council determined what is to be done with them?" Loris asked the Speaker.

"Despite our threats a century ago, it is abhorrent for us to kill our own," the Speaker said. "But how can we let them loose? Has their time in slumber made them more docile, tamed their bloodlust, made them more willing to follow the rules?"

"That is unlikely," growled a new voice. This was Yuris Dei, the Warden of the East. "They were savage before they went into hibernation. Now, they will be savage, angry and hungry for the hunt once more."

"They have been fed," Loris informed. "A caretaker hunts

down food and feeds it to the sleeping wards, as was stipulated in the original covenant. I appointed the current custodian myself two decades ago."

"Barely enough food to live on," Yuris Dei said, derisively. "Just enough to avoid death. You think they will awaken satiated? Do you think that their streak of rebellion will have disappeared? We did not solve the problem. We just kicked it down the road for a century. There is nothing that will curb their bloodlust. There is no Old Magick that can contain them. They will wake up and lay waste to the lands around them. Once again risking revealing our kind to the humans…to the Hunters. We shall all…"

"Nevertheless," interrupted the Speaker. "The covenant is the covenant. We are bound by the agreement. It is a solemn blood oath, sealed by Old Magick."

The wardens exchanged glances. Apprehension was etched on every face.

"Remind your fellow Wardens, Loris," said the Speaker. "Where are the Red Claws currently located?"

"In a small town in Georgia, Honored Speaker. It is called Angel Falls."

"And if they were to awake and, as your brother from the east fears, lay waste to the lands around them, where would they turn?"

After a moment's consideration, Loris said: "To Atlanta, Honored Speaker. It is a large city with a high crime rate, which would camouflage them, for a while at least."

"But the Hunters would soon take notice of the death pattern," Gehrig Tal said. "It is not a question of if, but of when."

A hush descended over the basement. It seemed everyone

was lost in somber contemplation.

"Very well," said the Speaker, finally. The weariness an trepidation could not be disguised from his voice. "We will consult with the High Chancellor on how to proceed. The Council of Elders will also travel to this Angel Falls to observe the situation on the ground."

He looked directly at Loris, an iron resolve gleaming in his eyes.

"Tell no one we are coming, unless it is absolutely necessary. The security of the Council is paramount. Prepare for our arrival in a few weeks."

Loris bowed. "As you wish, Honored Speaker."

The matter settled for now, the Conclave turned to less urgent business.

Loris sank down into his chair. If the Red Claw Family was allowed to awaken, it would surely bring every Hunter's eye to his region. It was inevitable. But he could take no action until the Council had made its decision. Loris was bound by his oaths. This left him deeply troubled.

Chapter 1

Nell was desperately trying not to think about the past few days. As she drove closer to her aunt's house, it became increasingly difficult.

Just a week ago she had been a simple college student at Vanderbilt University in Nashville, but her world had come crashing down around her. She now found herself ambling down the well-worn roads of provincial America.

Nell's first impression of the small town was it gave her the creeps. Of course, part of the creepiness might have been the time of day. She emerged from the two-lane highway and turned right at the sign that read 'Welcome to Angel Falls, GA: Population 2,380' just as the sun was settling into the horizon, spreading blazing rays throughout the sky and on the ground below as if it was trying to set it on fire.

After a while, the shadows began to lengthen and the entire town was bathed in a reddish-orange tint. She passed underneath a single traffic signal swinging from a wire and saw that the street she was on was called East Main and the one she was crossing was Arbor Avenue. Nell adjusted her grip on the wheel and eased off the gas a little. She took a moment to ponder how much her life had changed in such a short time.

Just a week ago she had been able to go down to Broadway after finishing studying for the day and listen to the country singers performing in the bars, the ones who would be on the radio in a few years. That was how it worked in Nashville. First, you paid your dues in low-rent honky-tonks around the state, half starving to death and using your meager income to pay for the most disgusting motels and items from the dollar menu at the low-end fast-food joints. Until you came to Nashville (if you had honed your craft well enough) and secured a spot at one of the downtown bars on Broadway. The waiting lists to perform were six months to a year long and the only pay you could count on was whatever you could collect at the end of the night in a pickle jar. Luckily, since it was Nashville, that could be $400 to $600 on weekdays and $1,000 to $2,000 on the weekends, depending on how good you were and how much alcohol and good cheer was flowing around the venue.

Even though Nell was studying corporate law at Vanderbilt, she harbored hopes of one day being good enough to play her six-string and sing in front of a real audience. But it seemed all her dreams had turned to ash.

Her father was paying her tuition and other expenses from a savings account he had started when she was just a baby. But because Nell was just an infant when he opened the account, it was in his name. Her parents were not rich — far from it. They both worked from home as realtors in the family business. The downturn in the US economy had hit the housing market hard and they were sometimes months behind on their bills. They tried to shield Nell from the extent of their financial woes, but when she called home she could hear the strain in their voices.

When they had died suddenly in a car crash, Nell had received word from the hospital. The bottom fell out of her world. Rushing home to organize their funeral and deal with their affairs seemed like a blur. Unreal. As the only child, she had counted on taking the entire burden on her shoulders.

What she hadn't counted on was the freeze that was put on her parents' bank accounts and estate after they died. They had apparently taken out a number of loans to pay for their business and living expenses, using the house as collateral. Now their remaining funds were frozen and the home was being claimed by creditors.

It meant that the latest quarterly tuition payment to the university hadn't cleared. Neither had the payment to the campus housing office. So Nell had nowhere to live and no classes to attend. Luckily, her mother's elder sister had reached out to her at the funeral and invited her to stay until things could be resolved with her parents' finances. Nell returned to Vanderbilt to collect her few possessions (mostly books, her beloved guitar and an ancient laptop) and set course on her battered phone for Angel Falls, Georgia, where her Aunt Laura lived.

As for her parents, the shock was still so raw that she hadn't even cried properly yet. It was as if it was the deaths of her favorite characters in a TV show that was teased by the trailer the previous week. *On the next episode of Nell's Life, she receives the worst news possible. So why isn't she crying? Why is she just driving numbly across the country? Find out next week...*

A pang of despair suddenly accosted her, forcing her to swerve as the raw emotion briefly convulsed her body. A pick-up truck in the adjacent lane blasted its horn when Nell's old car came too close for comfort. Nell meekly held up a hand by way of apology. The other driver, a boy with bad acne who couldn't have been older than eighteen, gave her the finger before speeding off. She couldn't really blame him.

Nell was struggling to maintain her focus as she drove. She gripped the wheel with more force, until her knuckles turned white. She then exhaled sharply and eased her grip, taking in both sides of East Main as she rolled through town slowly.

There was a cafe with peeling stucco and a fading sign that proclaimed it was called The Tiger Diner. The name seemed out of place for a drab concrete building in small-town America. Next to the cafe was a gas station with just three pumps, lined up like soldiers in formation. The garage behind it was empty, with the glass door closed and the panes thick with dust.

On the other side of the street was Henrietta's Antique Furniture, according to the ornate window lettering. An old man in suspenders was bent forward at nearly 90 degrees as he dragged a table that had been on display on the sidewalk back inside the store. Next door there was a dress shop with a hand-lettered sign that read 'We Do Alterations!' with a yellow smiley face next to it.

Further along was a small building that Nell thought must be a bookstore judging by the name, Tome Sweet Tome. Beside it was a squat, rectangular store with a small parking lot that had a lighted sign flashing 'Grocers-Mart'.

Nell had her aunt's address programmed into her phone, which was lying on the passenger seat next to the packaging for a chicken-salad sandwich that she'd had for lunch. When she bought her car, a well-worn Hyundai Accent, the used-car salesman had thrown in one of those phone-holders you attach to your windshield with a suction cup. But after nearly a year of hanging on through bumps and potholes, the phone-holder had begun to succumb to gravity and fell off at regular intervals. Now it was somewhere among the Land of Lost Automotive Knick-Knacks — also known as the trunk.

More small businesses popped up from the shadows on East Main as she pressed the accelerator to match her speed to the 35 miles-per-hour sign that was on the side of the road.

There were a few people out and about, but no one took an interest in her. Maybe they were just being polite and didn't want to outright stare. She couldn't imagine a stranger would drive into a town this small very often, and especially unnoticed. A small shiver ran down her back, but she couldn't say why. Something just felt slightly off.

At the end of East Main she followed her phone's GPS onto a road that turned upward into the hills. The business district, if you could call it that, was left behind, although she did encounter a few houses and a daycare (though it probably doubled as a residence) as well as a sign that told her that she could increase her speed to 45 if she wanted to. She did.

Mostly what she found along the winding lane, which Google Maps identified as Marsh Valley Road, were fields. Most of them contained wheat, corn, tobacco and other such crops. Some of them had cows. A few had horses. One or two were empty. She picked up her phone and flicked the voice commands back on. She had turned them off on the highway because the app was annoying her with alerts for every exit that she didn't need, but now she didn't want to miss her turn and end up on the property of an irate farmer.

As it turned out, she found her aunt's house easily, even though she had never been here before. Nell had grown up in Clarksville, Tennessee, and despite Georgia being only one state away, she'd never had occasion to visit. Aunt Laura had never married and liked to keep to herself. Not that she was unfriendly. 'Self-contained' was a better description. She didn't need the constant hubbub of other people. Of course, Nell had seen her aunt at family gatherings and such, but she was what Nell thought of as 'Christmas card family'. Family members that you remembered to send a Christmas card to, but didn't add to your gift list (or expect a gift from).

Her aunt's house was fairly modest. It was a two-storey home with white siding and black trim. The mailbox out front was red with painted sparrows. There was gravel on the driveway and a yellow pick-up truck that looked like it had been in its prime somewhere around 1986. In the yard, there were bird feeders and bird houses all over.

Nell parked next to the truck and stepped out. The gravel crunched beneath her shoes. She thought about grabbing her overnight bag, where she kept essentials such as her laptop, phone charger, tampons and the like, but she decided that she should first present herself at the door before dragging any luggage into her aunt's home. After all, maybe Aunt Laura had changed her mind. Perhaps she had felt sorry for Nell at the funeral but had since had second thoughts. The remote location of her home spoke volumes about her appreciation of solitude.

Nell closed the car door and marveled at how it was basically the only sound other than a few birds chirping and the wind gently rustling through the leaves of the giant willow tree in the yard. Her crunching footsteps broke the stillness as she threaded her way between her car and the yellow truck, and then became as silent as bare feet on carpet when she stepped onto the grass to cross to the front door.

She pressed the doorbell and heard musical chimes inside the house. After several moments the front door opened, slowly at first and then more quickly. The woman standing there was instantly recognizable as her Aunt Laura — white hair pulled back into a ponytail, sharp blue eyes and a thin, almost feline, body. She was slightly shorter than Nell and wearing jeans with a white roll-neck sweater.

"Nell, dear!" the woman said, opening the screen door and enveloping her in a hug. "I'm so glad you made it alright. I had the TV tuned to the weather channel to see if there were any problems along your route. But you got here. Do come in."

Relieved that she was still welcome, Nell entered the house. There was an underlying scent of 'Old Person' there. A hint of stale roses and mothballs. It was familiar to her, having visited her grandmother and several other elderly relatives, but it was only a faint under-current to the scent of potpourri and what smelled like fresh gingerbread cookies.

Once Nell was settled in the quaint, country-style living room, Aunt Laura served her gingerbread cookies (Nell's nose was on point) with a tall glass of milk. Despite feeling a little like a child given a treat, Nell ate gratefully.

"Such a sad ordeal," Aunt Laura said, sitting across from Nell with a cup of herbal tea. "They were so young, your mom and dad. They were…" She remained silent for a long moment. Then she continued, her voice choking in the back of her throat. "…basically in the prime of their lives."

Seeing her mother's sister express her grief, Nell felt something break deep inside. She had spent the past few days thinking of her parents' deaths in mostly practical terms. She had never allowed herself to examine it deep enough to trigger any intense emotions. But now, as she heard her aunt's voice break, Nell felt a barrier shatter in her as well. She began to cry — fat tears and heaving sobs that both exhausted her and gave voice to the roiling emotions she had been storing over the past few days.

Never again would she see her mother in the kitchen making coffee first thing in the morning. Never again would she hear her dad's electric shaver buzzing away in the bathroom. She couldn't even step foot in the home they had loved so much because the bank had basically taken over at this point.

Nell fell into her aunt's arms and they both cried for what seemed like an eternity. When they finally came up for air, the sun had gone down and beams of dark orange and purple were spreading through the living room.

"Did you get a look at the town on your way through?" Aunt Laura asked.

"The only street I saw was Main," Nell said. "It seemed kind of quiet."

"Yes, they do roll up the sidewalks around this time of the day in most of those businesses there," Aunt Laura said. "Safer that way."

Nell thought that was a slightly odd comment. Angel Falls didn't exactly strike her as a hotbed of crime.

"And Main is the majority of the town anyway," continued Aunt Laura.

She reached over and patted Nell's hand.

"Well, for however long you are staying with me, I hope you will enjoy it. I know it's not under the best circumstances, but I will really like having some company around here for a while."

Nell gave her a tentative smile. The cold truth was it didn't really matter whether she enjoyed it or not. For now, she was stuck, at least until the disbursement of assets from the will was finalized and the new semester started. However, in the present moment she felt such love for her aunt, who had taken her in when she had nowhere to turn, that for the first time in days she felt like she could breathe freely. It was true — there was nothing in the world like family.

***

Nell spent most of the next week mourning the loss of her parents. She spent days just crying her heart out. The sheer magnitude of her grief overwhelmed her and she found she could barely function as a person. Her aunt was always on hand with a sympathetic ear, a soothing back rub or a warm bowl of homemade soup.

On one occasion Nell was curled up in a ball on her bed crying. The strength seemed to have left her body. Aunt Laura must have heard her sobs. She gently knocked on the door before coming in and sitting next to her on the bed. Without saying a word she began stroking Nell's hair. After a while she started to sing in a soothing, melodious voice:

"The sun doesn't always shine
But as long as you are mine
I can face the fiercest storm
For you keep my heart and soul warm"

Nell raised her head.

"That's beautiful," she said, between the tears. "Where's it from?"

"Your grandmother, the one you were named after," said

Aunt Laura, still softly stroking Nell's hair. "She used to sing it to me and your mom when we were little girls. We all had to share a bed back then, so she made up songs to stop us bickering over who had more space. She could pluck melodies and words out of thin air. It was a gift."

Aunt Laura looked over at Nell's guitar standing in the corner of the room.

"She would have been proud of you, Nell," she said. "A lot of her lives on in you, as does the spirit of your mother. Her kindness and inquisitiveness about the world. So, in a way, they are both alive, and both oh so proud."

Nell had no words, so she simply sat up and hugged her aunt.

The days passed slowly. When she had no more tears left in her to cry, the clouds of despair parted ever so slightly and Nell found the mental space to look beyond her grief, if only for short periods. She began reading books on her eReader and practicing guitar in between contemplating her loss.

Eventually, the crashing waves of her grief abated to a steady background tide that ebbed in and out of her consciousness. Nell knew that tide would remain with her for life, but she was at least able to function again. Aunt Laura didn't have Wi-Fi and the 4G data signal was patchy where they were. Nell was curious to see what her friends were up to on social media and catch up with the state of the world. So she grabbed her laptop and drove into town, trying to find some place that had free Wi-Fi.

There wasn't a big coffee chain or anything like that, but she did find The Tiger Diner again. She parked in the lot across the street and went in, laptop in hand, and asked a young blonde girl in a safari-print apron if she could use their Wi-Fi if she bought something. The waitress shrugged.

"Sure hun. You can use it even if ya don't buy anything. The connection's pretty slow, but I can check my messages in between bussin' tables. Just don't tell the boss-man."

Nell thanked her and sat down on a stool at the counter. She opened up her laptop and connected to the Wi-Fi. There was no password. Nell tried to think of the last Wi-Fi hotspot that she had used with no password, or requirement to at least enter an email address so you could be spammed with ads later. She came up blank.

"I'm Hattie Lee," the girl in the apron said, coming over and pouring her a cup of coffee without asking. She handed Nell a menu and after a moment's deliberation Nell chose the healthiest thing that she could find — a chicken tender salad with ranch dressing.

"You just get into town?" the waitress asked, scrawling down the order on a green pad.

"Yes," Nell said. "I arrived a few days back."

"Oh yeah? Where from?"

Nell looked up from her computer screen. She was waiting for her newsfeed to load. Apparently this cafe had the slowest Wi-Fi in the state of Georgia.

"Um...from Nashville. I was a student at Vanderbilt," she replied.

"Well, dang!" the girl said, putting her hands on her hips.

Nell stared at her. It was such a strange reaction that for a minute she couldn't decide if the girl was making fun of her or not. There was no hint of sarcasm on the waitress's face, so Nell decided that she was genuinely taken aback.

"You don't get many students around here?" Nell asked, tentatively.

"Hell no," Hattie Lee said. "Most people stoppin' in here who ain't local are lost. They just wanna know the quickest way out of town. Whatcha doing here anyway?"

"I'm staying with my aunt for a while. I'm taking some time off school."

"Your aunt a townie?" the waitress asked.

"I guess you'd call her that. Her name is Laura Peters."

A spark of recognition lit up Hattie Lee's face.

"Sure, I know Missus Peters. I've never seen her in here, mind. But she's in charge of the Jaycees and my mom made me join this year."

Nell didn't know what the Jaycees were and she didn't ask. While she didn't want to be rude to the curious waitress, she was itching to get back to checking her social media. But Hattie Lee kept hanging around, right beside her.

"So, are you looking for work or anything?" the girl asked.

Nell looked up, opened her mouth to say 'No' but then happened to catch a glimpse of her car parked across the street. She *could* get a job. In fact, maybe she ought to get a job. Especially since her gas tank needle was hovering just above the red marker. She didn't want to ask her aunt for gas money. It already felt too much like freeloading. A job would also stop her moping around the house and perhaps take her mind away from her heavy thoughts.

"Maybe," she said slowly, still processing the idea. "What job?"

"Well," the girl said, gesturing to the 'Help Wanted' sign in the window that Nell hadn't even noticed. "The boss is looking for a swing shift waitress. That's 2PM to 10PM, when we close. You ever waitressed before?"

"Once," Nell said. "Sort of."

The 'once' had been when she had helped out at a friend's wedding. There had been some kind of dispute with the catering service, so some of the wedding party were tasked with passing out food and drinks.

"Well there you go," Hattie Lee said, brightly. "He ain't even looking for experience, but since you have some, he'll probably get you working right away."

Nell blinked. "Um…okay. How do I apply?"

The girl smiled and placed a hand on Nell's shoulder.

"Ain't no need for all that fussin'. Just wait here, hun. Ole Peck's in the back. I'll get him to come out and talk to ya."

The boss turned out to be an extremely overweight man in his mid-thirties wearing a grease-stained apron, which presumably at one point had been white, and a blue hairnet. He introduced himself as Rowdy Peck. Nell didn't know if 'Rowdy' was a nickname or his actual name, but he looked fairly docile and she couldn't imagine he had gotten it from his wild weekend activities.

"You know how to use a cash register?" he said, pointing to the ancient one behind the counter.

"Yes," Nell said, without hesitation.

In fact she had no idea how to use a cash register, but one look at the archaic machine told her that the calculator app on her phone was probably harder to figure out.

"Job pays $7.75 plus tips," he said, lowering his bulk onto the stool next to hers and taking a crumpled pack of cigarettes out of his apron's breast pocket. He extracted one and laid it across a half-full cup of coffee without lighting it.

"You a drifter?" he asked, eyeing her guardedly.

"Huh?" Nell shook her head. "No…no…I just moved here."

"No one moves here," the man said.

He picked up the cigarette and fingered it lovingly then put it down on the coffee cup again.

"My aunt lives here. Laura Peters. She lives off Marsh Valley Road. Do you know her?"

"Nope. Can't say I do."

Rowdy picked up the cigarette again and put it in his mouth. He took a drag of it unlit and then pulled it out.

"Can't smoke the damned things," he said, frowning. "Cancer of the lungs. I got two, maybe three years if I go lighting up. Maybe ten if I don't. Least that's what them medical folks tell me."

Nell was taken aback. People sure weren't shy in Angel Falls.

Rowdy stared at the cigarette for a long moment, sighed and then crumpled it up and dumped the loose tobacco and paper fragments into the coffee cup.

"Bring me some form of ID this afternoon," he said, snapping himself out of his reverie. "Wear sneakers or something comfortable when you start. Don't wear any damn heels. This ain't a strip club and no open-toed shoes on account of OSHA."

Nell made a mental note to Google 'OSHA' later.

"I'll have a shirt and apron for you," he continued. "You can wear jeans. Can you work a full shift off the bat?"

"Um…sure," Nell said. "Can't see why not."

He gave her a circumspect look.

"Okay, I'll give you a shot. Whatd'ya say your name was?"

"Nell. Nell Cartwright."

They shook. Peck's handshake was firm and his skin was softer than she had expected. He started to get up, but then sank back down heavily and looked directly at her.

"You got a car, Nell?"

She nodded.

"Good. You can park in the lot across the street in the day, but move it to the front of the restaurant after six. That's when the cops stop chalking tires and enforcing the parking signs."

He reached over and gripped her forearm. Nell inhaled sharply at the sudden move. She was on her guard.

"Don't be out after dark unless you're in your car driving home," he said, sternly. "Don't be walking around. Get me?"

His eyes were wide and his gray-green irises bore into her.

Nell stared back at him and nodded slowly, feeling rattled.

"Good," he declared.

He let go of her arm, pushed himself off the stool with great effort and then disappeared through the swing doors back into the kitchen. Nell finally let out her breath and stared after him, gooseflesh prickling her arm where his hand had been.

What is it with this town, she thought.

Chapter 2

Nell had been in Angel Falls for a fortnight. She had never had trouble making friends before or, at the very least, friendly acquaintances. But people in this town seemed wary of those who weren't born and brought up here. As a result, when she visited the shops or sat next to the stone fountain in the small town square she felt eyes on her from every direction. They felt to Nell like accusing eyes, telling her that she did not belong here.

So this morning before her shift she resorted to her other lifelong refuge, apart from music. One that she first relied on at school when she hadn't yet developed the social skills to make nice with other kids — the library.

Angel Falls' library was located a few blocks from the central square, housed in a rather impressive building for such a small town. The library had a set of stone steps that extended the entire length of the building, leading up to four granite pillars and a huge, ornately carved wooden door.

'Henry Freeman Memorial Library' said a small bronze plaque on one of the pillars. That might explain why the library was housed in a building far grander than the town's police department or courthouse. Whoever Henry Freeman might have been, he certainly wasn't short of a few bucks and evidently wanted to leave an indelible legacy in Angel Falls. For that, right now, Nell was grateful.

Nell passed beyond the pillars and through the imposing door into a small foyer. The library was instantly cool on her shoulders as she stepped inside. There were several posters on the walls, mostly geared towards kids. One read: "Today a reader, tomorrow a leader!" Another featured five preening boys who she thought might be in a teen band. They had books in their hands and appeared to be reading intently. The tagline read: "Reading Takes You in One Direction — Straight to the Top!" Nell groaned inwardly. She'd be surprised if these pretty boys had read one book between them. But maybe she was being too harsh.

There were two restroom doors flanking a small drinking fountain with a little step-ladder leaning against a wall. Presumably patrons could take the little ladder to help them reach books on the higher shelves. Nell wasn't sure this was wholly compliant with national health and safety regulations, but she reminded herself to adjust her thinking. Things were just a little different away from the big cities.

Directly above the fountain was a large poster showing how the library was divided, which Nell took a moment to study. She was impressed. While Vanderbilt's main library, where she had spent so much time this year, was bigger, Henry Freeman Memorial was far more impressive than any local library she had visited.

The poster identified the circulation desk, fiction and non-fiction sections, and various other library staples like the kids' area, reading room and periodicals. Nell decided to head straight for the fiction section to browse books from her favorite authors.

Though Nell owned an eReader, she had read everything currently stored on her device. Besides, she found that she missed going to a library and feeling the texture of physical books in her hands, particularly the reassuring heft of hardcover editions. She wandered the shelves, reading spines and pulling out books whenever she found an old favorite or something she had been meaning to read but never got round to. Soon, she had an armful of books balanced precariously against her chest as she ambled carefully down the aisles.

Worried that the books might come tumbling down to earth with an almighty crash (Henry Freeman no doubt tutting from beyond the grave) she decided the wisest course of action was to check them out before the pile grew taller.

At the circulation desk she had expected to find a grouchy elderly woman in a knitted cardigan. She had no concrete reason to jump to that conclusion, but her surroundings just seemed to give off that vibe. This library seemed so well organized, even though it appeared completely empty currently except for Nell, that she expected a fastidious jobsworth who looked as if they spent all their time maintaining it. Instead, she found a girl who couldn't have been more than two or three years older than she was.

She had a warm smile that created dimples on her soft caramel skin and reached up to her deep brown eyes. Her dark hair was braided and tied neatly behind her back. A nameplate in front of her read: Amara Dalmar, Head Librarian.

Nell lowered her stack of books to the countertop and pointed to the nameplate.

"Is this you?" she asked, hoping she wasn't being rude, but curious to know.

"It is," the girl laughed musically, her eyes lighting up. "I guess I seem kind of young to be the head librarian, huh? What it doesn't mention is that I'm also the *only* librarian."

Nell was astonished. How did she oversee the entire building?

"We also have some lovely volunteers who help out," added Amara, noticing Nell's quizzical look. "They actually put me to shame when it comes to organizing books and add to my collection of terrible librarian jokes. Do you know why I don't stock dystopian novels by George Orwell?"

Nell shook her head.

"Because they're *so* 1984."

Nell beamed at her. She couldn't help it. The girl's energy was infectious.

"I'm Nell Cartwright," she said, extending her hand before she had time to consider whether it was appropriate or not.

The girl reached out and shook it greedily.

"Great to meet you, Nell! How is it I've never seen you in here before?"

"I just moved to Angel Falls to live with my aunt," Nell said. "Her name is Laura Peters."

"Westerns-gardening-mysteries-and-ceramics," the librarian said, promptly. "Oh! Oh! And bird watching!"

Nell looked momentarily confused.

"Sorry," Amara said. "Those are the subjects she likes to read. I try to burn that stuff into my brain so whenever a new title comes in I can set it aside for someone who I know would really appreciate it."

Nell smiled. "Wow, that's dedication."

"Not really," Amara said. "It's my pleasure. I love these books like they were my own children — which didn't sound as creepy and weird in my head — so I appreciate others who love them too."

"Well," Nell replied. "You're talking to the right girl. Could I possibly check these out?"

Amara turned to the stack of books and started scanning them with practiced skill.

"Stephen Mercher old school. Piers Davies. Jaya Thorn. Harmony Constance number one. This is quite a selection you have here."

"They're some of my favorites that I haven't read in years," Nell explained. "Except for Harmony Constance. I try to re-read the entire series every year. It's like coming home."

"Sorceress Sisters!" Amara said, excitedly, holding her fist out for a bump. "I read all six books every year and then I hold a party, for one I might add, and binge watch all the movies."

She lowered her voice conspiratorially. "Don't tell anyone, but I would hit Constance with a Contemptible Curse for a shot at Seamus Sedgwick."

Nell laughed loudly. After a few seconds she realized that she was in a library and half-expected Amara to shush her. But the other girl was laughing just as hard as she was. Nell knew they would become fast friends.

***

Nell had taken her books home and immediately jumped into them. She had almost forgotten how great it felt to curl up in bed between the covers with a good book. Her aunt brought in a huge mug of chocolate milk and a plate of cookies.

"Ooh, this brings me back," said Nell, taking in the sea of cookies on the large plate. "I used to drive mom crazy. She always wanted me to have fruit or yogurt, or something equally healthy. But I put my foot down, as only a petulant little girl can. I wouldn't do my homework without chocolate milk and cookies on the table next to my books."

"I know," said Aunt Laura, with a playful smile. "She used to tell me all the time when I telephoned. That's why I brought them up for you."

She winked and left the room. Nell felt like her heart could burst. Munching cookies dunked in chocolate milk while reading fantasy fiction made her happiest she had been since her parents died.

Still, she had her responsibilities. Studying law hadn't allowed a lot of time for pleasure reading, but even now she had to postpone Harmony and Seamus rescuing Atticus Atlow from the forest goblin so that she could serve hearty fried food to the townsfolk. She got herself ready quickly and jumped into her car, setting off for The Tiger Diner.

Nell had worked six shifts at the diner so far. The money she earned had been paltry, but she was grateful for it nevertheless. On the first day she had made about a million mistakes, bringing the wrong food to the wrong people, spilling drinks and forgetting orders. She had made less than $5 in tips. Still, it brought her gas gauge up to one-eighth of a tank, and that allowed her to drive without having to ask her aunt for money. To Nell, it was a victory, however small.

She also discovered that she could eat at the diner without breaking the bank, which would help reduce the burden on Aunt Laura when it came to grocery bills. Nell felt guilty that she couldn't contribute much to the household costs, even though her aunt, bless her, never appeared put out by it.

Peck gave his staff a whopping 75% discount on any food they ordered and took it out of their paychecks. This was his cost on the meal, he explained to Nell. He didn't feel right making a profit from those who worked for him. It meant that with the diner's already incredibly low prices, compared to Nashville at any rate, she could order a giant burger and fries that she couldn't even finish for about a buck fifty.

Nell had also kept Peck's warning in mind, although she didn't really know why he was so adamant. At the risk of being called foolhardy, she was never one for being afraid of the dark. She had gone out at night alone in Nashville all the time. In fact, the best music could be found during the small hours in the bars along Broadway and the other venues scattered throughout the city. Nell had never felt fearful walking around at night. She conceded that in Nashville part of it was due to the throng of tourists that were ever-present day and night, but even further downtown like Church Street or at 3am on the Vanderbilt campus, she had walked by herself without feeling particularly paranoid.

But there was something different about Angel Falls. At just past 6pm on her first day at work she was so busy bumbling orders that she didn't even think about moving her car to the parking spaces restricted to 30 minutes or less during daytime hours in front of the diner. But Peck had apparently been serious because he stomped out of the kitchen and forced her to take a break long enough to move her car from the lot across the street. He wouldn't explain why when she asked, he just turned heel and huffed back into the kitchen after making sure she would comply.

A few days later, when Peck hadn't been in to remind her due to a medical appointment out of state, Nell had forgotten to move her car. So she was forced to cross the street into the lot after the diner closed. Streetlights illuminated the sidewalk, but the imposing lot, which was mainly only used in the day, stood dark and empty except for the familiar faint outline of her old car. There had been a prickle in the air that she didn't like. There was no chill outside, nor was there any wind, but as she crossed the sidewalk and stepped onto the tarmac of the lot both her arms broke out in goosebumps.

She felt eyes on her, but it wasn't like the guarded townsfolk sizing her up. This was different. These eyes weren't judging her — they were watching her. They were tracking her every step, creeping along her flesh, like a predator, completely silent but with a primal cunning. She imagined the glint of moonlight reflecting in sharp, animalistic eyes.

Nell shivered involuntarily and quickened her step. She reached her car and hastily shoved her key into the lock, heart pounding. She twisted the lock open then grabbed the handle as if her life depended on it, swinging the door open. She sat heavily in the driver's seat before quickly slamming the door shut and pressing down hard on the lock. She peered into the rearview mirror and her heart nearly stopped. There was a lumpy shadow in the backseat. Nell twisted her body round sharply. Then sighed with relief. It turned out to be her jacket, which she had thrown haphazardly across the back seat before her shift. After taking a deep breath she started the car and drove with the inside dome light on the entire time until she reached her aunt's house.

Nell didn't know if her reaction that night was due to what Peck had said to her, if he had somehow transferred his own strange foreboding on to her, or if there was actually something sinister lurking in the shadows. Either way, she decided there was no good reason why she needed to be walking around Angel Falls after dark.

As far as the waitressing went, she had improved a great deal since her first day. She rarely mixed up orders now, and (nearly) always brought everyone their correct drinks. She had learnt to basically attach a pot of coffee to her hip because it was what most people wanted. She had also learnt the art of calling orders into the kitchen using the shorthand terms unique to The Tiger Diner. The cooks no longer regarded her with quizzical exasperation whenever she approached the serving window.

However, waiting tables was a lot more physically demanding than Nell had ever imagined. For one thing, there was no rest. Towards the end of her first few shifts she felt like she was dancing barefoot on a stage while someone underneath kept aiming a flame at the soles of her feet. But thanks to an inspired recommendation from Hattie Lee, she had purchased a pair of gel insoles from the drugstore, which positively transformed her into a new woman.

Nell brought her thoughts back to the here and now as she slowed her car and entered the parking lot across from the diner. She maneuvered into a spot as close to the entrance as possible, just in case she again forgot to move her car after six. She took a quick look around at the few other vehicles dotted about and bushy scrub at the back of the lot. Everything was still. No movement. Yet Nell was still a little spooked by the memory of her flesh crawling as she felt a presence here. She quickly hopped out of the car, locked it and hot-footed it out of the lot and across the street.

She entered the diner just before her shift. Despite filling her belly with oatmeal cookies just an hour ago, she found she had room for a grilled cheese. A girl needed her strength when she was working on her feet, she reasoned. As usual, the food was marked down and Nell stuffed an IOU note into the register. Peck worked on an honor system when it came to staff perks. Nell found it both quaint and endearing.

After dusting crumbs from her top, Nell grabbed her notepad and pencil and started her shift. A few moments later the door opened with a tinkle and a group of railroad workers shuffled in and headed towards a large corner booth. Nell grabbed the right number of coffee cups and filled a pitcher of water. When the men were seated, she went over.

"Hey guys, how was work today?" she asked, brightly.

"Not bad," a stout man named Eddie Haskell replied, taking a cup and pushing it forward to indicate he wanted a fill of coffee.

The town had become decidedly friendlier towards Nell since she had begun working at the diner, to the point where she barely felt any whispers when she went into the shops.

"Say, when you gonna run off with me to Mexico?" Eddie asked, to the mirth of his crew.

"Don't you have a daughter a year older than me?" Nell replied. "How would she feel about me being her stepmom?"

The other men guffawed. Haskell flushed.

"Well, you certainly know how to ruin a good fantasy, Nelly," he conceded, looking sheepish.

"Besides, I don't think I could handle a rough and tough fella like you," Nell added, feeling a little sorry for the workman and trying to help him save face.

Haskell brightened.

"You ain't the first to be intimidated by what ole Ready Eddie has to offer, and won't be the last, my dear," he replied, the mischief back in his eyes.

"Now what can I bring you good folks?" Nell asked swiftly,

moving matters on.

They placed their orders and Nell went over to the kitchen window to inform the cooks and hand over the ticket.

She turned around to find a young man lugging a huge flight case through the door. She watched as he approached the back of the diner, deposited his load and then went back outside. Nell observed as he continued to lug in cases. No one else seemed to find this out of the ordinary, so she finally went into the kitchen to ask who he was.

Charlie Miller, the swing shift cook, looked out to see what she was talking about.

"Yeah, that's Devan. He does open mic here on Wednesdays most weeks."

"Open mic?"

Angel Falls never ceased to surprise.

"You know, where people come and play songs and shit," Charlie said.

He clapped a hand over his mouth. "Goddammit!"

Nell laughed. Charlie had a two-week-old baby at home and was trying to remove the more colorful words from his vocabulary, mostly without success.

Nell went back out to the dining area and made her rounds with the coffee pot while she surreptitiously watched the young man bring in more equipment. He wore a tight black T-shirt and closely-fitting jeans, which accentuated his firm body. But it was his face that Nell found fascinating. He had dark olive skin and black hair with full lips and large hazel eyes, which appeared almost luminous when they caught the light. The name Devan didn't offer much of a clue as to his background. Nell couldn't place him, but he certainly appeared unique among the folks of Angel Falls.

When everything had been unloaded from the gray van that Nell now saw was parked across the street, he came back in and waited by the counter. Nell finished her rounds and started a new pot of coffee, feeding scoops of grounds into the vintage machine.

"Hi," Nell said, catching the boy's eye.

"Hi there," he said. "Can I get a Sprite?"

"Sure," Nell replied. "Erm, do you usually have to pay, or is it on the house?"

"Well, it's usually free," the boy said. "But I'll pay if you want me to."

"No need," Nell said, with a smile. "All good."

"You're new," the boy said. The end of the sentence was lilted up like a question, but it could easily have been a statement.

"Brand new," Nell replied. "Open mic, huh? That sounds fun."

She poured him a Sprite and added some ice.

"Thanks," he said. "I'm Devan."

He held out a hand.

"Nell Cartwright."

She shook his hand. It felt warm, his grip firm. She instinctively looked into his face as she shook, locking on to those iridescent eyes.

"It is fun, at least I think so," Devan continued, then proceeded to drain half his soda. He must have been parched from his exertion.

"Do you play or sing?" he added.

Somewhat distracted by his presence, she blurted out the truth, which she normally would have been reticent to admit.

"I play guitar a bit and sing."

"Yay! Fresh talent," Devan exclaimed, holding up a hand for

a high five.

Nell awkwardly high-fived back, wishing she had kept her mouth firmly shut.

"You up for a song tonight?" he enquired, casually.

"Oh, God no!" Nell blurted out, horrified by the prospect. "I only play where me, myself and I, and perhaps a few house plants, can hear. I'm strictly an amateur."

"You should hear some of these guys croak out their numbers," Devan said, grinning. "It might give you a new perspective on 'strictly amateur'. Anyway, nice to meet you Nell. I've got to get set up."

Devan opened up the cases and began to prepare his equipment while Nell pulled three orders from the kitchen that were ready to go out. She took them to their respective tables and continued pouring coffee, taking orders and delivering food to patrons while the open mic was set up. Apparently, it had been scheduled to start at 6pm because approximately twenty minutes before that time she started noticing people coming in with guitars, keyboards, black cases adorned with bright stickers and generally the kind of stuff that you didn't normally see at a diner. Many of them ordered just a coffee or a soda with no food. It seemed Nashville wasn't the only place where aspiring musicians had to pinch the pennies.

Nell found herself with a little free time due to the lessening need to ferry food, sauces and cutlery to people that were eating. Instead, she found herself merging with the crowd, taking in the proceedings. The people coming in were definitely younger than the normal patrons of the diner. They were filling the place up. Open mic was apparently pretty popular in this town. Perhaps there simply wasn't much else to do.

"Hello everyone!" Devan said in an exuberant voice over the microphone. "I'm so glad you're all here, looks like we're in for a good night. Last week I took down the names of those who wanted to perform today. I'll call them off and, if you don't get cold feet and bolt for the door, come on up and show us what you've got."

A few whoops and claps rippled through the crowd.

"In the meantime," continued Devan. "If your name isn't on my list yet, just grab me and I'll see if I can squeeze you in. As soon as we get through those who've booked we'll move on to the B list, time permitting."

He motioned to Nell.

"Nell here has you covered for food and drinks and Charlie in the kitchen will do his damnedest not to give you food poisoning."

"I heard that, you little shit-squeak!" came the cry from the kitchen. Promptly followed by "Goddammit!"

More claps and giggles rippled through the crowd and Nell smiled. Devan called up the first act, an older man who looked to be in his sixties. He was carrying, of all things, a set of bagpipes. Perhaps this was going to be a long shift after all.

Nell noticed the boy in the black leather coat long before he got up on stage. She was attuned to anyone sitting at a table without food or drinks on it, in case they needed service. When she had approached him he had simply asked for a glass of water. As the evening progressed and the various acts took to the stage, her eyes kept coming back to him. He hadn't touched the water.

She studied him for several moments without him noticing. Finally, he glanced in her direction and she flushed, her eyes bouncing off to the ceiling in an effort to pretend that she hadn't been staring.

There was nothing specific she could put her finger on that made him stand out from the crowd. Even so, he did, as if he had some kind of aura that couldn't be seen but sensed nevertheless. But there was also the fact that he was extraordinarily handsome. His dark brown hair was pushed back, forming a slightly messy yet stylish quiff. His cheekbones were prominent and matched his square jaw. His eyes were the deepest blue, which stood out in contrast to his light skin. For some reason Nell was drawn to his hands, which were slender and almost feline. He wore a thick leather coat, so she couldn't judge his frame, but she imagined that he was athletic rather than bulky. She felt a heat rising in her face, and perhaps elsewhere. Her cheeks flushed red.

Flustered and self-conscious, Nell quickly busied herself with her duties, but kept a furtive eye on him as she served coffee and the occasional piece of pie to the attendees. She was watching to see when he would go up to perform. She assumed he would because he had shoved a hardbody guitar case underneath his table. Only a little of it was visible but, being a guitar player herself, Nell had recognized it easily.

The night wore on, and the clock crept closer to nine o'clock. Finally, at twenty minutes past, Devan grabbed the mic and motioned in the stranger's direction.

"Okay, folks. A rare treat. We have Christopher performing for you once again. Let's give it up for Christopher!"

Nell put down the cheeseburger and fries that she had been preparing to deliver back on to the counter. Whoever ordered it could wait a few minutes. She watched the boy in the leather jacket go up to the front with his case, from which he extracted a gorgeous maroon and black electro-acoustic guitar. The scattered spotlights reflected on its shiny body.

Christopher hooked up his guitar to the cable provided then slid onto the stool in front of the microphone.

"Hello," he said shyly.

He took a deep breath and then strummed a chord, adjusting some of the pegs to fine-tune the sound. Then he began.

When he started to play, Nell forgot everything else around her. He was picking out a complex pattern that she couldn't even follow. His slender fingers danced across the fretboard, rapidly picking out notes, while his other hand delicately strummed the strings to make the guitar almost sing. The closest thing Nell's brain could compare it to was flamenco music, but this was less aggressive with more emphasis on melody and rhythm. Every note was in its right place, forming a cascade of sound. Nell was powerless to do anything other than listen to him play. Then he began to sing.

She was surrounded by pure bliss. There were at least five patrons who would have appreciated a coffee refill, one person still expecting a cheeseburger and fries, and another who was waiting for a milkshake that had just finished mixing in the machine. None of them, including Nell, gave a single thought to food or drinks. The boy in the black leather jacket sang with the assured voice of someone twice his age, and at least four times more talented than anyone appearing on those tacky singing competitions on TV.

The entire room was transfixed, seemingly hypnotized by the rhythm of the guitar and the accompanying sound of Christopher's silky voice. Nell sunk down and put her elbows on the counter, just inches from the cooling cheeseburger and fries, her fists pressed into her cheeks.

Devan stared open-mouthed from behind his portable

mixer, a finger still attached to a knob that he had finished turning a while back. Everyone else was frozen, as if this were a TV show and someone had pressed pause on the remote. For four minutes or so this continued until the boy's fingers plucked the last note and it echoed through the speaker system, before slowly fading away.

Nell started to come back to herself, pulling away from the cheeseburger that was now wafting into her nostrils. No one was clapping. That particular action took several moments as the crowd recuperated from the spell cast by the song. Then thunderous applause echoed through the diner with everyone cheering and thumping tables. A few hoots of appreciation pierced through the clamor.

Nell thought that the boy would blush, considering how shy he appeared to be, but his cheeks remained as pale as ever. He quickly packed up his guitar and went back to his table while the crowd reached out and touched his jacket as he passed like he was some kind of guru.

"Nell, we need to ship these orders," came Charlie's cry from the kitchen, finally breaking Nell's reverie and transporting her firmly back to reality, where she was a diner waitress with a stack of orders to go out.

"On it, Charlie," she called out. "Just got a little backed-up out here."

"Well, get movin' darlin', the food's getting colder than a witch's tit," came the reply. Followed by the customary: "Godammit!"

When the night finally ended, Nell turned off the lights and went out into the cold air, using the key that Peck had given her to lock the door behind her. She had moved her car in front of the diner earlier in the evening. As she walked the few steps to the driver's door she caught a shape out of the corner of her eye. Her heart jumped into her throat and her stomach turned over. She whirled around, hands placed defensively in front of her.

The boy in the black leather jacket was leaning against the glass of the diner with his black guitar case a faint shadow behind him.

"God," Nell said, clutching at her chest. "You scared me."

The boy stood there for a moment and then stepped forward so that he was more visible under the street light.

"I'm sorry," he said. "Are you new in town?"

Nell stood by her car door and quickly inserted the key, making sure she heard the locks open as she twisted it. It wasn't that she was particularly threatened by the boy in the black jacket. She didn't feel any ill intentions from him. But she couldn't shake how eerie this town made her feel.

"Yeah, I just started working here," she said, turning back to face the boy.

"You play guitar," he said. It wasn't a question.

"Uh…yeah..I mean sort of. I'm just an amateur. Not like you. I don't get why you don't have a record deal."

"A record deal?" He appeared confused.

"Yeah, you know, a contract to produce an album, get your music out there. You are amazing."

"Thank you," he said. "You should be careful out here at night."

"Is this town haunted or something?" Nell said, trying to keep her voice light even though she was a little annoyed with yet another cryptic warning. "You're not the first person to tell me that."

The boy in the jacket nodded.

"It's good advice. I'm Christopher Deverell by the way."

"Nell Cartwright."

"I could tell from your eyes that you are a musician," he said. "You were following my picking and strumming patterns."

"Yeah." Nell said. "Got me. Where did you learn to play like that?"

"Practice. Lots and lots of practice. Do you work every Wednesday, Nell Cartwright?"

"As long as old Peck will have me," Nell said.

"Then maybe I will see you again."

The boy nodded curtly then started walking up the sidewalk, the click from his hard-soled shoes echoing along the street.

"Do you need a ride?" Nell called out, on a whim.

"No, thank you," he said just before he turned the corner into the alley beside the diner.

Nell quickly jumped into her car and drove off, looking into the alley as she passed it. The boy had entered it only a few seconds before. But there was no one in sight. Strange, she thought.

Chapter 3

Christopher Deverell exited the alley swiftly and went up a side street. He heard the sound of the girl's car starting up, but he was already gone, moving with the speed that had come with the rest of his abilities: the increased strength, sharper vision, heightened senses and the complete cessation of the aging process, of course. Also, he had gone into what he thought of as his stealth mode, so his movements were virtually silent.

There were other benefits to being a vampire, but there were also disadvantages. While he could hypnotize an entire room by playing guitar and singing, he had no way of knowing just how talented he was. People were mesmerized no matter what. He had been learning to play the guitar for just over three years. There was a lot of downtime when you were a caretaker. He wished that he could sometimes play without his vampiric aura casting out, but it was completely automatic. Oh well.

Christopher was caretaker of the Red Claw Family. That meant that he had been turned specifically for that purpose. He had no sire — none that he knew of anyway — and he had no family. He was a ward of the Council. Who did the job before him, he did not know. All information was on a need-to-know basis.

He barely remembered his former life. It had been twenty years ago, but it was as hazy as a dream that's about to fade. He remembered living on the streets, a 22-year-old without a purpose or a job. He remembered eating at soup kitchens and trying to procure pot, pills or whatever else would get him high and help numb the pain.

He also remembered that night in the alley. He had been hanging out near a bar that was closing in the hopes of bumming a smoke from someone. Then he remembered being attacked from behind and dragged into a dark corner to die with what felt like stab wounds in his neck.

Of course, he hadn't died. Instead, he found himself quite alive and vibrant, with all of the mortal addictions of his body having disappeared. No longer did he crave getting high. No longer did he care about finding drugs or getting drunk. He had no desire whatsoever to smoke cigarettes. In fact, he felt stronger and healthier than ever before in his life. His vision was enhanced. He could see farther and more clearly than before. He could identify sounds that were hundreds of yards away. He could detect scents that he had never even noticed before and his dexterity and strength had increased dramatically.

But there were things missing as well. While the darkness gave with one hand, it took with the other. He recalled feeling overwhelming sadness when his younger brother Gabriel had died from leukemia when he was six. He remembered that sadness, but he could not recreate it, could no longer feel it in the depths of his being, where it had always resided. The tears and torrent of emotion were no longer there. It was as if some ethereal surgeon had removed that section of his brain, or perhaps soul. There was now a ... now a what? Stillness, detachment, coldness — there was no way to describe that absence accurately using words.

But he had sensed something subtly shifting when he met the girl in the restaurant. There was something about her. She had somehow provoked a nerve and the slightest trickle of emotion had begun to run through his system. It was like a small candle in a giant cavern, yet it was there, casting a faint light. He had not felt that way for years, and had no explanation.

Christopher moved quickly through the streets, mostly taking the alleyways. The alleys were his tunnel system through Angel Falls. He could see them in pitch black as clearly as a mortal might see them on an overcast morning. He could hear sounds that even dogs might miss and was silent and swift as he moved adroitly on the balls of his feet.

The Red Claw estate was five miles from the outskirts of town, but once he reached the fields covered with tall stalks of corn he could let his feet go free and they would swiftly take him there. The guitar case he carried was no burden and he could reach speeds of twenty or thirty miles an hour without breaking more than a few stalks of corn. These were his gifts. These would be his gifts for eternity.

He had never questioned his fate. The road he was on before he was turned only had one ultimate destination. He considered himself one of the lucky few. He would never have to go through the arduous aging process like mortals did. He would never have to deal with Alzheimer's or heart disease. He would never have to succumb to a cruel blood cancer that would hollow him out from the inside, as it did to poor Gabriel. Christopher Deverell would never die.

Of course, that meant that he had to live in the shadows (well, most of the time) and certainly never hunt anywhere near Angel Falls. The Council of Elders took care of the property taxes and had set up a talisman that made anyone without the constitution of a vampire feel completely ill at ease when they approached the estate, unless they were invited. The taxes kept away the law and the talisman kept away the curious. It was a simple system that had worked for as long as Christopher had been caretaker, and apparently for decades prior to that.

Christopher made it to the estate in record time and vaulted over the wall. The tall stone wall was another barrier that kept the outside world at bay. While an ordinary person might need a rope and about fifteen minutes to scale it, all Christopher had to do was jump up and grab on to the top to hoist himself over. There was no fear or thought. He traversed the wall with ease and landed catlike on the grassy ground below.

The estate was located on twenty acres with the center portion containing the main mansion housing the Red Claw brood. Christopher went straight there, a shadow along the winding gravel road, quickly reaching the door. It swung open as he approached. Old Magick still had a place in the new world.

His heightened senses were always struck by the musty smell inside, which seeped into every corner and crevice of the imposing building. He made sure that the door swung shut again. Old Magick had never failed before, but it was force of habit. He wandered towards the hibernation chamber, which had previously been the atrium of the grand house. Inside were dozens of Red Claw family members, each resting in a stone box that had been imbued with the dormancy enchantment. They were wrapped in their Family ceremonial robes, featuring an ancient ornate script that Christopher could not decipher. Plastic tubes ran into their arms for feeding.

Christopher always found it slightly jarring looking at these preternatural beings in their ceremonial splendor, but with cheap plastic cannulas attached to their bodies, as if they had somehow wound up in the local emergency room with a mortal complaint of chest pain or feeling a bit dizzy. But his opinion on the matter was irrelevant, as long as he kept them alive, if barely. The taste of mildew ran across Christopher's tongue, decaying flesh reached his nose, the constant drip of blood acted as a ticking clock.

He stared at the stone crypt of Zachariah, who was the head of the Family. Next to him was a Red Claw named Klaus. Both looked the same as ever. Still. Suspended. Frozen in time. Loris, the vampire who had turned Christopher, had briefly described the Family's inglorious history when Christopher was first given his duties all those years ago. Loris had also tried to explain some facts about the vampire race, to orientate Christopher into his new existence. He mentioned something about wardens, the High Chancellor, Magisters and other such esoteric stuff. None of it was particularly relevant to him.

The feeding was his main job. Each month he would procure four humans and suspend them one at a time so that their blood slowly drained into the dozens of IV tubes. Under normal circumstances, the blood of a human could sustain one vampire for a week. But these vampires were drip-fed slowly, giving them just a trickle of sustenance to keep them alive. Any more than the Council stipulated ran the risk of disrupting the enchantment and awakening the brood. That would be bad. Very bad. It was a fine balance, one Christopher had learnt to navigate over the past two decades.

This was his destiny, until such time that the Council deemed the Red Claw Family could awake. He didn't see that happening anytime soon. It was a solitary, monotonous existence. Most of the time he was okay with it, finding escape in reading and learning new things, such as the guitar. But recently he felt the urge to be out in the world, to take (calculated) risks, hence his two appearances at the diner. Now, with these strange emotions evoked by the human girl, he wondered if something grander might be at play here, subtly directing his actions. Or perhaps he'd finally gone stir crazy and was inventing a fanciful narrative to justify his brash, if not downright reckless, actions. But something about her spoke to him. To Christopher it felt elemental. It felt ancient.

Chapter 4

Over the next two weeks Nell had become something of a whizz at waitressing at The Tiger Diner. She had mastered the art of holding four plates at a time, devised a mental shorthand to remember everyone's drinks and had learnt the names of many of the regulars. Most of them were older folks, and she had to fend off flirtations from many of the men, but she didn't feel out of her depth anymore. She had also worked through two more open mic nights, but hadn't seen the boy in the leather jacket again.

She also tried to muster up the courage to perform herself, even if all she did was a cover version. The assorted performers with their varying levels of talent assured her that she wouldn't be the worst they had ever heard. But during both open mics her guitar had sat silently beneath the counter next to the cash register, even though the other waitresses would have gladly covered her for a few minutes. She just couldn't bring herself to go up there in front of all those people.

At the following open mic, she arrived at work, put on her apron and began her shift. She was passed the baton by Hattie Lee, who sweetly wished her a good shift in her thick Georgia accent before running out to her boyfriend's car and jumping in.

Nell grabbed a fresh pot of coffee and began making her rounds.

"How are you youngsters today?" She asked a group of seniors, who were arguing animatedly about some government policy.

Charles Unger, a retired mechanic and the oldest of the bunch, looked up at her.

"Well, if it isn't the prettiest waitress at the Tiger. I'll take a shot of coffee, my dear."

"Now, Mr Unger," Nell said, chidingly. "I happen to know that you said the very same thing to Hattie Lee yesterday."

"That's because the prettiest is whoever's holding the coffee pot," Unger chortled. The rest of the table chuckled as well.

Nell went around the table and poured them all coffee.

"Can I get you something to eat?"

"Only if you got cherry pie on offer," said one of the men down at the end, with a smirk.

Frenchie Brand, the sole female in the group and a recent widow, smacked his shoulder hard.

"You behave yourself, Frank Gilbert," she reprimanded.

Nell had learnt that "cherry pie" was a reference to sex in this part of the world. She could do nothing but ignore it. For one thing, the group always tipped well. For another, they were from a different time. They had never heard of the #MeToo movement and considered provocative banter with the waitresses just one of the perks of being a regular at an establishment.

Nell went around the diner, stopping at each table to check on people, take orders and pour coffee.

About half an hour later, the bell over the door jangled and in came Devan, lugging a large flight case. He hefted it to the usual spot at the back and greeted Nell with a huge grin.

"How's waitressing?" he called to her.

"No complaints, so far. How's hosting?" she called back.

"Not too bad, I must say," he replied, before walking back out to collect the remaining cases.

She poured him a Sprite with ice and set it on the counter. After a few minutes of lugging equipment, Devan came over and sat down at the counter. He gulped down about three-quarters of the Sprite in one go.

"Thirsty work?" Nell asked, smiling.

"Sure is," he said, wiping his mouth with the back of his hands and shooting her another grin. "Say, how old are you, Nell?"

"Twenty. Why?"

"You want to go out with me sometime? There aren't a lot of girls my age around town. They've mostly gone off to college or fled to a big city."

"How romantic," Nell said, hands on hips. "You sure know how to charm a girl, telling her she's your only option."

He blushed, but only slightly. "Erm … that's not what I meant."

Nell smiled to show that she had been (partly) kidding. Then she shrugged. "I'll think about it." In fact, she didn't know what to think at all.

"Fair enough," Devan said, not pressing the issue. "Okay, I've been hydrated, now it's time to get back to pulling the wagon."

He got up and began running cables to connect microphones and speakers to the soundboard.

Nell watched after him, curiously. The curiosity wasn't for him, it was squarely aimed at herself. Ordinarily she would have instantly said yes to going out with a guy as cute as Devan. In fact, she wasn't really sure why she had hesitated now. Was it the boy in the black jacket? He had never demonstrated any romantic feelings. In fact, he had never demonstrated any feelings full stop, come to think of it. He was a complete stranger to her. She didn't know his age, where he lived or where he had gone to school. She didn't know if he was a happy, laid-back person or someone prone to anger and brooding. She knew nothing about him. Yet, there was something about him. She was drawn to him in a way that she had never experienced before, and they had barely exchanged twenty words. It was all a little crazy.

Nell cleared her head by focusing on her duties. She wiped down tables, took orders and made polite chit-chat with some of the regulars. The open-mic crowd were starting to filter in now, with their assortment of cases and eager expressions. She passed close to the entrance and glanced at the nearest table to see if it needed a wipe down. Her breath caught in her throat. He was there. The boy in the black jacket. He was facing away from her, but she could tell even from the back it was him. The jacket was a major clue, of course, but it was also his dark hair that cascaded down and ended neatly at his neckline.

She suddenly knew something for certain. He could sense her staring at him. He even knew it was specifically Nell. For some odd reason, she could sense him sensing it.

Oh, for God's sake Nell, she chided herself. *That doesn't make any sense. Get a grip.*

Gathering her courage and feeling her heart speeding up in her chest, she came around the table and looked into his blue, piercing eyes. His skin was pale, his lips a deep red, almost as if he was wearing lipstick. She had never been this close to him before.

"Hello, Nell Cartwright," the boy said, softly. "I see you brought your guitar this week."

Nell was taken aback. How could he have known? But before she could ask he pointed to the barely visible case near the cash register.

"I'm assuming that is yours?"

Nell nodded.

"And are you going to be playing this week?"

"I…I don't know yet," Nell said. "What about you, Christopher Deverell?"

"I'm flattered that you remembered my name. Yes, I plan on giving it a go."

"Can I get you a coffee or something?" Nell asked, hoping to quickly gloss over the subject of her playing.

"No, thank you. I'm content to just sit and watch," Christopher said. "Is that okay?"

"Sure," Nell replied.

She looked up and saw that someone at a table across the diner was trying to get her attention. Still, she lingered.

"Maybe we can talk later," she ventured.

"Sure," Christopher said. "I would like that."

"Me too," Nell replied.

She busied herself with taking orders and carrying out food and drinks. Every now and then she would throw a quick glance at Christopher, and she had that same uncanny sense as before, that he could tell she was staring at him. But he didn't turn around to look at her. He kept staring straight ahead as the open mic was set up.

Nell tore her gaze away and looked around. She noticed

Devan again, and this time he had been looking at her. However, unlike all the other times, there wasn't a cheerful expression on his face. He was frowning and there was something in his eyes that seemed to signal warning or foreboding. But it only lasted a millisecond. It might even have been her imagination. Devan grinned at her again and kept working on the tangle of cables by his feet.

Nell found that she was sweating even though the air conditioner was on full blast in the diner. There was a swirl of emotions in the air and she was feeding into it, not exactly sure what was going on. Had she really seen a scowl on Devan's face? She tried to shake off the weight of emotion that had attached itself to her and took a fresh pot of coffee around the diner, offering refills.

Eventually the open mic started and many of the same people that she had seen perform before got up and did their thing. Some of them were fairly talented, some of them were just beginners and, honestly, some of them were plain painful to listen to. However, she clapped enthusiastically at the end of each song and all the performers looked pleased as they made their way back to their seats.

"We've only got a few more on the list," Devan said into his microphone, a little feedback echoing back from the speakers. "But I happen to know that our illustrious waitress Nell plays guitar! I've been trying to talk her into coming up here, but so far she's refused. Now I'm calling her out! Come up and play for us!"

The crowd swiveled around to stare at her and many of them cheered. Nell glared at Devan, frozen like a deer in headlights. She wanted the ground to open up and swallow her whole.

Her eyes still locked on Devan, she shook her head. She

didn't want to get up there when she wasn't ready, and she certainly didn't want to be called out in front of the entire diner. Finally, she said loudly, her cheeks bright red: "Not this week, folks. We don't want your orders getting cold. Maybe next week."

"Okay, fine," Devan said, a little petulantly. "Next week then. We'll hold her to that." He looked at his list. "Next up then we have....Christopher."

Nell looked over at Christopher, who was pulling his guitar case from beneath the table. Then she looked back at Devan. The way he had said Christopher's name reminded her of the scowl she thought she registered on his face earlier. Were they enemies or something? Was it simple jealousy? It felt like something deeper.

Still, Devan moved aside politely enough when Christopher came up and even helped him position the microphone like he did with the other singers. Christopher sat down and snapped a capo onto the second fret of his guitar's neck.

"This is something I finished yesterday," he said. "I hope you like it."

He began to play and sing and, just like before, Nell found herself slipping away into a kind of reverie as the music cascaded through the speakers and into her ears. She caught the words of a verse.

In my world of darkness
Everything is just one shade
Nothing shines, nothing brightens
In this darkness I have made

He went into the chorus with a flourish on the guitar strings.

Like the first air that was breathed
Like the caged bird that has been freed
The swell of the ocean, the roll of the waves
The feeling of saving ... and of being saved

Nell and the rest of the patrons in the diner were transfixed once again by his sublime guitar playing and singing. The spell lasted the entire length of the sweet ballad until the last note faded. Everyone looked as if they were slowly coming out of deep hypnosis. Even Devan looked as if he had been under anesthetic for the past few minutes and was languidly emerging from the haze.

"Thank you," Christopher said into the silence around him.

The audience began to clap and many of them stood to give him an ovation. Nell had seen this rapturous response before, the last time Christopher had performed, but it was still incredible to watch. His song had affected her (and apparently everyone else) far more than any other performance tonight.

Christopher left the stage. She wondered whether he would go back to his seat or just leave straight away. Instead, he surprised her and came to the counter where she stood. He carefully placed his guitar case between two stools and then sat on one himself.

"Hello, Nell," he said. "What did you think?"

"Are you freaking kidding me?" she replied. "It was incredible. It was better than incredible. I wish I could play like that. Damn."

Christopher smiled.

"No one judges their art more harshly than the artist," he said. "Perhaps you are not giving yourself enough credit. I have doubts, too."

"That's crazy," Nell said. "You're like the best." She realized how that sounded and reeled back. "One of the best performers I have ever heard."

"That might be exactly what people will say about you once they hear you play," Christopher replied.

That was sweet, Nell thought.

She came down to rest on her palms on the countertop in front of him, so they were face to face. The lights above were bright.

"After all, why bring your guitar if you don't want to play it," Christopher continued.

At first, Nell simply looked into his eyes and nodded. Then she noticed something. An inkling she had earlier in the evening seemed to be confirmed. Christopher's skin appeared to be covered by some kind of makeup. She didn't know why he would be wearing makeup, and she half reached out a hand to touch it.

Christopher jerked away, forcefully.

"What are you doing?" he shot at her.

"Sorry," Nell said. "It just…it looks like you're wearing makeup."

Christopher immediately got up from the stool and grabbed his guitar.

"I have to go," he said, tersely.

"Wait, I didn't…" Nell started, but Christopher was already out of the door.

She watched him move swiftly past the window, nothing more than a shadow in the night.

***

Later that night, Nell reached her aunt's house with Christopher still on her mind. Aunt Laura was in the living room reading a book. Nell could see it was entitled 'Contemporary Ceramics'.

Nell said hello and sat down on the couch beside her.

"It's late. I'm glad you're back," said Aunt Laura.

"Why, what's out there?" asked Nell, playfully.

"Oh, ghosts and ghouls, and all manner of things that go bump in the night," said her aunt.

Nell chuckled. Aunt Laura patted her hand.

"How was your day, dear?" she asked.

"Oh, not bad," Nell said, not wishing to burden her aunt with her tribulations.

"I see you took your guitar again. Did you perform?"

Nell shook her head.

"No, I'm afraid I chickened out, again."

"I wish you'd let me know," Aunt Laura said, yawning.

She put down her book and stretched.

"One of these days you're going to get up there and blow them all away, and I'm going to miss it."

Nell blushed then patted her aunt's hand back.

"I promise I'll tell you the minute I know for sure I'm going up," Nell said, smiling.

It felt good to have family around her again. When her parents had been killed, Nell felt like the bottom had fallen out of her world. The two people who loved her most had simply gone. Vanished. Never to be seen again, apart from in memory. No one could ever replace them. But in Aunt Laura, Nell had found the empathy and affection that she had so sorely been missing.

Not only was her aunt allowing Nell to stay at her house

at no charge, she was also giving her plenty of space to deal with her parents' passing without pressuring her about going back to school or getting a proper job. She supported Nell's decisions and even gently encouraged her to perform at the diner. Nell felt her heart swell with love and gratitude. She instinctively roped her arms around her aunt in a warm hug.

"I'm not sure what that was for, dear, but it is greatly appreciated," said her aunt, who hugged her back warmly. They both went to bed soon after.

In her room, Nell turned off the light and crawled under the covers. After about twenty minutes of turning this way and that she accepted that sleep would not come easily tonight. She found her mind drifting back to the mysterious Christopher. What was with that guy? He was quiet, barely showing any emotion or cracks in his stoic veneer. When he said that he sometimes doubted his talent, it was hard to believe. He was probably the most talented guitar player and singer that she had ever seen, in person at any rate. The way that he was able to transfix a crowd was magical. It was almost otherworldly.

As she thought about Christopher and his delicate fingers strumming the guitar, she found her own fingers creeping down below the sheets. The tension of the day was begging for release and she needed a helping hand, as it were, to find sleep.

She didn't know what it was about Christopher that drew her, especially as there were so many questions surrounding him. Was he really wearing makeup? If so, was it a fashion statement? Was he some kind of emo, goth or just an enlightened metrosexual about town? Whatever the truth, she couldn't deny that her body responded to him. She felt something awakening when she looked into his crisp blue eyes.

She hadn't been able to do anything about it at the diner but now, in the solitude of her attic bedroom, she slowly moved her fingertips as she pictured his face.

Her breath quickened as she pondered the enigmatic boy who she had barely interacted with, imagining his lips on her neck, his body pressed against hers. A tingling heat was building in her body. She began to breathe more heavily, sucking in each inhalation as waves radiated out from her center, building and building. She continued to picture Christopher in her mind. She had no idea what his body looked like. He always wore that leather coat. She tried to picture what was underneath it. He had worn dark jeans each time she had seen him, and she tried to picture what might be underneath them, as well.

Just as she was approaching the point of no return, another image crowded into her mind. It was Devan, grinning as he glanced at her across the diner. She recoiled in shock. What was he doing in her fantasy? She had been focusing on Christopher. Up until this moment she hadn't thought about Devan at all, especially not in *that* sense. He was a nice guy, and definitely cute, but her desires were centered around Christopher. So why had Devan entered her head?

The heat of the moment was lost. Any thoughts of sweet release were quite a distance away now. Any thoughts of sleep were even further away. Her pounding heart slowed to normal speed as she lay there confused and frustrated.

She got up from the bed and went to the window. She stared out at the tall trees that filled her aunt's large backyard. There were plenty of long shadows, but nothing appeared out of the ordinary. In fact, she wasn't quite sure why she was looking out of the window in the first place. Then, an idea flashed into her mind. It was indescribably crazy. But she was ready to throw caution to the wind. This evening had turned out to be bizarre all round, so why not top it off?

Nell undid the catch of the window and opened it fully. It was a balmy night and a soothing breeze came wafting in. She shimmied out her pajama bottoms and underwear before pulling her oversized Vanderbilt-U T-shirt overhead and throwing it on the bed. She stood completely naked.

Grabbing a towel, she carefully climbed out of the large window, feeling the rough tiling beneath her bare feet as she gingerly traversed the roof. After finding a spot out of view of her aunt's bedroom window, she laid the towel down and sat. This was her definition of crazy. She was in her birthday suit, sitting on the roof of her aunt's house, bathed in the bright glow of the full moon and perhaps even visible from Marsh Valley Road, which ran adjacent to the house. But somehow, it felt like the perfect place to be in that moment.

She leaned back and felt the tile slightly dig into the skin of her upper back through the towel. But she didn't mind. A light breeze brushed over her body. She heard crickets chirping. A canopy of stars speckled the inky-black sky above her. Her senses were heightened. She felt at one with the landscape, earthy and elemental. She arched her back, a tingling of desire rekindled in her flesh. She didn't know if it was because she was out in the open and completely exposed, giving her a rush of excitement, or if there was some other reason. For once she didn't question it. She simply submitted to the moment and the will of her body.

Her fingers began to explore again. She felt the familiar ripples of pleasure coursing through her body. Slowly at first, then building in vigor. The feeling was more intense than before. In her room she had been underneath her duvet, one part of her brain conscious of the fact that her aunt was close by and slightly mortified that she might be overheard. Now, she was alone and completely exposed to heaven and earth. The thought thrilled her. Her fingers began to work more furiously. She closed her eyes.

There were competing pictures in her mind. She started with an image of Christopher, his stoic presence and handsome face. But she also found herself seeing Devan. He popped into her mind like one of those boxes at the end of a YouTube video, covering the image you were just concentrating on. Except instead of feeling annoyed, she felt aroused. This was uncharted territory. She reminded herself to forget analyzing for once, and just go with the flow.

The moon and stars, gentle breeze and landscape of majestic nature all fed into her luscious delirium. Soon she was roiling with energy, which she released into the universe with a spasm of her body and protracted moan.

It took several minutes for the trance to fade, but she slowly emerged from the haze. She found herself lying on rough tile that dug into her skin in various places. She heard a noise and looked around wildly, but there were no cars passing on Marsh Valley Road. She sat bolt upright and scanned her surroundings, wrapping the towel tightly around her body. She was suddenly self-conscious and anxious.

The yard was dark and filled with shadows. She hugged herself and shifted her gaze from tree to tree. Was there something out there? Or someone? Had she really heard a noise? She suddenly came fully to her senses. What the Hell was she thinking? Why had she been compelled to come out onto the roof of all places and, well, do that? She cringed even thinking about it. Nell Cartwright was many things — an honor student, a terrible dancer, a 90s sitcom aficionado, a passable cook and a closet believer in astrology. But one thing she most definitely was not, well up until now at least, was a freaking exhibitionist.

Suddenly, her attention was diverted to one of the large oak trees standing in the yard. A shadow darted out from behind the thick trunk. Two yellow eyes glinted in the moonlight. They seemed to look at her as the shadow moved across the yard. The…thing…whatever it was quickly concealed itself behind another tree. Nell rubbed her eyes and began shaking involuntarily. What on earth had that been? Was it a raccoon or some other creature? It seemed bigger. A deer?

She continued to stare at the tree for several seconds. She couldn't take her eyes away. She couldn't blink. Her heart was pounding in her chest and a cold sweat broke out on her forehead. The formerly soothing breeze now chilled her and the hard tiles were becoming increasingly uncomfortable.

Ever so slowly, Nell stood up, never taking her eyes off the tree. She began to creep backwards across the roof without breaking her gaze away from the ominous trunk. If she lost her footing she might end up falling and breaking her neck, but she couldn't look away. The creature might have been the size of a large dog or even a small horse. It was hard to judge from this distance. For the moment, the yard was still and free of movement.

Nell continued walking backwards and, mercifully, made it to the window without mishap. When she felt the sill bumping up against her backside she swiveled round and climbed in as quickly as possible. She slammed the window shut and fastened the catch.

Nell jumped into bed. She buried herself beneath her duvet and covered her head, in case the yellow-eyed thing had crept up to the window outside. Her heart was beating like a drum and her entire body was charged with apprehension.

There had been something out there. The question was what. And did it have something to do with why people in this kooky town were warning her against being out after dark? If there were bears, coyotes or wolves running wild, why didn't they just say? A little plain speaking wouldn't go amiss.

This entire night had gone from strange (with Christopher's apparent makeup) to downright bizarre (her unexpected exhibitionism) to off-the-charts freaky just now. Nell curled herself into a ball and tried to regulate her breathing. Eventually, she was able to muster up enough courage to pull the covers down. Her eyes scanned every inch of the room. It looked the same as always. There were no unnerving new shadows or strange faces in the window. Nothing out of the ordinary.

After several more moments of looking around, Nell got up and put on her discarded night clothes. She then grabbed her rucksack and took out her laptop. She found a few DVDs in the front pouch and selected Friends Series 8, Disc 1. She sat up in bed with the old computer perched on her lap and tried to lose herself in the innocuous melodrama of the six familiar characters. The creepy feeling still lingered, but the raucous laugh track and ditzy humor helped distract her mind.

Sleep finally came to claim her, and there were dreams. Dreams followed by nightmares.

Chapter 5

It was exactly four weeks from the eerie night on the roof before Nell saw the boy in the black jacket again. She had seen Devan several times at the diner. He was there most Wednesdays for open mic, and never passed up the chance to ask her out. She always made some excuse and demurred, but with the promise of future consideration when he looked crestfallen. She couldn't get his scowling expression out of her mind whenever he asked.

Nell brought in her guitar for each open mic with every intention of finally saying yes and getting up to perform. Yet each time she failed to do so, telling herself the diner was too busy, or Peck might not be cool with it and she shouldn't get on the wrong side of the boss.

At the next event Christopher resurfaced. Nell actually saw him enter the diner this time, which was something she hadn't witnessed before. He was usually just there, like an apparition that had materialized out of the ether. He walked in and went straight to his regular seat by the entrance, gently placing his guitar case under the table.

Nell took a deep breath. She was apprehensive due to the way their last interaction ended. But she decided to bite the bullet and went over with a menu and pot of coffee in hand.

She already knew that he wasn't going to order anything, but it had become a habit to take those things over when she approached a fresh customer.

"I have been remiss," Christopher said when she arrived at his table, no hint of animosity in his voice.

"Howdy stranger, what do you mean?" Nell asked.

"You work for tips. I have given you nothing."

"Oh, don't worry," Nell said. "I don't really serve you anything, so I wouldn't feel right."

"Still," Christopher said.

He pressed two bills into her hand. When she looked down she actually had to do a double-take. Sitting in her palm were two hundred-dollar bills.

"No! This is too much!" she protested, mouth open.

"Please," he said. "Take it. I would feel so much better about coming here if you did."

Nell looked at him for a long moment. This was almost four times the amount she made in tips a day. She didn't want to accept it, but she didn't really know how to refuse without causing offense. Also, a part of her was elated because now she could pass the money on to her aunt to help with the house costs. She shook her head and tucked the bills deep into her pocket

"Thank you so much, Christopher," she said. "I really appreciate it."

"Listen," she added, swiftly. "I'm sorry about the last time you were here. I shouldn't have…I mean…why you decide to…well…it's your business…and…."

"I have anemia," Christopher interjected, saving Nell from her verbal flailing. "Sometimes it makes my skin too pale and I wear covering."

"Oh," Nell said, berating herself internally for making a big deal of it. "I'm sorry."

"It's okay," Christopher said. "You were curious. That's understandable. I was just a little...well, embarrassed."

Nell bit her lip.

"Tell me, Nell, are you going to play this week?" he added, hastily. It seemed Christopher was now the one who wanted to move the topic of conversation on.

Nell stared down at her work apron and the half-full pot of coffee in her hand.

"Um...I don't know."

"Well," Christopher said. "I have decided that unless you also perform, I won't be playing this week."

Nell glared at him, mouth open again. It was becoming a habit.

"But...that's like... blackmail... everyone is waiting to hear you."

"Maybe everyone is waiting to hear you, also. You have a voice, too," Christopher said, softly.

Charlie in the kitchen shouted that two orders were ready to go out. Nell had to return to her duties. But she found herself mulling Christopher's last phrase over and over again.

After she finished sending out the plates and did a fresh coffee round, Nell made a quick phone call after remembering something before coming back to Christopher's table. She took the seat opposite him. He raised his eyebrows.

"You're seriously not going to perform?" She asked.

He looked at her evenly.

"Not unless you do."

"Well," she said, a little petulantly. "I can't today. I promised my aunt she would be here the first time I played. She's not answering so I can't tell her to come down. It means a lot to her, and to me. I want to keep my word."

"Keeping your word is important," Christopher said, approvingly.

"Yes," she said, her voice defiant. "It is to me."

"Then you give me your word," Christopher said. "If I go up and perform today, then you practice with me this week and next Wednesday we perform a song together."

Nell stared at him, fighting the overwhelming urge to hang her mouth open like a trout yet again.

"Okay, fine," she said, finally, aware she needed to get back to her job. "I guess we can learn a song and I'll go up with you."

"And play?" he prompted.

"Yes, and play. I wasn't just going to stand there like furniture!"

"And sing?"

"I don't sing very well," Nell said, the familiar insecurity returning.

Christopher hesitated, appraising her with his sharp eyes.

"Okay, playing is a good start," he finally conceded.

He seemed pleased, even though he simply leaned back in his chair without changing his expression. He pulled out a pen from an inside pocket, scribbled an address on a paper napkin and handed it to her.

"This is where you can meet me. Is tomorrow okay?"

Nell considered.

"Sure. It's my day off."

"Very good," Christopher said.

He then smiled and held up a hand in the traditional high-five pose. Nell cracked a smile back before doing the decent thing and slapping his palm, so he wouldn't be left hanging. Christopher deftly interlaced his fingers with hers, so they were now holding hands. His skin was slightly cold to the touch but not unpleasant. Christopher squeezed gently. Nell squeezed back in reciprocation, her smile widening. Their touch lingered before Christopher unexpectedly brought her hand to his lips and kissed it gently.

"I look forward to seeing you," he said, before releasing his grip.

Nell beamed back. She couldn't help herself.

Later in the evening, he got up and performed. His playing had the same effect as every other time. The entire crowd was enraptured, hanging on to every note. After the customary thunderous applause Nell found herself thinking that if she were to play with him she might somehow diminish the performance. That she would dull Christopher's light with her shadow. Her old patterns of thinking were hard to break.

Still, she had given her word, and that was something that the boy in the black jacket seemed not to take lightly.

Chapter 6

At noon the next day Nell went to the address that Christopher had written down for her. It was a small, nondescript house about four miles out from The Tiger Diner. There was no car in the driveway. She had assumed Christopher owned a vehicle, even though she had never seen him get into one, but it appeared she was mistaken. She wondered how he traveled to places that weren't really within walking distance, such as the diner. Maybe he took an Uber, or perhaps he had a bike.

Nell went up the narrow concrete steps, taking in the mailbox, which was simply marked with a large 6, the number of the house. She knocked on the unremarkable wooden door. She noticed it had no glass, just a tiny spy hole three-quarters of the way up. After nearly a minute, the door opened and there was Christopher, dressed in his usual dark jeans with a black long-sleeve T-shirt. He looked at her for a long moment, then peered behind her before pushing the door open so that she could enter.

She wasn't sure what to expect when she entered Christopher's house. After all, he gave nothing away. Unfortunately, neither did his house. It was furnished sparsely. There was a red fabric couch with an end table on each side. Matching lamps stood atop of both. These weren't ornate or decorative light fixtures, just plain plastic swing-arm lamps like you'd find in any office. There was an old-fashioned television that looked like it had come from a thrift store and a large coffee table, with no sign of wear and tear on its pale wood surface. On the mantle above the small fireplace, which didn't look like it was used, were three photo frames.

As she crossed into the living room, Nell glanced at the images in the frames. There was a woman in a white dress, a smiling girl holding a green balloon and a hipster-looking guy cradling a baby in his arms.

"Are they your family?" she enquired, casually.

Christopher shook his head.

"Those came with the frames. I'm afraid I haven't had a lot of time for home decorating."

Nell nodded politely, but thought how strange it was to have pictures in your living room of people you didn't know. Surely the first thing you did when you bought a frame was to replace the stock image inside. Who just placed them on display?

She put her guitar case down on the hardwood floor and sat on the couch.

"You live here by yourself?"

"Yes," he said, sitting down next to her.

"What about your parents?"

"They died."

"I'm sorry," she said, her thoughts involuntarily turning to her own loss. The raw emotion began to well from the pit of her stomach. "Was it recent?" she asked, her voice slightly unsteady.

"Many years ago. Now it's just me."

He studied her face, noticing the quiver in her voice.

"I can relate, sadly," she said, taking a deep breath. "I lost both my parents this year."

Concern crossed his features.

"Both? Was it sudden?"

"A car crash," she confided, feeling the despair rising up to her chest.

Christopher cupped both his hands over hers. His skin once again felt slightly cold to the touch.

"I'm so sorry, Nell. That must have been awful for you."

He was only a foot away from her. She could smell him. Unlike most guys, he wasn't bathed in cologne or aftershave. Instead, his smell was old-fashioned and musty – strange but not altogether unpleasant. She traced his lips with her eyes and then moved up to his straight nose before finding his sharp blue irises.

"Are we going to play guitar?" she asked softly, holding back the sting of tears and not wanting to spiral down into her well of grief.

They had both leaned in closer. It might have been unconscious on his part, but Nell had done it on purpose. Her emotional state had served to strip away a layer of reserve. She felt he understood her loss. Now their faces were just inches away. She tracked the outline of his strong jawbone and noticed the empathy in his eyes.

He was always so stoic and unreadable. But there was little trace of that reserve now. What she saw in his eyes was perhaps a dawning memory or emotion. That outer veneer that had been impenetrable for weeks now seemed more fragile.

"Yes, the guitar," he breathed, finally pulling away, but slowly as if he was fighting a magnetic pull. He stood up and looked around, his eyes finally alighting on the stairs.

"I'll be right back."

Nell sank back against the couch. She had been so sure that he was about to kiss her. They had only been an inch apart. An involuntary jerk from either one of them would have pressed their lips together for their first kiss. Nell hadn't dared to lean in. But she furtively hoped that Christopher would.

She felt flustered and was in need of water, so she got up and went to the kitchen. She began opening cupboards looking for a glass. There were no glasses to be seen. In fact, there was nothing in the cupboards whatsoever. They were all completely empty. Perhaps he bought bottled water.

She went over to the fridge door and pulled it open, followed by the freezer compartment on top.

They were both empty. The refrigerator wasn't even plugged in. No light came on when she opened the door and when she reached her hand inside the interior was at room temperature.

It was as if whoever lived here, if anyone actually did, had no need to eat. In fact, they had no need for anything, including a glass of water. But how could that be? If Christopher truly lived here, there would be signs of, well, living. There would be coffee grounds on the counter, washing liquid near the sink, crumbs near the toaster, marks on the coffee table.

She hadn't been in the bathroom yet but she was fairly certain that there would be no shaving cream in the cabinet or remnants of stubble in the sink. She would find it bare and unused, like everything else here. The house was like a vacant property that had been perfunctorily decorated for potential tenants to view. If you did nothing more than glance around, then you might believe someone was in residence. But look deeper and it was obvious that no one was living here. It didn't make sense.

Nell went back to the couch and sat down heavily. Just then Christopher came back downstairs with his guitar case in hand. Nell's first instinct was to ask about the kitchen, but she stopped herself. She didn't want to betray the fact she had been snooping. Besides, his house was his business. Perhaps he was just exceptionally clean, or had some kind of OCD about his things. There was probably a perfectly reasonable answer here. If she asked him for an explanation and he gave her one, it was true she would feel better, but then he might see her as a busybody. So she kept silent and smiled as he pulled his immaculate maroon and black guitar out of its case.

"Ready to rock?" He asked.

Nell nodded and brought her wooden acoustic guitar out of its case. It looked a little sad compared with his gleaming axe.

"This is one of the simpler songs," he said. "I'll go through the notes."

Christopher began to play. He was years ahead of her in technique and skill. She studied him intently as his fingers flew along the strings. She tried to make sense of which string acted as the bass beat and how the rest of the composition was weaved around it using the remaining strings. Nell thought it would probably take her a week to learn it. Still, she kept up to the best of her abilities, mirroring his finger positions as well as she could. Slowly but surely, she learnt the basic components of the song as Christopher went through it several times.

Even here, in this apparently un-lived house with its empty cupboards and stock photos in the frames, she felt hypnotized by the music. There was that familiar aura that she had felt in the diner whenever Christopher played. She didn't understand how it worked, but she knew at a primitive level that it wasn't exactly normal. But, as the notes rang out to form an intricate canopy of sound, she found herself sinking into it like a warm blanket.

"How do you play like that?" She asked, softly. "How do you…I don't know how to describe it. It's like a spell."

"It is one of my gifts," he said. He looked down at his shoes. "I think you know by now that some things about me are not exactly…usual."

Nell remained silent.

"There is something you should know about me, Nell."

He took a long breath, still looking down. He seemed to be torn.

"What is it?"

There was another protracted pause.

"I don't know how…the time is not right," he said, finally, with a heavy sigh.

An awkward silence ensued. He must be painfully shy, Nell thought, not unkindly. Perhaps that was what he was trying to express. Maybe it was up to her to move matters along. This was unfamiliar territory for her. She wasn't at all sure how to proceed. She fidgeted with her fingers. Her heart raced and her breathing was quick. Before she could second-guess herself, she decided to take a leap into the unknown.

"Does the thought of being close to someone scare you?" Nell asked, tentatively. "Is it fear of rejection?" she added.

He looked pensive, vulnerable. Nell's heart was drumming in her chest. Her palms felt clammy. But she collected her courage and met his eyes.

"I like you Christopher," she said. There, it was out in the open. "You're unlike anyone I've met before, but there's things I need to know about you."

More silence. Nell frowned.

"Is it me?"

"No, not at all," came the swift reply. He searched her eyes. "Did you know that the song I played yesterday was about you?"

Nell's eyes widened.

"About me? But…you barely know me…I barely know you."

"I know what I feel," he said. "And I haven't felt for a long time."

Nell pondered his last phrase, which by ordinary standards was odd, yet it made sense to her after getting to know Christopher. He hadn't said 'I haven't felt that way for a long time', but instead 'I haven't felt for a long time'.

There were a million things she wanted to say, but none of them seemed right at that moment. She wanted to ask about the house. She wanted him to expand on his feelings for her. She wanted to know what it was that he needed to tell her about himself. The questions swarmed inside her like angry bees. She opened her mouth twice to speak but nothing came out.

Eventually, Christopher put his guitar aside and gently took her hands again.

"I have duties to attend to, Nell," he said, regretfully. "But we will meet on Wednesday, for the song."

Nell didn't protest. She felt bewildered and emotionally exhausted. She simply packed up her guitar and allowed him to escort her to the door. They both went out to the porch and stood facing each other. Nell looked into his eyes. She tried to decipher what was hidden there, but came up short again.

He gripped her shoulders and squeezed. Then he slowly leaned in and gently kissed her on the cheek.

"Until Wednesday, Nell," he said softly.

Slowly, he lowered his hands until they were gripping hers and squeezed. Then he turned and went back into the house.

Chapter 7

Christopher sat heavily on the sofa, raising his hands to his temples. He was changing. There was no denying it now. Ever since that first trickle of rekindled emotion when he met Nell, his feelings towards her had been growing stronger and stronger. For someone in his position, that was a very dangerous predicament to be in.

For a long while now he had never particularly considered humans, except as a food source. He had gone to the open mic sessions and played his music, but it had been for himself, to have some brief respite from the monotony of his existence. He wasn't in it for the applause or adulation of the mortals. Their opinion meant nothing to him. He felt nothing for them.

But he couldn't honestly say that was the case now. He regarded this particular human as more than just potential prey. That was dangerous. Moreover, what he had done today, inviting her to the house, was monumentally reckless. What did he hope to achieve? What kind of future could they possibly have? It was simply absurd. But it appeared the old saying was true: the heart wants what the heart wants. Even if that heart resides in an undead body.

He could still feel her presence in the house. Her scent lingered in the air. He knew she had been rummaging around in the kitchen earlier. Even though he was upstairs at the time, his enhanced hearing picked up every detail. She undoubtedly knew something was amiss. Nell was no fool. He could sense her demeanor had shifted when he came back downstairs. He could hear the blood rushing in her veins as her heart thumped away in her chest. She was anxious. Who could blame her? It must have looked like a decoy house where the sinister owner lured innocent victims to their grim fate. He was surprised she hadn't bolted for the door.

Sensing her apprehension almost broke him. He couldn't bear for her to think of him unkindly or, worse still, with fear. It was why he was on the verge of telling her who he really was and, more importantly, what he really was. But he managed to pull back from the brink.

Now he sat with his head in hands, his mind in turmoil. Since he was turned he hadn't been one for brooding or deep introspection. He had accepted his fate with a certain serenity. He enjoyed his gifts and knew his previous mortal life was taking him up a dead-end road. But now he looked at this new reality in a harsher light. The purpose of his existence seemed hollow and futile.

Each month, a crew dispatched by the Council of Elders would show up in a van to take him into Atlanta to track down fresh food for the Red Claws. The Council had already researched the prey, using plants placed in the shady underbellies of the city. This was Christopher's one stipulation upon accepting the appointment — that the killing was not indiscriminate. The Council reluctantly agreed, but only because they could see how it would also benefit them.

So the victims were lowlifes and criminals. While you could argue that no one deserved to have their life simply snatched away from them, these individuals would probably be the most suitable candidates for such a fate. They were the rapists who waited in dark alleys. They were the drug dealers who eagerly peddled their wares to children. They were the addicts who violently assaulted and robbed innocent passers-by to sustain their habit. They were the gang members who went around terrorizing business owners and took payment-in-kind with fingers and ears when not enough cash was forthcoming.

They were the type of people who were expected to show up in homicide reports, individuals who no one would miss or mourn much when they were gone. The Council saw the wisdom in targeting them to camouflage its activities, even though it involved dedicating extra resources to scrutinizing and stalking the prey.

Leather straps had been attached to large metal hooks in the ceiling above the atrium of the Red Claw mansion. It was Christopher's job to hook up each victim in turn over the course of the month. He would strip the body of its clothing, place IVs into the arms and hang it upside down, so the dangling limbs were at the lowest point of the suspended body. Gravity pretty much did the rest.

The blood drained from them over a period of days. It was collected in a large mechanical device that continually mixed in an anticoagulant and then ever-so-slowly circulated the blood to the sleeping residents via the IV tubes. The container's mechanism kept the blood warm and thin, as if it was still in a human body. This kept the food supply fresh. Christopher took what he needed from this community pool. He fed every couple of days. It didn't disturb him. He knew where the blood had come from.

He took stock of today's date. The van would be coming in

just a few days' time for the next run. Christopher would do what needed to be done. The cycle would continue. He didn't dread the task. The only thing he dreaded was the thought of Nell finding out what he did.

The house he sat in now was simply a shell. He didn't live there, but often spent time there when he didn't want to be in the nest. He had rented it using a portion of the money allotted to him by the Council. Each month, after the deed was done and the van was about to leave the mansion, he would receive a thick stack of bills in an envelope. At first, he had simply thrown the envelopes in a drawer as he barely put a dent in their contents. After a while, he decided to use the money to rent a house. He wanted a haven of his own, away from the oppressive gothic mansion. Somewhere simple where he could practice the guitar or pursue any other interests. It was his little secret, a small symbol of independence.

He rented the house directly from the owner, using his old ID and offering to put down a hefty six-months' rent up front. All his payments were in cash so the owner, a retired fire-fighter, spied a way of keeping his income out of the hands of "Uncle Sam's Henchmen" as he called them (more commonly known as the IRS). Few questions were asked after that. Christopher left his payments in the mailbox on the first of each month.

Eventually, he knew he would have to tell Nell the truth about himself. He had been so close today. Instead, he had told her it was not the right time. But the truth was, there was never going to be a right time.

Chapter 8

Two days after her visit to Christopher's house, Nell was back to the grind at The Tiger Diner. She served the regulars, gratefully collecting her tips and making sure that everyone had their fill of the jitter juice.

When her shift ended, she counted up her tips and filled out her time card at the counter before popping it underneath the cash tray in the register for Peck. After the last of the customers trickled out, she locked the front door and began the process of cleaning the restaurant so it would be spic and span for the breakfast service. As the late-shift waitress, she took care of the front of house while the cooks tackled the day's grime in the kitchen. Right now it was only Charlie Miller on duty as he'd let young Dwayne Redmond off early to catch a movie with his girl. Charlie had a coarse demeanor, but he was a softie at heart.

Nell busied herself wiping down the tables, made sure that the sugar, salt and pepper shakers were full, replaced the ketchup and mustard bottles that were running critically low, and ensured each table had a sufficient supply of napkins stuffed into the square metal holders. Then she cleaned the counter top and surfaces behind it, scrubbed out the coffee pots in the large metal sink and sent the last load of dishes through to the industrial dishwasher in the back. Finally, she swept the floor.

When all the tasks were checked off, it was dark outside. But this wasn't unusual for Nell. She had moved her car to just outside the diner earlier in the evening, so it was just a case of locking and leaving.

She put the broom back into the storage cupboard and called out into the kitchen to say goodnight.

"Same to you, Nelly. Get on outa here now," came the reply from Charlie.

Charlie always went out the back exit because he parked in the alley behind the diner. There was only one parking space back there and, as he had seniority, it was his domain. Nell didn't begrudge him the spot. In fact, she probably would have refused the space anyway if she had been offered it. Deserted alleyways in the dark of night weren't exactly her idea of fun.

She left through the front door and then locked up behind her. There was no metal security grill to pull down or fancy alarm system to punch a code into. This was small-town America and folks generally looked out for each other. She saw the lights go out in the kitchen through the door's glass panel, meaning Charlie had left. The entire restaurant was now plunged into darkness. She took a breath and turned around. Her car was exactly where she left it, waiting at the curb. It felt eerie tonight. A giant moon hung overhead, casting a spectral glow across the town.

Nell quick-stepped to her car, unlocked the door and got in. She put the key in the ignition and turned it. There was no response. She turned the key back to the off position and tried once more. Again, instead of the throaty sound of her motor chugging to life, she was met with deathly silence. The engine remained cold and inert.

"What the hell, Hydie?" she complained to her usually faithful Hyundai, using her pet name for it.

She began to check the gauges and switches. She looked at the steering column then realized immediately what had happened when she saw the position of the headlights indicator. When she had driven to work in the afternoon there had been a cloud of mist in the air, probably from water spraying at nearby crop fields. Due to the reduced visibility she had turned her headlights on to be more conspicuous to oncoming traffic. She had forgotten to turn them off when she had parked her car. It wasn't something she usually did when arriving at work so it slipped her mind. During her shift the headlights had slowly drained her battery.

Using hope more than logic, she turned the key a few more times. The engine remained resolutely silent. She slapped her hand on the steering wheel and berated herself for her being so absent-minded.

Then she thought of Charlie, who had left only a moment ago via the back door. He might not have driven off yet. He would probably have a pair of jump leads, or could help give her a push-start or something. If all else failed, surely he'd give her a lift home. He wouldn't just leave her stranded.

Wasting no time, Nell got out of her car and darted around the side of the diner to the alley. She was praying she'd see Charlie's pickup still there, running with its headlights on. Instead, she was greeted by an empty space. A white painted rectangle on the ground indicated where her last hope had been only moments ago. She must have just missed him. Just her luck.

A noise echoed from nearby. It was like a branch breaking or a dry leaf crackling underfoot. Nell turned her head quickly to scan her surroundings, but saw nothing. There were shadows in the alley, but nothing appeared to be moving.

Relax, she told herself. *Don't let your imagination run away with itself. Wolves and coyotes avoid built-up areas, and it's unlikely to be a bear.*

Nell turned around and began retracing her steps. The same noise sounded again. This time directly behind her. She froze. Her heart was in her throat. She slowly looked around again.

This time she noticed a shadow that stood out from the rest. The other silhouettes appeared ordinary — the contours of nearby street lights and the straight angles of surrounding buildings. But this one was far from ordinary. For one thing, it was almost human shaped. But it couldn't possibly be a person. The body would have to be at least ten feet tall and unnaturally thick. Her eyes widened. She thought she could make out limbs.

Nell froze in place, her body seemingly unable to move a muscle as her brain scrambled to process what she was seeing. She took two gasping breaths before squeezing her eyes shut and opening them again. She willed her body to get moving. Mercifully, it obeyed.

Nell began to walk on wobbly legs back to the front of the restaurant. She resisted the urge to flat-out run, because she didn't want to trip and fall in the dark. With each step she took, it seemed as if there were echoing steps behind her. Surely it was just the acoustics of the enclosed alley. But she wouldn't look back. She couldn't even if she wanted to. She kept her eyes fixed on the glow of street light directly in front of her where the passageway ended.

Nell finally arrived at the sidewalk and broke into a jog.

She reached her car in a few bounds and hastily unlocked the door. She threw herself inside and slammed the door shut, hitting the "LOCK ALL" button at the same time. She heard the reassuring thunk of the locks go down. Thank God there was just enough juice in the battery for that function.

She stared out her windshield, her chest rising and falling rapidly with ragged breath. There was nothing there. There was no giant shadow coming after her. There was no hairy monster outside her car. There was only an empty street bathed in the glow of amber lamps and diffused moonlight.

She recalled the lumbering shadow in the alley. It was just her imagination. It had to be. What did they call it? Paridola? Paredoma? When your mind sees a random pattern and tries to make sense of it by turning it into something it isn't. That was all that was happening here. It had to be. The fact that she had been scared out of her wits certainly didn't help her brain to process external stimuli accurately.

She let out a long exhale. While she wasn't in danger, she was still stuck here. Being locked in her car meant she was (relatively) safe, but what now? How did she get herself out of this predicament?

She had to bite the bullet and call someone for help, at this late hour. What other option did she have?

The first person she thought of was Christopher. Weren't they kind of friends, or more even, now? But she never took his number. Up until two days ago he'd only been a rather mysterious acquaintance, so she had never asked.

She scrolled through the contacts on her phone and found her aunt's number. It was just after 11pm. Urggh. She hated to do this. Especially after Aunt Laura had done so much for her already. Besides, she would be asleep, which made matters worse. But she was family and would (hopefully) understand why she was being dragged out of bed in a situation like this.

Nell winced then pressed the dial icon next to the contact name and put the phone to her ear. It rang several times. Then it went to voicemail.

"Hi Aunt Laura," she said into the phone. "It's me, Nell. I'm really sorry to call you this late. I'm kind of stranded in town at the moment…outside the diner. My car's got a dead battery and I…um…can you just call me back, please…if you get this?"

After she left the awkward message she waited a couple of minutes and then called the cell phone again. It rang several times and then went to voicemail once more. That most likely meant her aunt was fast asleep. Aunt Laura only had a cell, having got rid of the landline she said she never used, and the handset was probably not in the bedroom. She had a spot on the breakfast bar where she often left it to charge. If it was there she wouldn't even hear it from the bedroom, especially if she was sound asleep.

Nell kept scrolling through her contacts. She only knew a handful of people in Angel Falls and didn't have many numbers. She had Hattie Lee and Rowdy Peck in her contacts, but wasn't particularly close to either of them and didn't think they'd appreciate being called at this hour. It just didn't feel right to burden them.

However, if she didn't get assistance she would have to stay in her car until the morning, when she could ask for a lift or perhaps find a bus. The other option was trying to walk home. While it could be done, it wasn't a particularly enticing choice, considering her aunt lived more than four miles away.

She looked out of the windscreen again. Her heart nearly stopped. The strange shadow was back, now just at the mouth of the alley. Nell was certain it hadn't been there the last time she looked out only minutes before. Was it because the moon had moved position and the angle of the shadow had shifted too? No, that didn't seem right. It wouldn't have just appeared complete like that. But there it was again, hulking and murky black, arms and legs seemingly sprouting from an unnaturally immense body. She suddenly recalled primal yellow eyes appraising her as she sat on her aunt's roof.

Nell nearly dropped her phone because her hands were trembling so badly. She gripped the device in both hands, looking from the screen to the shadow in case something sinister leapt out from the dark. She scrolled through her contacts trying wildly to find someone.

She was about to finally call Peck when she came across another name. She had only met her once, yet she had felt an instant connection with the ebullient librarian and they had exchanged numbers. If she hadn't been in full-blown panic mode, Nell might have hesitated to call her in the middle of the night. It wasn't as if they had a history together or an established friendship come to that — but Nell *was* in full-blown panic mode. Her heart was pounding in her chest, her palms were sweating so badly that the phone was slipping and every slight noise was making her jump in her seat. She hit call.

As Nell brought the shaking phone up to her ear, she looked back at the shadow. It wasn't in the same position as before. It had moved closer to the car. Was she imagining it? She didn't know and she didn't care. Right now, all she wanted was to hear another human being on the other end of the phone. She begged every deity she could think of to make Amara answer her call.

The phone rang and rang. Nell never took her eyes off the shadow. Just when she was sure the call would switch to voicemail, she heard a faint voice.

"Hello?" The speech sounded groggy.

"Amara?" Nell's voice was tinged with unmistakable panic. "This is Nell Cartwright...the girl you met at the library...Ms Peters' niece. I'm so sorry to wake you, but my car's broken down...and I'm getting pretty scared."

"Nell?" Amara's voice was more resolute as she shook off the sleep. "Nell, where are you?"

"In front of the diner where I work...The Tiger Diner on East Main. My car won't start and it's dark and there are shadows and..."

"Say no more," Amara said, her voice laced with concern. "I'm on my way. Give me ten minutes."

Nell hung up the phone and stared out of the windscreen. Mercifully, the shadow was in the same position it had been the last time she looked. It was perhaps ten feet away from the car. But Nell was convinced that it had moved before. She waited, staring at it, unmoving in her car and unable to do much more than breathe.

The minutes ticked by. Each one seemed to last forever. She kept glancing at her phone's time display for the briefest second before staring back up at the shadow. Each time she glanced down it seemed like the clock was running slower. The last two times she looked the time hadn't changed at all. It coldly read 11:33pm, taunting her. It was like the passing of a second had grown into a minute and a minute had grown into an eternity.

Suddenly, headlights splashed onto the street ahead and a car came into view. Nell almost cried out in relief. Her hammering heart finally slowed a little. She began to breathe easier and when she looked out into the darkness, she couldn't see the shadow at all now. It seemed that in between registering the car lights and looking out of the windscreen again it had simply disappeared. Perhaps it had never been there. Imagination was a powerful thing. Pareidolia — that was the word! Seeing things that weren't there. Nell remembered carelessly throwing her jacket in the back of her car just a while back, and later thinking something sinister was lurking in the shadows.

Amara pulled up in her little Mini just in front of Nell's car, then got out and came to her window. She had thrown a long brown coat over her pajamas and was still wearing slippers. She must have dashed out of her house right after the phone call ended. Nell was overcome with gratitude, and relief. She scrambled out of her car and threw her arms around Amara, not caring a hoot whether it was over the top.

"Hey, it's okay," Amara soothed, hugging her back.

After a long moment the librarian slowly pulled away, studying Nell's face.

"You must've been really frightened."

"You have no idea," Nell said. "I'm not usually a scaredy-cat, but I thought there was something out there. This shadow…it seemed like…it was moving."

"The mind can play tricks," Amara said.

"Yeah," continued Nell. "That must have been it."

Amara stroked Nell's hands, remaining quiet as Nell caught her breath.

"Do you have jump cables?" asked Nell. "My battery is dead."

"Dad said I should never leave home without them," Amara replied. "I guess he was right, after all. I'll go get them."

Amara hooked up her car battery to Nell's, and then went back and revved her engine to get the juice flowing. After a few minutes, Nell tentatively turned her key in the ignition. She heard the engine catch and sputter, but then it quickly died again. After around five more minutes of charging, Nell crossed her fingers and once again turned the key. The engine caught and then roared into life. Nell gave a thumbs-up through the windscreen at Amara, who returned the gesture along with a broad smile. After a few more minutes Amara got out and began disconnecting the jump cables.

Nell went to meet her.

"I don't know how to thank you."

"That's what friends are for," Amara said. "If you hadn't called me I would've been pretty disappointed when I heard about it later."

"You're my savior," Nell said. "I don't know what I would've done if you hadn't..."

Amara waved away the thanks, as if what she had done was nothing particularly special.

"Any time. It's no big deal, really. Sorceress Sisters stick together."

Amara took Nell's hands again.

"Go on home now, Nell. Get some sleep. You look exhausted."

"That's the best suggestion I've heard all day," Nell replied.

The two women hugged again then Nell got into her idling car. She put it into gear and drove off, with Amara following behind her for several blocks. Nell wasn't sure if the librarian was taking her normal route home or if she was just ensuring Nell's battery was holding up.

After a few more minutes Nell saw a flash of headlights in

her rearview mirror before Amara peeled off onto one of the side roads, waving enthusiastically through her windscreen.

Nell continued straight on and took the exit for Marsh Valley Road. She reached home without further incident.

As she collapsed onto her bed, she recalled the image of the strange shadow. She slept with the lights on that night.

Chapter 9

Nell didn't have work the next day, so she bought a large bunch of flowers in town and headed to the library. She showed up just after it opened and Amara greeted her with a warm smile from behind the main desk.

"Nell! Are you feeling better after last night?"

"Yeah," Nell said, sheepishly. "I actually feel pretty silly now, jumping at shadows. I'm sorry I dragged you out. Home was only a few miles away. I could have walked."

Amara frowned.

"Actually," she said. "It's probably better that you weren't out after dark. It's not a good idea."

"Why does everyone keep telling me that?" Nell asked, mildly exasperated. "I've heard it from at least three other people, including my boss. Are there dire wolves wandering around or something?"

Amara gave her a half smile.

"No dire wolves as far as I know." She lowered her voice. "But some years ago there were some odd killings in the area. They took place before I came to Angel Falls, and were pretty brutal from what I read. The authorities thought it might be some kind of wild animal attack and the bodies…." She shuddered involuntarily. "Let's just say there wasn't much left."

Amara went quiet for a moment and then clapped her hands together.

"But that's not why you came in here. You came in for some lovely books, right?"

Nell held up the bouquet with a smile.

"I actually came in to give you these, my hero," she said, handing over the colorful flowers.

"For me! Wow, you shouldn't have," said Amara, receiving the bouquet with a wide grin and sparkle in her eyes. "They're beautiful."

She took a long inhale of the fresh scents.

"You've just done what no guy has ever done before," she added, before leaning forward and hugging Nell warmly.

"Really?" said Nell, still clinging to Amara. "Someone as lovely as you. I can't believe it."

"Sad but true," said Amara. "I live alone, but have my books to keep me company on a lonesome evening."

"Amen to that, sister," said Nell, grinning. "And books don't snore, or elbow you in the ribs at 3am."

"Or leave the seat up," added Amara. "Or find someone else to rifle through their pages behind your back."

They both chuckled loudly.

"Speaking of books, are you sure I can't help you find any, since you're here anyway?" asked Amara.

Nell's thoughts involuntarily returned to the strange shadow that she had seen last night. It seemed the experience was still weighing on her mind. Then she remembered something Amara said just moments ago...'The authorities thought it might be some kind of wild animal attack'.

Could it be possible that she was being stalked by the same...

thing…that was implicated in the attacks? And was any of this related to the feral yellow eyes she saw from the roof of her aunt's house? She was probably adding two and two together and making five, but if she really was in danger she at least wanted to be armed with a few facts.

"Well…" she began, tentatively. "You know how you said there were some murders locally years ago. Do you happen to have any clippings or newspaper articles from the time?"

Amara blinked at her.

"I was thinking about paranormal romance recommendations, or dystopian sci-fi, shifter fantasy, that kind of thing," said the librarian. "Are you sure you want to read about all that real-life unpleasantness?"

"I was just thinking back to that shadow yesterday," Nell admitted with a sigh. "It could almost have been a beast or something."

"Oh Nell," said Amara, sympathetically. "You were in a heightened state. Fear does strange things. You're not going to do yourself any favors by filling your head with theories like that. You might never sleep again, even if I checked out *The Expanded History of Igneous Rocks* for you. And yes, that is an actual book."

Nell smiled, wanly.

"You're probably right, Amara," she said. "But please humor me. I don't think I'll be able to sleep without having looked into it now. It'll be like an itch that I haven't scratched. It's just the way my mind works. It can't deal with unknowns, or stuff that's left hanging."

Amara shrugged.

"The killings stopped a while back. Looking at those old news stories now isn't going to bring you much comfort."

Nell noticed the librarian studying her face, no doubt taking in her dejected expression.

"Still, I am a librarian," said Amara. "Which means I am here to serve. So your wish is my command."

She gave a bow. Nell smiled.

"We've got those newspaper files on microfiche. I'm afraid we haven't digitized the archives so you'll need to use your old-fashioned peepers to search for the stories. You're going to have to go through pretty much the past several decades, because the attacks were spread out. But they would have made the front page in a quiet area like this, so perhaps start there."

"Bring it on," said Nell, rubbing her hands in a theatrical gesture. "I'm up for a challenge."

"That's the spirit!" said Amara. "I'd better get your lovely blooms in some water and then I'll pull out the SCC reels for you."

SCC turned out to stand for Spalding County Courier, the local newspaper. Amara set up the machine at the back of the periodicals section and Nell began to go through newspaper after newspaper trying to find information on the killings. Amara had written down a few years for reference that she thought might be useful, but Nell didn't skip anything. She started with the January 3, 1960 edition and went forwards from there. She checked every front page of every newspaper (luckily the Spalding County Courier was a weekly publication, rather than a daily).

After two hours, Nell's mind was a whirl of information. Unfortunately, none of it was about macabre deaths. Who knew so much could be written about peanuts, pecans, blueberries and spring onions. Yet anything that affected the crops was hot news in the Courier. It seemed the local populace was also obsessed with minor-league hockey, football and baseball, as well as hiking and all things out-doors.

When Nell finally looked up from the viewer she could see ghost images of headlines and newsprint floating on the white back wall of the library. She needed to take a break. There were a few older folks in the room reading newspapers and magazines, so she stood up and gently stretched a bit. If the room were empty she would have opted for star-jumps and perhaps an air-squat or two.

She shook out her hands and then got back to it, sitting down and planting her eyes onto the viewer screen. Her fingers gently rotated the metal dial, which advanced the microfiche reel and brought up new editions of the Spalding County Courier. About 20 minutes later she hit pay dirt.

The front page on May 2, 1971 screamed:

MYSTERIOUS BEAST LEAVES HIKER IN SHREDS

The story read:

A local hiker was mauled to death in a suspected animal attack while traversing the Long Pine trail on the outskirts of Angel Falls.

Police have named the deceased as Edward McTavish, a 44-year-old father of two from Orchard Hill. His badly mutilated body was discovered by another hiker, Emmeline Merritt, 27, two days ago at around 3.40pm Eastern Standard.

Emergency services were able to identify the body from the driver's license Mr McTavish was carrying.

Wildlife experts from East Griffin Forestry Commission have no explanation as to what kind of creature could have inflicted such extensive injuries. Some locals have speculated that it was a bear protecting its territory, while others have pointed the finger at a pack of mountain lions.

Edward Copeland, an assistant professor at The Georgia College of Anthropology, said there had been no previous sighting of either species in the vicinity of Long Pine. He added that the teeth marks more closely matched that of a canine. However, due to the size of the indentations and extent of damage to the body, he was at a loss to identify a likely culprit.

The story went on to detail the various cuts and wounds to the victim's body as well as gauge more reaction from baffled locals. Sadly, it also included reaction from the victim's devastated wife and family. Nell read the article several times, shaking her head. She felt for Mr McTavish's children, having herself experienced the pain of suddenly losing parents. This tragic event must have been the talk of the town back in '71, she reckoned. Nell made a note of the article's date in her pad then twisted the metal dial on the reader to continue scanning pages.

She stopped again at October 2, 1982:

WOMAN SLAIN AT HOME IN GRUESOME ATTACK, POLICE MYSTIFIED.

The article described an attack in a woman's home with the same hallmarks as the 1971 slaying. The victim, 36-year-old Marsha Dunn from Angel Falls, had been ripped apart in exactly the same gruesome manner. Police linked the killing to Edward McTavish's animal mauling eleven years prior.

However, what they were at a loss to explain was how a pack of mountain lions or an angry bear had entered Ms Dunn's apartment on the 14th floor of a high-rise building, with no discernible signs of forced entry.

The only theory they could come up with was that some sicko had discovered the mutilated body in the wild and then dragged it up to the woman's apartment in order to... Nell shuddered to even consider that part. However, the hypothesis was full of holes. How did the sicko know where she lived? Even though the death occurred before the era of widespread CCTV cameras, how did the perpetrator ever expect to take her home without being spotted? And why even bother? Why take the risk when he could have just acted on his twisted impulses when he first discovered her? As an explanation, it was a non-starter.

Other reports implied the killing was part of some kind of satanic ritual. However, that theory gained even less traction. Angel Falls wasn't exactly a hotbed of Devil worship or cult activity. What's more, there was no evidence of another person being present in the apartment. Ms Dunn lived alone and there were no fingerprints that pointed to another human being. There were some hair fibers that were collected, but when the lab results came back they were inconclusive. The hair appeared to be both human and canine. Police put it down to contamination of the samples.

Nell had spent more than three hours with her eyes fixed on the microfiche monitor. She heard a rustle on the table just beside her. When she looked down she saw an opened brown paper bag with two croissants inside. A coffee cup was placed next to it and when Nell traced the hand holding it upwards she wasn't surprised to see Amara's smiling face.

"Brain fuel for our super-sleuth," said the librarian, before squeezing Nell's shoulder and then turning heel and heading back to the circulation desk.

Nell grabbed a croissant and stuffed it into her mouth, savoring the flaky texture and buttery taste. She washed it down with a gulp of the strong Americano coffee. It hit just the right spot. She felt blessed to have met such a gracious soul as Amara.

Nell continued searching the archives in between bites and sips. She was on a roll now and came across more cases. Each one seemed stranger and more unlikely than the previous one. There were a total of six victims over a period of twenty-two years. Then the unexplained killings stopped in the early nineties. Police hadn't uncovered a single plausible lead in all that time. At one point, the Sasquatch Society of America even contacted local law enforcement to see whether it could lend its expertise. Bigfoot aside, the accepted theory was that whatever feral animal or pack of animals had been responsible, it or they had left the territory in search of a new hunting ground.

Nell settled back in the chair and blinked rapidly, trying to get her eyes accustomed to the lighting of the reading room once again. She thought about all the tragic deaths but, much like the police at the time, couldn't fathom any of it. But one thing stood out to her and it made her heart pound in her chest like a freight train. There had been at least two mentions of a hulking shadow prior to the murders taking place. These had been reported by witnesses who saw the victim before their grisly end. This fact scared Nell witless. Had they seen the same apparition that she had last night?

Nell switched off the microfiche machine and brought the

box of reels back to Amara.

"How was it?" The librarian asked. "Did you find what you were looking for?"

"Honestly," Nell said. "I'm more scared than ever now."

"I told you they were brutal," Amara said. "Do you want me to recommend a good book to make you laugh? You've got to try *When Winter Ends* by Kara Kenyon."

"I don't think that's going to cut it," Nell said.

Her mind flashed back to Christopher. His strangeness and the eerie feeling she got when she was in his house. Was he somehow linked to the shadow and the dark subject matter she had just spent the best part of the day researching?

"Let me ask you something," said Nell, on a whim.

"Anything you want," replied the librarian.

"Suppose that I were trying to identify a condition"

"Condition?"

"As in a...syndrome or disease."

"O-k-a-y," said Amara, slowly. "You're in a curious mood today, Nell, but I'll play along. What kind of disease?"

"The symptoms include pale skin, like skin so pale you need to cover it with makeup just to look normal. No apparent consumption of food or drink."

Then she remembered something else. When Christopher had cupped his hands over hers.

"Also, skin that feels cold to the touch," she added.

Amara looked amused and raised her eyebrows.

"And I'll bet you've never seen them under direct sunlight, right?" she said, playfully.

"Well no, I can't say I have," said Nell, looking confused. "But what has that got to do with anything?

"You're just messing with me, right?" replied Amara.

Nell shook her head.

"No, I'm serious."

Now Amara was the one to look incredulous.

"Well," she said. "If this isn't an elaborate joke, then I suggest you need to be looking in the fiction section. Start with Sheena Marshall if you want a more modern take."

Nell just stared at the other woman for a long moment. Sheena Marshall? Then it clicked.

"The vampire author?" she said.

The suggestion was so outlandish that she had never considered it. But now that it was out in the open, it didn't seem so far-fetched. Of course, Nell didn't believe for a second that Christopher was actually a vampire. But perhaps he was one of those people who lived as if they were. YouTube's algorithm had suggested a video on the topic not so long ago and she couldn't resist the click. This wasn't mere cosplay, the people interviewed actually slept in padded coffins, made up their skin to look deathly pale and even drank each others' blood during their play rituals. Was Christopher part of the vampire subculture? It might explain a great deal.

"Ok, humor me," said Nell. "How can I find out more?"

"Well," said Amara, still quizzical. "Are you looking for a horror novel or a factual book, like the history of Vlad the Impaler, who was supposed to be the inspiration for Dracula."

"Mostly the second," Nell said. "But maybe a couple of novels too, if you can recommend any good ones."

"There's always the classic by Stoker," said Amara. "Philip Kline has a very decent novel called *Night Brood*. Sheena Marshall starts off strong but the later books are pretty meh."

She kept thinking.

"There's the *Red Sunset* series, which had the teenies flocking to bookstores, which I guess is great in itself, but the books are a little…sappy…shall we say. What's all this about, anyway? You're a paragon of mystery today."

Nell quickly scrambled for something to say. A college assignment? Creative writing course? Pet project? But when she glanced at Amara, she saw the selfless woman who had rushed out in the dead of night to rescue her from the diner, who brought her food when she hadn't even asked. Real friends don't lie to each other. Full stop.

Nell took a deep breath and then began.

"So, this is going to sound uber-nutso, but there's this guy…"

She went on to describe Christopher, from their first meeting at the open mic evening to the strange encounter at his mystery house.

"You don't seriously think he's a…"

"Of course not," Nell interjected. "But that's not to say *he* doesn't think he's one."

Amara looked more bemused than ever. Nell explained her, admittedly unorthodox, theory.

"Do you think it was him last night in the shadows watching you?" Amara asked. "Perhaps it's part of his vamp role play. You know, the paranormal seduction of an innocent damsel. A wannabe vampire can't just ask a girl to the local Italian, where's the supernatural allure in that?"

It seemed Amara was enjoying this perhaps ever-so-slightly.

"I don't think so," Nell said. "The shadow I saw – or I thought I saw – was bigger…"

She suddenly felt self-conscious and silly for having started this conversation.

Amara sensed her unease.

"I'll point you towards those books," said the librarian, more earnestly. "At the very least you'll learn a thing or two, which is never a bad thing. Reading takes you in one direction..."

"Straight to the top!" Nell finished.

The moment of light relief was welcome.

Nell spent the rest of the afternoon studying vampires in the library. She confirmed that Vlad the Impaler had been an actual person and the inspiration for Dracula. In reality, he was a brutal leader who slaughtered his own people and had a reputation for abhorrent cruelty. She also learnt of the many myths in fictional vampire lore. For example, their skin sizzled and burned off their bodies when exposed to direct sunlight. Also that they were repulsed by garlic, which would have been a shame, as Christopher would never get to try her roasted spinach and garlic orzo. It was the one recipe in her culinary arsenal that she thought she had mastered.

If her hunch about Christopher was correct, why was he pretending to be a vampire? What did he get out of it? There was no doubt in her mind that she had feelings for him. But how did you fall for someone that might be a plain wack-job. Okay, that was perhaps a bit harsh. Someone who...lived an alternative lifestyle, shall we say. Why pretend to be something else? Especially when that something is an undead creature that only exists in the pages of fantasy books?

She pulled a small notebook and pencil out the pocket of her jeans and began writing. She titled the page:

'More things that don't make sense about Christopher Deverell'

Then continued writing underneath:

- *Face and hands completely pale. Almost white. Not sure about*

rest of body.
- Has no food at his weird house. Doesn't eat or drink?
- Odd hypnotic effect when singing, or playing guitar. Natural talent? Something else?

Nell was at a loss as she looked over her list. She wasn't certain that she accepted Christopher's explanation that he had a medical condition affecting his skin. She wanted to believe him, but there was so much other weirdness about him that didn't help his cause. Luckily, she hadn't been caught snooping around his kitchen when she came over to his place. But why maintain a shell of a house with bad furniture, no food and generic pictures on the mantle? It was hardly decked out like a bachelor pad and he had made no moves to try and bed her, so it was unlikely to be his private love nest. What was its purpose?

She turned to the next item on her list. The hypnotic effect when he performed. Nell knew from her own experience that listening to music could put you into a trance-like state. The songs she loved most evoked strong emotions in her and stirred clear memories of the first time she heard the tracks. But with Christopher it was different. She recalled the way the crowd at the Tiger became fixated on him. All talking and even movement ceased. It seemed like he enraptured the audience, mind, body and spirit.

She tried to think back to what she was feeling and thinking when he was playing, but came up blank. It was as if the music transcended thought. There was just the song washing over her. She recalled feeling like she was waking up from a pleasant dream when the last notes faded and the song came to an end.

There had to be an explanation to all this weirdness, but everything seemed just out of reach. She put the pencil down and closed her notepad. Then she leaned back in her chair and rubbed her temples before folding her arms in her lap. She just sat there, letting her mind wander as she looked around the old-fashioned library.

As the sun nearly completed its journey across the sky and began throwing out golden-reddish rays, Nell had one last idea. It was something she should have done ages ago, in fact. She dashed back to the reading room and sat at one of the ancient PCs lined up at the back that offered free internet browsing.

She searched for Christopher Deverell. She tried multiple spellings but only one entry came up. It was a missing person's post from two decades ago by the Atlanta Mercy Mission homeless charity. Beneath the brief description, which stated his age as 22, was a picture. When she studied it, her mouth hung open in shock.

In the image he looked tired, with bags under his eyes and a weary expression. But otherwise he was the exact same person that had been coming into the diner and playing guitar. If the post was correct, he would have to be at least 42 years old now. But he hadn't aged a single day from the time the picture had been taken. Not one line. Not one wrinkle. Not one blemish. He was almost a carbon copy of the image on the screen.

Things had just escalated from the surreal to the downright chilling.

Chapter 10

Nell scanned the entrance of the diner. The place was packed as customers crowded in for the open mic night. Lively chatter and the chinking of cutlery on plates reverberated around the heaving venue. Nell felt hot and was rushed off her feet with orders. But she made time to steal glances at the entrance every so often.

A part of her didn't want to witness that familiar silhouette coming through the door. Seeing the taught, slender body holding the guitar case would mean two things, both frightening in their own way. The first was she would have to make good on her commitment and perform tonight. A promise was a promise. The second was that she would have to come face to face once again with a man who, it seemed, was timeless.

As if by divine synchronicity, Christopher came through the door, guitar case in hand. Nell froze. Her breath caught in her chest. She stared wide-eyed at his face, studying every detail her eyes could take in at this proximity.

After coming home from the library the day before, she was sure she must have been mistaken. The image on the screen couldn't have been Christopher as he is today. She was simply misremembering his real face and overlooking the subtle signs of aging that had to be there.

But right here, right now, as she stared at him in the flesh, the truth hit home. He was so eerily similar to the picture taken over two decades ago. His skin was unwrinkled, unblemished, unlined. The eyes were sharp with no hint of creases around them. A passage from her favorite poem, 'Time Lies Eternal' by Laurence D. Chandler, came unbidden into her mind — *'Neither current nor tide, neither conceit nor pride, the hands remain still, the old laments wane, we all must succumb, yet still you remain'.* A shiver made its way down her back.

Half an hour later Nell sat frozen in front of the crowd, her fingers curled into the shape of the first chord and pressed down on the strings of the guitar. The microphone in front of her felt like a giant bug's eye that was callously scrutinizing her. She had promised Christopher she would perform with him and there was no way out of her obligation. She had given her word. So she had followed him up to the front of the packed diner and sat down on the stool next to him. She stole sideways glances at him, studying his face carefully, in case she had missed something before. Some flaw, rumple or line. She hadn't.

The crowd was friendly and most of them knew her by now. She spotted Aunt Laura, who gave her a doting smile and wave from her seat near the front. However, that didn't lessen the icy terror in her heart. Part of it was what she had discovered at the library yesterday. All of the unanswered questions about Christopher Deverell. But much of it was plain old stage fright.

When she looked up into Christopher's youthful face, which was giving her a reassuring smile, she almost convinced herself that there was a reasonable explanation for what she had uncovered. She vowed to confront him about it later. But right now, she had something more pressing and somehow even scarier in front of her. Playing to an audience. Christopher adjusted the microphone and brought it level to his mouth.

"Hello everyone," he said. "Some of you know me, but this week your lovely waitress Nell is going to join me." Even his speaking voice was musical as he conferred with the audience.

The crowd began to applaud loudly. This didn't help Nell's nerves one bit. She couldn't seem to nod her head in acknowledgment. It was as if her neck was trapped in an invisible brace that kept her immobile. Her heart was beating in her chest so loudly that she fretted it would be picked up by the microphone. Her hands began perspiring and she was worried that her fingers would slip off the strings, messing up the chord patterns.

Then Christopher played the opening notes and she forgot about everything. She felt a warm current spread down from the top of her head and run out through to the soles of her feet, which were propped up on the metal ring of the stool.

She knew the song. They had practiced it several times at his house. She had practiced on her own as well. She began to play, matching his movements with a fluency she had never achieved during rehearsal. She was able to keep up with his complicated picking pattern and when it came time to sing the first verse, she found herself leaning into the microphone to harmonize with Christopher, even though singing wasn't part of the agreement. It just felt so natural to be doing it.

Together they were exuding some kind of new energy, amplifying and accentuating the aura that Christopher cast out. It extended from them in waves, starting with the people in the front of the room and then permeating all the way to the back. Even Charlie Miller and Dwayne Redmond in the kitchen leaned against the small window where the orders were shipped and watched with glazed expressions. For the duration of the song the two cooks didn't have a single care about what was charring on the grill behind them.

When Nell and Christopher finally finished the song, there was a stunned silence that seemed to stretch for an eternity. It went on and on and all Nell could do was look out at the crowd as faces slowly started to reanimate. It was as if someone had plunged their souls back into their bodies and they had arrived on the mortal plane once again.

"Please give it up for Nell," Christopher said, pointing an arm in her direction.

The applause nearly brought the roof down. Feet stomped and shrill whistles pierced the raucous clapping. Devan gave Nell a double thumbs-up and wide grin from the sound desk. Christopher placed a hand on the small of her back and gently rubbed in a circular motion. Nell briefly wondered how cold his hand would feel if he was touching her bare skin.

The ethereal spell of the music broken, Charlie pointed to the orders stacking up at the serving window. Nell went back to work, but not before receiving a warm hug from her Aunt Laura, whose eyes were moist.

"That was simply wonderful," she said, clearly emotional. "It reminded me of my mother. You have that special touch, Nell. It seemed to skip me and your mom, but I see it in you. I hear it in you. It was almost like she's still here with us."

Nell couldn't even imagine higher praise.

"That's the best compliment I've received in my life," said Nell, blushing. "Thank you so much Aunt Laura."

They hugged again before Aunt Laura said she wanted to head home before it got too late. Nell wished her a safe journey.

About an hour later when Nell was brewing a fresh pot of coffee, Christopher came and sat at the counter. The diner was buzzing with a larger evening crowd than usual, even for an open mic night. The din of conversation and laughter served as permanent background noise.

Christopher leaned in.

"You were wonderful up there," he said, his mouth close to her ear.

"I was only following you," Nell replied, having to raise her voice to be heard. "I was just trying to keep up."

"You did far more than that. You were the star of the show," he said.

She looked into his eyes thinking about what to say next. She wasn't really interested in talking about the song. It was over. There were so many more pressing matters swirling around in her head.

What are you pretending to be? Why is there a picture of you from two decades ago that states you were 22? Where do you really live? What do you really do? Why doesn't your house have any food or dishes or cups or real pictures in the frames? Are you a crazy person? Am I a crazy person? I would have to be to get involved with someone like you. Yet here we are.

The questions churned in her brain but she didn't ask any of them. What kind of opener do you choose when what you really want to ask is, 'Why are you living a lie?' Finally, Nell bit her lip and pulled away from the counter to grab the coffee pot and make her rounds. She felt Christopher's eyes burning into her back as she left him sitting there.

***

At the end of an exhausting shift Nell stepped out onto the street. She closed the diner door and turned the key in the lock before slipping it into her pocket. When she turned around she found Christopher waiting for her. Déjà vu. Yet this time she wasn't surprised. In fact, she would have been surprised if he had not been there. He was leaning in the exact same spot as before, blended into the shadows. She remembered what Amara had said yesterday and examined his body's outline critically, to see if he could have been the shadow in the night. She didn't think so.

"Hello Nell," Christopher said, softly. "You have questions for me, don't you?"

She looked up into his eyes but resisted being drawn into those deep blue pools.

"That's perhaps the understatement of the century," she replied.

There was a noise. It seemed to come from the parking lot across the street, towards the back near the bushes. Christopher's head jerked towards the sound. His eyes narrowed and he inhaled deeply. They both scanned the lush foliage. Nell couldn't see anything out of the ordinary. Christopher finally looked away, but she could see unease on his face.

"So..." He paused. "Questions."

"I just need to know...I just need to know who you are," Nell blurted out. "The pictures in your house... Nobody just leaves the shop ones in the frame. Those pictures were dusty, so they've been there a while. Then I try to get a glass of water. There's no food or silverware or cups or dishes or spoons...." Her voice was rising in both volume and pitch. "... or anything else in your house that shows you live like a normal human being. And how do you explain the fact that..."

There was another noise from the bushes, like a low scraping sound. They both snapped their heads around. This time the sound was accompanied by movement. The foliage swayed in the darkness. Nell thought she could make out a shadow. Christopher instinctively placed his body between Nell and the parking lot.

"I will answer your questions, Nell," Christopher said, urgently. "But not here, not now. It's not safe." He paused again, looking behind him across the street. "Do you believe that I have feelings for you?" He placed his hands on her shoulders.

Nell nodded.

"Yes, that's one thing I do believe," she said.

"Do you think I have feelings for you?" she asked, tentatively.

"I know you do," came the unequivocal reply. "I feel them washing over me."

Christopher stepped forward and wrapped his arms around Nell, reeling her in for a tight embrace. Nell rested her head against his chest and roped her arms around his torso, squeezing him back. She lifted her head to look into his eyes. Christopher leaned down and planted a soft kiss on her lips. Nell reciprocated, feeling herself melt into his touch. Christopher gently pulled away before looking around again. He began guiding Nell towards her car.

"We cannot talk tonight, as much as I want to be with you," he said. "I have an...errand...and you must go."

"Christopher," Nell replied. "These questions. They *need* answers. I don't think I can..."

"I swear," he interrupted. "You will get your answers. But please get in your car now. It's not safe out here."

Nell gave up arguing and unlocked her car. She got in and rolled the window down.

"When will I see you again?"

"I will find you. I must go now, and so must you."

Nell started her engine and put Hydie into gear.

Christopher grabbed his guitar case, which was leaning up against the restaurant window, then swiftly made off. He turned into the alley beside the diner.

Nell pressed on the gas pedal and drove up to the mouth of the alley. She peered in and saw him disappearing around the corner as he left the passageway. She was surprised by the distance he had covered in what seemed like only a moment.

She drove on and turned at the end of the road. She went up a block, and then another, on her usual route home. She suddenly caught sight of Christopher crossing the street. He was moving fast.

Curious to see what he was up to, she began following him using the smaller roads. The streets here were empty at this time of night and she encountered no traffic. But she soon found that he was moving too fast, traversing playgrounds and parking lots. She couldn't keep up.

Then she noticed another set of headlights that appeared to be traveling in his direction. This was odd as everything in this small town was shut at this late hour. The lights were two blocks over and moving much faster than she had been. Was this why Christopher was spooked? Was the other car following him? Was he in danger?

She hesitated at an intersection and then made an impulsive decision. Instead of rejoining East Main and heading towards Marsh Valley Road, she pressed on the gas and began following the tail lights of the car up ahead. As she drew closer she realized that it wasn't a car at all, but a black van.

After a while the van joined Martin Luther King freeway on the outskirts of town. Luckily, there were still plenty of cars on this road so she could disguise her surveillance by keeping a few vehicles behind. She kept the box shape of the van and its distinctive thin rectangle tail lights in her sights, paying close attention to where it turned so she could make the same maneuvers, all the while maintaining a discreet distance.

They drove for a few miles before the van eventually turned right onto an unlit dirt lane. She followed directly behind it. She had no choice as no other cars had taken this route. However, she maintained enough of a distance to (hopefully) not raise suspicions. She had no idea where she was. She also had no idea where Christopher was. However occasionally she thought she caught movement out of the corner of her eye in the cornfields adjacent to the road. But she couldn't be sure.

After about half a mile the van slowed. Nell automatically slowed as well. She watched as the van turned onto a sloping gravel drive. It stopped at a set of immense metal gates that were at least fifteen-feet tall. The gates were set in an imposing stone wall of the same height that ran all the way around a plot of land.

Nell watched as the gates slowly opened. No doubt someone in the van had a radio fob key. The van passed through the threshold and was lost to her view. The gates began to slowly swing shut again. Nell couldn't see or hear the mechanism that was moving the huge iron gates, which struck her as odd. Perhaps it was hidden in the ground.

She turned off her headlights and crawled along the lane in her car, stopping as close to the gates as she dared before killing her engine. She looked through the wrought iron barrier at the building beyond. She hadn't known houses like this existed here. House was actually the wrong word. This was a mansion. There was no other way to describe it. The van sat idling outside the grand entrance of the gothic residence. No one got out.

Nell saw movement again out of the corner of her eye. Suddenly Christopher burst out from the cornfield. She recognized his silhouette and the guitar case strapped to his back. If he was headed for the house then the people in the van were waiting for him. She had no way to warn him.

'Shit,' she whispered, panic rising.

She expected him to come around to the gates. That way he would at least notice the van and have a chance to run if he needed to. Instead, he sprang into the air and grabbed the top of the wall, then deftly hoisted himself over before disappearing out of view. Nell was dumbstruck. How could he possibly jump that high? It defied logic — and probably gravity.

Nell's heart was thumping loudly in her ears.

A moment later she saw Christopher's silhouette again through the iron gates as he leapt down into a crouch. He stood up and began walking. He didn't pause or seem alarmed at the sight of the van idling at the top of the driveway. In fact, when he approached the vehicle he went around to the driver's side window to exchange words. After a minute or two he slid open the side door of the van and got in. He wasn't being abducted, that was for sure. He had entered the van willingly.

The driver started to make a three-point turn in order to exit through the gates. Nell swiftly realized that the van's headlights would illuminate her car as it came out. She quickly started her engine and hit the gas pedal. For once she was grateful that Hydie was a rickety old model. Newer vehicles had sensors that would automatically switch on the headlights when it was dark. Hydie didn't, so she was able to stay incognito. Nell hurriedly drove about twenty meters past the gate and turned into the cornfield, crushing stalks as she vacated the lane and switched off her engine. She turned around and stared intently out of Hydie's rear window.

The van came out of the gates and turned left back onto the dirt lane, away from her. Nell took a long breath. Now she had to make a quick decision. Was she going to make a third impulsive choice tonight?

Following the van again might place her in harm's way. It might also somehow compromise Christopher. He obviously didn't want her to know what he was up to. Plus, this was his business, she had no right to intrude into his personal affairs. The sensible course of action was to turn back the way she came and head on home.

She turned her car around and drove back down the lane. She soon spotted the distinctive tail lights of the van and resumed following it from a safe distance. Nell had been sensible all her life. Frankly, it was overrated. Nell kept her headlights off, making Hydie close to invisible in the murky lane.

Christopher had said he had an errand to run. Maybe this was what he had been referring to. While she had no business following him to see what he was up to, she was going to do it anyway. Nell needed answers. She needed them now. This seemed like the only way to get them.

The van was pulling further ahead now, but Nell was loath

to go any faster in the narrow lane with her headlights off. The other vehicle quickly reached the end of the lane and turned right onto the freeway, heading away from Angel Falls. If Nell didn't do something now she was going to lose it.

She turned her headlights on and pressed her foot down. When she reached the end of the lane she peeled out into the traffic on the freeway, earning herself an irate honk from the car she had just cut in front of.

She put her foot down and stared frantically at the cars ahead of her. The van was nowhere to be seen. Just when she thought all hope was lost, she spotted the thin red tail lights about five cars in front as the road curved. She breathed a sigh of relief and nudged up her speed. Hydie protested by roaring and shaking. Nell stroked the steering wheel with one hand.

"Easy girl," she said, as if she were riding a horse.

She watched the van like a hawk, desperately trying to keep up in her old car. The other driver took the US-41N interstate turn off. Nell followed suit. She fell in three cars behind the van and maintained that distance for about 40 minutes. The van then merged onto the I-75N. According to the sign, they were heading for Atlanta.

About twenty minutes later the van finally took one of the downtown exits. Traffic was becoming more heavy now and the streets of Atlanta were illuminated by bright overhead lights. She followed behind for a dozen blocks until the traffic thinned out. This area of town gave her the creeps. It was the seedy side of the big city, with lots of liquor shops and convenience stores with metal bars on the windows and trash strewn by the doorways.

The van pulled into an alleyway. Nell quickly found a parking space on the road close to it. There was a meter flashing red and she fed some of her tip money into it. She didn't know if they checked meters at night, probably not, but the last thing she wanted was to get her car towed and get stranded here. She opened her boot and pulled out the hoodie she kept for emergency breakdowns, when she might find herself stuck in the car without heating. Vanderbilt-U was emblazoned on the front.

She pulled the hood over her head and walked up the sidewalk towards the alley. She ignored the other people weaving across the street, many of whom were drunk or no doubt high, and concentrated on the passageway in front of her. When she arrived, she peeked around the corner and saw the van idling in the alley with exhaust smoke pluming out the back and its brake lights on.

She ducked behind a dumpster and crouched down. It had a paper sign attached to it that read 'Property of Little Bangkok restaurant'. The smell of cooking oil and old meat filled the air, turning Nell's stomach. But she held firm as she covertly observed the alley.

After a few minutes, someone came out of a corrugated metal door and stepped into the alley. Their face was illuminated as they lit a cigarette. Nell could see it was a muscular man with a shaved head and large spider's web tattoo on his face. He walked over to another door and pounded on it. The metallic thumping echoed through the alley.

"Time's up, hommie," he shouted.

There was silence for a minute and then the door opened with a loud creak. A short, bald man wearing glasses and a crumpled suit came out. He glanced nervously at the intimidating smoker and then scurried down the alley. He passed Nell without noticing her and scuttled away into the night.

Meanwhile, the stocky man had opened the door wide and stood in the doorway.

"Hurry yo' ass up, bitch," he said to someone inside. "You ain't made shit tonight."

Moments later, a woman walked out. She was tall, black with long curly hair. She wore a tight white halter top with denim shorts and very high heels.

"How many more till I get some, Vinnie?" She asked the man, her voice edged with desperation.

"Bitch, you still ain't worked off the last baggie. I ain't no fuckin' charity."

He grabbed her by the hair and shoved her in Nell's direction.

"Get your stank ass back out there. Hit up Cheshire Bridge."

She tottered off down the alley as the pimp took a long drag of his cigarette.

At the same time, Nell saw the side door of the van slide open silently. She watched as a pair of slender legs exited the vehicle. They were dressed in familiar dark jeans.

Nell held her breath as her heart began to beat faster in her chest.

The pimp had just now realized that there was a van stopped in his alley with the motor running. He started walking towards it, holding up a hand.

The figure in black slowly crept around the back of the vehicle. Nell could make out the feet in the gap under the van. Vinnie was oblivious. Nell's heart began hammering now. She could hear the blood whooshing in her ears.

"Yo, you looking for girls?" shouted the pimp. He came closer to the vehicle.

Nell never even saw Christopher strike. One second he was out of sight behind the van and the next he was on top of Vinnie, pinning him to the ground. It happened in a split second.

"What the fuck, man?" said the shocked pimp, looking up into Christopher's face.

Nell suddenly felt unsteady. She reached out and gripped a handle on the side of the dumpster to balance herself. It felt greasy to the touch, but she didn't spare a thought for what manner of filth might be smeared on it. Her attention was solely on the scene unfolding in front of her.

Vinnie tried to struggle free but Christopher held him firmly in place as if he were restraining a toddler.

"I don't got no money on me," pleaded Vinnie. "We stash it in the back."

The grimy alley was illuminated by bright streetlights. Nell could see everything perfectly.

Christopher leaned down.

Nell felt like her heart was about to burst out of her rib cage. She tightened her grip on the metal handle. A bead of sweat ran down from her forehead into an eye, making it sting. Yet she couldn't flinch away from the sight before her.

Christopher sank his teeth into the man's neck. Vinnie tried to struggle but to no avail. His movements became more and more labored as Christopher remained attached to him. Finally the pimp stopped moving altogether. Christopher stayed in position for several seconds and then pulled away.

The pimp was frozen. The same was true of Nell, who was rooted to the spot like a statue. Her eyes wide, barely taking in breath. Her frazzled brain finally came to the realization that the pimp was now either unconscious or dead.

She watched in utter disbelief as Christopher sprang to his feet and slung the big man over his shoulder as if he weighed no more than a bag of feathers. He approached the side door of the van and rapped on it with his knuckles. Someone inside slid the door open and Christopher deposited his prey inside. The van shook as the weighty body landed on the floor. Christopher looked around briefly before climbing in and shutting the door behind him.

With Christopher and his victim out of sight, Nell finally broke out of her stupefied state. She gulped for air as her body demanded oxygen. She closed her eyes and willed her heart to slow down. After taking a few ragged breaths she suddenly realized that the van would pass her as it exited the alley. She needed to disappear. Now. She crept backwards onto the road, but bumped into someone behind her.

She whipped around and saw a skinny black man with a scruffy white beard and torn overcoat.

"Hey honey, you after some feel-good fenty?" he asked with a crooked smile.

He noticed the logo on her hoodie.

"I can do you a students' discount," he added. "My stuff's top of the line."

With her heart in her throat and adrenaline coursing through her veins, Nell shook her head and pushed past him, walking quickly back towards her car.

"Mind yo manners, bitch," came the shout from behind her. "You ain't better-un-us."

Nell heard the van back out of the alley. She pulled her hood down low over her face. The van's engine roared and then began to fade as it drove past her into the Atlanta night.

Her hands were trembling so badly that she almost couldn't

get the key into the lock of her car. Finally, she got in and slammed the door shut, thumping down the 'LOCK ALL' button.

Every nerve in Nell's body was on fire. She felt nauseous. She had never in her life witnessed anything so horrifying. Her mind replayed what she had just seen. That was no role play. No one was taking part in some kind of horror re-enactment by a kooky sect. She recalled Christopher lifting the thickset pimp as if he weighed nothing. She then remembered his impossible leap over the wall earlier in the evening.

He wasn't pretending to be a vampire. He wasn't mentally ill, as she feared. That left only one explanation. Her heart thundered. Sweat ran down her face. She glanced in the rearview mirror and noticed tears were spilling from her eyes. They weren't tears of sadness. They were tears of sheer terror.

Chapter 11

When Nell awoke the next morning, her first thought was that last night had been an awful dream. A wave of sweet relief rushed over her. It had to be a dream. There was no such thing as vampires, and the quirky boy who played guitar at the diner where she worked had categorically not attacked a pimp in an Atlanta alleyway and taken his body away in a black van.

But as the hazy veil of sleep lifted, more and more details of the previous night began to coalesce in her mind. She realized with a jolt that it couldn't have been a nightmare. If it was, she would be losing details, not remembering more of them as the seconds ticked by.

It had been real enough. Her now fully awake mind couldn't argue with the fact. While she couldn't alter any of it, she did have the power to decide what to do next.

She certainly couldn't see Christopher again. He was darkness personified. An accursed undead creature. Should she start wearing a cross around her neck? Did that actually work? She tried to recall her research at the library, but drew a blank on the topic of crucifixes. She desperately thought back to what she had read. She had definitely seen in one of the books that consuming a dead person's blood would poison a vampire, but was it a myth or fact? And by 'fact', all that meant was an accepted concept in fictional lore. More to the point, how was she going to get hold of blood from a dead body? It was all so ridiculous, yet terrifying. She tried a different approach to rationalize her thoughts.

Perhaps she hadn't seen what she thought she did in the alley. Maybe Christopher was part of some kidnapping gang that targeted criminal networks, because they usually had large amounts of ill-gotten cash. Perhaps last night he was holding a syringe between his teeth to keep his hands free for restraining the victim. When he had bent over the man's neck, he could have quickly injected him with the fast-acting sedative. As for the seemingly superhuman jumping and lifting, perhaps Christopher was just really fit and pumped some serious iron at the gym. But when Nell considered all the other weird things about him, she knew she was simply deluding herself.

The thing was, she didn't want to believe that Christopher was evil. Nothing in how he had behaved with her had seemed malicious or malevolent. In fact, he had always been annoyingly prudish and straight-laced. But wasn't a dual personality the very definition of a psychopath? She couldn't unsee what she witnessed last night. And what she had witnessed was a cold-blooded killer in action. Even though the pimp didn't illicit a great deal of sympathy from her, murder was murder.

Nell stayed in bed for a long time. She felt safe here with the purifying daylight streaming through the window and the blankets wrapped around her. She knew her aunt was puttering around downstairs, probably cooking up something nice for breakfast. Maybe she could just stay in her room forever. That would be nice. But she had a job to go to and, the harsh truth was, Christopher could track her down any time he wanted. From what she had seen of his abilities, hiding was not an option, which left only one course of action.

Chapter 12

Christopher procured the final victim just before dawn. The mansion's large underground garage now housed four bodies, which lay in repose on the bare concrete floor. They would be kept in cold storage until the last of the current batch was fully drained. Then one of the new bodies would be thawed and prepared for the feeding.

When a vampire bites its victim, the prey becomes subdued very quickly due to a sedative in the transmitted venom. The delivery mechanism is via the lateral incisor tooth and not the canines (or fangs) as espoused in popular fiction. The venom acts on the cytoplasm inside the victim's cells and creates an 'incorruptible corpse' — flesh that will not suffer the decomposition or necrosis that affects a normal cadaver. The freezing helps to keep the blood fresh while the venom ensures that plasma and platelets do not degrade in storage.

The two operatives from the Council helped Christopher haul the bodies from the floor to the industrial freezer in an adjacent part of the cavernous garage complex. In a few days' time, when the large female body currently suspended unceremoniously above the hibernation chamber was fully exsanguinated, Christopher would have to climb the ladder and release the leather straps wrapped tightly around her swollen ankles. He took a moment to remind himself who the plump woman presently dangling upside down forty feet in the air was.

Her name was Wilma Anne Pruitt and she was a babysitter who, rather perversely, hated children. But she was also an accomplished manipulator who could easily win the trust of unsuspecting parents with her sweet and virtuous persona. While Wilma detested infants, she loved money. She earned a very healthy side income by selling illicit images of the little ones she should have been protecting on the dark web. When her 'clients' asked for videos rather than pictures, Wilma didn't hesitate to agree — for a very hefty price, of course. The money she could now earn from her side-hustle would eclipse her income as a babysitter. It was a no-brainer (for someone with the moral compass of Wilma). She bought a top-of-the-range Android phone to capture the highest quality video. She wanted to keep her customers happy and coming back for more. Wilma never got the chance to use the expensive Samsung handset. Christopher sealed her fate while it was still in the box.

Her obese body, so ruddy and flushed in life, was now almost completely white. The only red left was a bit of blush on her cheeks. She had been the last of the four from the previous month, but now there was a brand-new supply, and thus the cycle continued.

After completing the customary tasks of heaving the four bodies to the freezer and handing over a thick envelope stuffed with cash to Christopher, the two Council employees were ready to leave. They both gave Christopher a curt nod and headed for the van.

The driver suddenly turned back before pulling another

envelope from his inside pocket.

"I almost forgot. I was also told to give you this," he said.

He handed over the thin envelope.

"What is it?" asked Christopher,

"I was not made aware of the contents. Instructions, I'd assume," came the brusque reply.

"Thanks," said Christopher.

The driver left with his colleague.

Christopher thought about opening the letter, but he was exhausted after last night's culling. It could wait. Besides, the Council never did anything in a hurry. He needed rest. He stuffed the letter into a pocket of his jeans and made his way back to the main house, where he ascended the grand staircase.

The Red Claw mansion had a total of eight stately bedrooms, but the space Christopher had chosen for his retreat wasn't actually a room. Instead, it was the attic space. He had dragged a lumpy mattress up through the crawl space, along with a selection of books and a candle-lit lantern. He could have claimed any of the immense rooms in the house, but chose not to. This had been a family home before it had been taken over for its current purpose. Generations had lived, loved, slept and probably ended their days in these rooms. Christopher felt like an interloper. He thought he sullied the history and collective memory of the house.

The attic space was his domain, an area that hadn't been inhabited before, so he could claim it as his own without the burden of guilt. When he was staying at the colossal mansion, something he avoided as much as he could, this tiniest of spaces was his refuge.

Christopher sank down on the mattress and entered a

soporific trance. Vampires don't require sleep as such, but they do need infrequent periods of catalepsy to allow the body to replenish its vital force. Christopher had drained a little blood from each of the four victims he procured last night, so he had enough nourishment for the time being. However, it was the trance state that signaled to the undead flesh that now was the time to assimilate the nutrients in the ingested blood.

As the intricate corporeal process ran its course, Christopher's mind flashed back to Nell and he felt the familiar shuddering sensation that he associated with his rekindled emotions. His eyelids twitched involuntarily. His mind's eye pictured the four bodies strewn across the concrete floor of the garage earlier today. All of them deserved it, he reasoned. All of them had spent the precious gift of life hurting others around them and bringing misery and darkness to the world. He was doing the human race a favor. At least that's how Christopher justified it to himself. But, as he thought of Nell, he wondered what she would make of his line of work, on a philosophical level at least. Would she agree that the world was a better, safer place without them, or did she hold the view that redemption was always possible?

Christopher didn't know the answer, but he would soon have occasion to find out, because he wasn't going to be able to keep this a secret. It was either come clean or let Nell go. He wasn't prepared to do that. Let the cards fall where they may.

Chapter 13

Nell gathered her courage and walked up to the small house.

In the end, it hadn't taken very much prompting for her to leave the refuge of her bed that morning. She had succumbed to the siren scent that never failed to lure her out — the smell of frying bacon wafting into her room. She imagined it paired with a couple of eggs over easy, toast slathered with her aunt's homemade blueberry jam and a tall glass of fresh orange juice. She suddenly felt hungrier than she had ever been in her life. Who knew mortal terror was good for the appetite. She got up and padded downstairs in her pajamas, tying her hair back with an elastic band on the way.

The eggs were scrambled, but apart from that everything was perfect. Aunt Laura had also made fat sausages that spurted and crackled in the pan as well as fried mushrooms, which were freshly picked from her garden. Nell ate until she thought she might burst. Her aunt looked on, pleased that her niece was so enamored with her efforts. Nell gave her a warm hug of appreciation before helping to clean up the dishes.

She went back to her attic room and began pacing the floor. Was she actually contemplating following through on her plan? Willingly entering the lion's den, so to speak. Her thoughts were all over the place since the spine-chilling events of the previous evening. But one thing stood out as she walked back and forth on the well-worn carpet and considered her options over and over again. There was nowhere to run. Nowhere to hide. She was sure of that. After the resignation to the fact came the anger. Why the hell should she run and hide, anyway? She had finally found peace with her aunt, made a friend in Amara and had built a life here. Though it wasn't a particularly remarkable life, it was hers, and it meant something.

Now here she stood in front of the austere little house.

Nell straightened her posture and marched up the narrow concrete steps. She passed the unremarkable mail box and knocked on the plain wooden door. Then she held her breath.

There was no response from inside so she knocked again, this time with more force. A minute went by, then two. She leaned over to look through the window of the living room. Everything looked precisely the same as the last time she had been here. The red couch with the small tables at either end. The functional lamps perched atop each one. The unused coffee table. It seemed no one was home, if you could call this bare-bones house a home.

Nell descended the steps and wandered around the side of the property, but the windows were set too high up for her to see into. Frustrated, she came around the front and marched up the stairs again. She pounded on the door with the side of her fist then placed an ear up to the cold wood. She listened out for any sounds — the creak of stairs, the closing of a door, any noise that would betray the fact that someone was there. She heard nothing.

He wasn't home. But was this really his home? What about the massive property out past the cornfields? Could that sprawling estate possibly be his true residence? Well, Nell was going to find out. She had come to get answers. She thought back to the car journey last night when she had followed the van onto the dirt track. The roads had been dark, but Nell was sure she could retrace the way to the grand house. She turned around to go back to her car, a renewed purpose in her step.

Her heart nearly stopped in her chest. Her skin broke out in goose flesh. Standing at the end of the drive was Christopher, looking up at her with a grim expression.

"Nell," he said. "What are you doing here?"

She tried to speak, but the newly-formed lump in her throat prevented anything from coming out.

Finally, she was able to squeak out: "I need to talk to you."

He stared at her for a long moment.

"Let's go inside," he said.

He passed her on the steps and unlocked the front door.

The decision to follow him inside wasn't easy. Nell knew first-hand what he was capable of. Yet here she was, on the cusp of willingly entering his den. Her feet felt like they were encased in cement blocks. Her heart was racing. But she reminded herself that there was nowhere to hide. If he wanted to find her, she was certain he would.

She forced herself to move forward and followed Christopher inside. Once past the threshold, she headed straight for the red couch and sat down heavily, worried that her knees might give out. Christopher pulled a cheap-looking metal dining chair from the kitchen and sat opposite her. He interlaced his fingers on his lap and looked directly at her.

"Ask your questions, Nell," he said, gently.

Nell swallowed and took a breath. She had no idea how to

begin. But the minute she opened her mouth, words came out, and tact and subtlety flew straight out of the window.

"I know about you," she stated, matter-of-factly.

He studied her.

"And what is there to know?"

Nell could feel the weight of his stare. She tried to shift her gaze away, but the pull was too strong. She was locked onto his sharp eyes.

"You're a vampire, and I can hardly believe I just said that with a straight face."

Christopher said nothing. He just kept looking at her, calmly.

"I saw you. Last night," continued Nell, finding her voice. "I followed you into Atlanta and I witnessed you murder that man in the alley. I saw you drink his blood."

Christopher's stoic exterior cracked. He looked taken aback.

A long paused ensued. Finally, he spoke.

"Assuming that what you have said is true, what are you going to do about it?"

She wasn't expecting that reply. She had anticipated a range of responses from Christopher when she imagined having this conversation. She had expected him to flat-out deny it. She had expected him to express shock and outrage at being accused of being a dark creature of the night. She had expected him to laugh in her face. She had not expected to be put on the defensive herself.

"I don't know," she said, feeling a little stupid.

"Does it change how you feel about me?" Christopher asked.

"Duh," said Nell, actually flabbergasted. "What do you think?"

He looked pained. Nell could see despondency in his eyes.

It threw her, seeing such depth of emotion in Christopher. She could sense he was growing into his feelings, discovering, or perhaps the correct word was rediscovering, a fire that had dwindled into a mere flicker. To Nell, it was almost mesmerizing.

Christopher suddenly stood up and began pacing the room. The intangible connection between them was broken and Nell found herself taking several deep breaths. She wasn't entirely sure if she had inhaled the entire time their eyes were locked.

"For what it's worth," she added, trying to temper her previous antagonism. "I don't think you're evil. Like in evil for the sake of evil. That man you attacked, I know he wasn't exactly in line for humanitarian of the year."

Christopher ceased his tramping and sat down again.

"I will tell you everything, Nell," he said. "I am going to share with you what no one else knows. No one human, at least. But you must promise me you will maintain your silence. You told me once that keeping your word was important. I am going to hold you to that now."

"I think it's pretty unlikely I'll be sharing any of this," said Nell. "I'm not especially coveting a one-way ticket to the nut house."

She realized she was being unnecessarily caustic again.

"Ok, you have my word," she said, more evenly.

"It is true that I am a vampire," Christopher began. "I was turned about twenty years ago. I think you know by now that I have a range of abilities that aren't exactly normal, by human standards at least. I think you are also aware that I can hold mortals under a type of spell. Though this isn't always intended on my part."

Christopher reached across and took her hands. His fingers

were slightly cold, which wasn't unexpected.

"I had no choice last night," he almost pleaded. That impassive aloofness was totally gone now. "You have to believe that, Nell."

She said nothing, but didn't retract her hands, either.

"I have been tasked with overseeing a Family of vampires by the ruling body of our kind," he continued. "They have been placed into a type of hibernation because they are too vicious for this world. I am responsible for feeding them, primarily. You've seen for yourself how that is achieved."

He looked down, then squeezed her hands, before meeting her eyes once more.

"However, I do not kill innocents. The pr…victims…are carefully chosen. I would never just take a random life. These are bad people, who have done bad things, and they will keep on doing bad things, unless they are stopped."

"By you," exclaimed Nell. "But what gives you the right to act as judge and executioner?"

Christopher sighed heavily before continuing.

"If I don't…perform this duty…then someone else will be recruited to do so. From what I know of my kind, it's probably unlikely they will have the same qualms over who is sacrificed."

Nell thought about the horrid man in the Atlanta alley and weighed it against all she knew (and felt intuitively) about Christopher. She looked up into his face. He looked almost broken.

"This is way beyond my pay grade," she said. "An avenging angel of the night who has to feed a horde of ruthless bloodsuckers. You couldn't even make this up. It's going to take a while for this to sink in."

They were both silent for a long moment.

Nell recalled her impromptu vampire research in the library.

"So garlic, crosses and sunlight. You can't stand them?"

Christopher smiled faintly.

"Folklore," he stated. "Myths and wishful thinking from a frightened populous in the late middle ages. And before you ask..."

He walked over to the fireplace before waving at the round mirror hanging just above it. His reflection waved back at him enthusiastically.

"When something isn't understood, superstition is quick to fill the void," he said. "It brings comfort in an uncertain world and allows mothers to sooth their children at night."

"But you are immortal?" asked Nell.

"True," he said.

"So you're immune to death?"

"Not quite," he answered. "Sever the head from the body or drain the blood and we cannot live."

More silence filled the room.

Nell then asked the question that had been nagging at her ever since she had learnt of his true nature.

"You said you had feelings for me, but how can that be? I thought your kind had no feelings, especially for humans. Aren't we just mobile protein shakes to you?"

Christopher reached out and placed his hands on her shoulders, pulling her in slightly. Nell was a little taken aback by the move.

"That is something that I cannot answer, Nell," he said, fixing her with a solemn look.

It intrigued her to witness the range of emotions he was now able to muster.

"It eludes and confounds me," he continued. "For two

decades I have felt nothing. No guilt, no shame, no hate, no envy, no greed, no love, no lust. I simply just was. But lately, especially after I met you, things are coming to the surface. I am at a loss to explain it. But I believe you are the catalyst."

The first thing Nell thought was that this had to be a line. It was so ridiculous, so completely outlandish, not to mention cringeworthy, that it couldn't be real. But then something sparked in her memory. She recalled reading a throwaway passage in one of the books on vampire lore she had skimmed at the library.

"I might possibly be able to shed some light on that," she ventured, instinctively moving closer to him.

Christopher stared at her, incredulous.

"Really? How so?"

Nell held up a hand, as if to defend herself.

"Look, it's probably nothing. Just a line or two in a kooky book about prophecies and folklore, not the most reliable source of information. It was about a vampire who was turned against his will who would go on to cleanse the world, or something equally melodramatic. I remember it involved him slowly returning to human form, experiencing raw emotion again and whatnot."

Christopher was silent.

"Were you turned against your will?" Nell inquired.

He remained quiet.

"I'm just trying to help," she said, holding her hands up. "Don't shoot…"

"Are you sure that's all there was?" Christopher interjected. "You cannot remember anything else?"

"No, there was barely anything there. It was one small entry among a whole list of supposed revelations and foretellings. I had been reading a bunch of books and my brain was pretty frazzled by that point. You said yourself that there's a lot of nonsense out there about...your kind."

Christopher's face was the most animated she had ever seen it. He had an eager expression. He squeezed her shoulders.

"This might be significant, Nell. Can you find out more?"

She took a breath.

"I don't see how. I would need books a lot older and more detailed than the one in Henry Freeman Memorial. That was literally all the information they had."

Christopher contemplated, then came to a decision.

"I can get you access to a library, an ancient one filled with volumes on the preternatural," he said.

Nell's interest was piqued, but she hesitated.

"And why exactly should I help you?" she said. "We've just established you're a murderous vampire. It's not the kind of revelation that generally elicits a great deal of sympathy."

Christopher placed his hands on her knees and gently pressed. Nell thought she could get used to this tactile side of Christopher.

"There's absolutely no reason," he admitted. "All I can say is this is important to me, Nell. I feel something is happening and it's bigger than me. I need to know what and, more importantly, why. I need you. We *must* try. Even if we are just clutching at straws. You said you followed me yesterday. Did you make it to the nest?"

"Nest? I passed a lot of trees, which nest in particular?"

"Sorry, I'm not being clear," said Christopher. "The big house, it's where the Red Claws are located."

"Erm yes, I know the one," she admitted, a little sheepishly.

"Good. Can you meet me there tomorrow, in the afternoon?"

Nell shook her head.

"I have to work tomorrow, Sundays are busy for us." She hesitated before adding: "But I can come either before or after my shift."

"It is better you come before," he replied, visibly relieved. "It's not wise to be out in the dark."

Nell threw her hands up in the air.

"Great," she said, exasperated. "Now I get to hear it from a bona fide vampire!"

Christopher gave her a quizzical look.

"Never mind," she said, resigned. "This is probably the dumbest thing I've done in my life, and I bought the Baywatch 9-series box set — at full retail price, but I'll be there. I can't resist a mystery, or a library."

Chapter 14

The next day Nell awoke feeling lighter than she had the previous morning. While it was now beyond doubt that Christopher was a vampire, and the fact still astounded her, two things gave her some comfort. One, she herself was not in any mortal danger from him. As selfish as that sounded, self-preservation was an innate instinct. And two, he was not a merciless killer who preyed on innocent people. While his justification for terminating morally repugnant individuals was still sketchy in her mind, he at least showed he was operating with a conscience.

Moreover, the mystery of what was happening to him and why was not only intriguing, it was irresistible. As she had told Amara previously, Nell had to scratch the itch of curiosity when it arose. Her mind couldn't leave things dangling. It was just the way she was hard-wired.

Christopher had also confirmed that he had feelings for her. At the risk of coming across like a first-grader with a crush, that fact still warmed her. Deep down, everyone wanted to be wanted, she reasoned. When she had discovered he was a vampire, she had assumed his so-called feelings were just a ruse to hide his true agenda, which probably involved his teeth, her neck and a delectable cocktail of warm blood. But now, she was sure his feelings were genuine. She saw the pain in his eyes when he thought he was being rejected. However, what kind of future could they possibly have? That was a question for another time.

Nell sprang out of bed and got herself ready, kissing her aunt on the cheek on the way out of the house. In the light of day, the mansion was fairly easy to find. She just had to ensure she didn't miss the turning for the narrow dirt track that led up to the grand house. As she approached the tall metal gates, they glided open slowly. She figured Christopher must have been watching the security cameras. At this close proximity she still couldn't hear the motor mechanism that was moving the heavy iron barriers. Perhaps it was a silent technology.

As she drove up the gravel drive and approached the entrance to the property, Christopher came out to meet her.

"Welcome," he said, as she got out of her car. "I thought you might run for the hills after yesterday."

"I can't say it didn't cross my mind," she said. "Would it have done me any good?"

She studied his face.

"I'm glad you are here," was his only reply as he reached out and hugged her.

Inside, the house was just as magnificent as it appeared from the exterior. It had a classic, almost medieval styling with plush furniture and rich carpets. Though there were plenty of signs of wear and tear if you looked closer. She had no idea how many rooms it contained, but she passed at least six on the ground floor spread along a wide corridor as they made their way to the library.

They descended a set of stone steps at the end of the passageway. This took them to a smaller corridor. The walls here were also stone with what looked like gems inset in the masonry. They glimmered as Nell walked past. The walls were cool to the touch as she put her fingertips on the stone and trailed them along the passage. Finally, they came to a set of large dark wooden doors. Christopher grasped the handles on either side and opened them.

Nell's breath caught in her chest. She looked out on a colossal library with shelves that seemed to go on and on. The library must have been the height of the entire house. Huge wooden ladders on horizontal rails lined every shelf. She craned her neck up to take in the sheer scale of the room. She couldn't even begin to fathom the number of books that were here. A giant oak table stood regally in the center of the room, surrounded by twelve lavish leather armchairs.

"Wow," Nell breathed. "This place is incredible."

"The Red Claw Family is one of the oldest in existence," Christopher said. "While it spawned butchers and conquerors, it appears the Family also had scholars. They have been building this collection for hundreds of years. It's their collective knowledge and ancestry."

"There are tens of thousands of books here," Nell said. "Probably more. How do I pin down one specific prophecy? I don't even know where to start."

Christopher looked at her and shrugged.

"I don't know, Nell. I have never used this library."

Nell took a step forward. She took a deep breath as she scanned the rows and rows of volumes. She then turned to Christopher.

"I can't do this alone. I have to call someone for help," she said.

His face instantly dropped. She could see the apprehension

in his eyes.

"You don't understand," he said. "No one else can know. Even you are not supposed to be privy to our existence, let alone be standing where you are right...."

"She already knows," Nell interrupted.

His mouth dropped open.

"Well not knows outright," she clarified. "But she was the one who first brought it up. I told her your...symptoms, thinking that it was some kind of disease. She was the one who suggested that you were a... well... you know."

Christopher frowned.

"You cannot say it. Do I disgust you that much?"

"No!" Nell said. She moved closer to him. "It just...takes some getting used to...you have to concede that much, Mr Vampire."

She kissed him on the cheek. His face softened.

"Besides," she added, gesturing around her. "I have no chance of finding anything on this prophecy without her help. The person I have in mind is an expert on organizing and filing books. It's her job."

"And you trust her?" asked Christopher, looking troubled.

Nell thought about all the selfless things Amara had done for her.

"Probably with my life," she replied.

Christopher sighed deeply.

"Bringing someone else in could put them in danger."

Nell raised her eyebrows.

"You never said I was in danger!" she shot back.

"I won't let anything happen to you, Nell. You have my word," he reassured. "But this endeavor is not without its risks. You need to understand this, and so does your associate, before any decision is made."

"I understand," Nell replied.

"Good," Christopher said, looking troubled and now also looking drained.

Things were moving fast and in unexpected ways. Lately he hadn't been feeding as regularly as he normally did. The events and new emotions surrounding Nell had disrupted his pattern. But fatigue now suddenly caught up with him. He felt unsteady on his feet and swayed a little.

Alarmed, Nell grabbed him and wrapped her arms around his torso.

"Christopher," she breathed, searching his face.

Christopher berated himself for not feeding before Nell arrived. How stupid could he be? He had to take better care of himself.

"My energy is low," he said, resigned. "I need to feed. I'll be back with you in just a few minutes."

"I want to see," said Nell, without missing a beat. She hugged him tighter.

"What?" He shook his head. "No, absolutely not. You don't want to see me feed. I can't have you thinking of me as... as..."

"As a vampire?" she said.

"As a monster," he replied.

She placed a hand against his chest.

"I want to know who you really are, not just the kooky guitar guy," she said. "Or there's not really a future for us." She could feel his body, taught and firm. "Also if, as you say, I'm potentially putting myself in danger by helping you, then don't I deserve at least that much?"

Christopher sighed. Things were spiraling out of his comfort zone and it unnerved him. But he didn't have a convincing argument, especially as she was going out of her way to help him.

Nell followed him back upstairs to the long corridor. About halfway down he opened a set of doors. For the second time that day, Nell's breath caught in her chest.

In front of her was an expansive atrium with a grand set of stairs set just behind it. In the center was a stainless-steel machine with dozens of tubes sprouting from it. Each tube went into a stone casket that contained a body wrapped in some kind of shroud. A thicker tube sprouted from the top of the strange device. Nell followed it upwards. Her hand automatically flew up to her mouth. Suspended upside down just below the ceiling was the naked body of a heavyset woman. Thick leather straps were wrapped around her broad ankles. Her skin was almost pure white. She was obviously dead.

"You were not meant to see this," said Christopher, almost apologetically.

"That woman," Nell said, averting her gaze from the bloated corpse. "Tell me she really…"

"She did," Christopher finished for her. "She really deserved it. The world, and many of its children, are better for it."

Nell left it at that. She didn't want to know the details.

Christopher approached the metal machine, which let out a steady low hum.

"The blood is treated with an anticoagulant," Christopher explained. "That way, it can be dispensed over an extended period of time."

"What did they do?" Nell asked, her voice cracking a little as she looked out over the scores of stone boxes spread across the wide expanse.

"They could not control their bloodlust, and this put all our kind in peril," Christopher said. "I have only been a caretaker for twenty years, but they have been asleep for far longer."

"And do you feed on… well…" She gestured upwards without looking.

In answer, Christopher walked over to a wall and picked up a length of clear tube that was resting on a shelf.

"You said you wanted to see," he said, with a wry smile.

She wasn't so sure now.

He attached the tube to a nub on the machine and then opened a small valve. The tube slowly turned crimson as blood flowed along its length. She watched Christopher place the end in his mouth, his Adam's apple bobbing as he drank. When he was satiated he turned the valve off before removing the tube from his mouth. He staggered slightly, as if he had just drunk too much alcohol. Nell went to him and offered a shoulder.

"It's okay, just the initial rush," he said. "So, are you well and truly disgusted now?"

"Well yeah, a little," she replied, candidly.

Just then the machine made a loud grating sound as if cogs inside were jamming. The harsh noise reverberated around the wide expanse of the atrium. Nell looked alarmed.

"It's okay," said Christopher, placing a hand on her back. "It does that from time to time. The mechanism needs flushing out." He tilted his head up in exasperation. "But in the name of the Omni-Father, why did it have to happen now?"

"Can you fix it?" asked Nell.

"Yes," replied Christopher, his brow creased. "But it might take a while, and time is not on our side. You need to be out of here as quickly as possible."

He glanced back at the machine, looking more perturbed

than ever.

"Okay," he said, having come to a decision. "Call your friend if it will make researching the prophecy quicker. Make a start in the library and I'll join you as soon as I'm done here."

He leaned in and embraced Nell tightly. She hugged him back, reveling in the sturdiness of his body and firm grip of his hands on her back.

"Thank you again for helping me," he said. "It means everything."

"Do what you need to do here," replied Nell. "Then come back to me."

"There's nowhere I want to be more," he said.

He reached up a hand and tenderly caressed her face before releasing her from his grip and walking over to the machine.

Nell quickly made her way back out of the atrium. She sat heavily on a thickly cushioned green chair in the corridor and contemplated. Should she really involve Amara in this? Was she finally asking too much of her friend? Christopher had said that it might be dangerous, but they only needed to locate a book or two. How dangerous could that be? The catatonic Red Claws weren't a threat, since they had been asleep for at least twenty years. Amara had told Nell to call on her for anything she needed. In fact, she even said she would be disappointed if Nell didn't.

Before she had time to second-guess herself, Nell whipped out her phone, went to her recent call list and tapped on Amara's name. She pressed the phone to her ear. Amara answered on the third ring.

"Hey Nell, nice to hear from you, everything okay?"

"I'm fine," replied Nell. "But, and I have no right to ask this of you yet again, I have a favor to request."

"That's what Sorceress Sisters are for, remember," said Amara, with a smile in her voice. "Anything I can do for you, I'd be glad to."

"Okay," said Nell, taking a sharp intake of breath. "So, you remember that guy. The, um, weirdo from the diner I told you about."

"Count Chocula," Amara said. "The mind-bending, calorie-dodging, guitar whiz who's hot, and cold at the same time. How could I forget?"

"Yes, that's the one," said Nell, dryly.

"What about him? He hasn't hurt you, has he?"

"No, no, nothing like that," said Nell. "Look, this is going to be hard to believe..." She gripped the phone tighter. "I mean... unless you were there...and saw what I saw... well...then..."

"You sure everything's okay, Nell?"

"Yes, yes, sorry, I'm rambling now...the favor. I need you to help me find a book or books. In a library. But not your one, lovely though it is. This is a secret library...in a big house."

"Secret library?"

"Yes, only he said it might be dangerous, but I'm not quite sure how."

"I'm a little worried about you, Nell," came the reply. "Text me your address and I'll be right there."

Nell didn't know the address so she had to give directions instead. Then she went out of the front entrance and stood on the gravel. She had time to think in the fresh air as she awaited Amara's arrival. Nell had told her friend nothing that made any sense, just spouted gibberish. Amara was probably concerned for her mental health at this point, which would be understandable.

About twenty-five minutes later, Amara showed up in her

little Mini. She entered through the gates, got out of her car and walked up to Nell, giving her a hug.

"Wow, big house is kind of an understatement. I had no idea this was here," said the librarian.

"You should see the inside," said Nell.

Amara studied her face, looking concerned.

"So, what's this about, Nell? You mentioned the guy?"

"You're never going to believe me," Nell said. "I've seen the proof and I'm still having a hard time accepting it."

"Try me."

"Okay…so the guy…Christopher Deverell to be precise… well…he's not pretending to be a vampire. He actually *is* a vampire."

She looked at Amara for a reaction. She was expecting her to laugh or perhaps look up the number for the nearest mental institution. She did none of those things.

"You believe me?" asked Nell, not convinced.

"I believe that you believe it," replied the librarian, sympathetically.

"Fair enough," said Nell. "But there's more."

She filled Amara in on the details of her courtship with Christopher and the prophecy she had read about in Henry Freeman. She described the ancient library, the Red Claws and that fateful night in downtown Atlanta. The words spilled out of her. It was actually a relief to tell someone else, to organize her jumble of thoughts in coherent sentences. It seemed to give the impossible a tangible logic that could ground it in reality.

Amara weighed Nell's words.

"I've lived in Angel Falls for a while now," said the librarian. "That experience forces you to keep an open mind. Things are just a little off-kilter here, that's why I wanted to look out for you."

"I know it's a lot to take in at once," said Nell. "I can still hardly believe any of it...and that's after seeing it for myself."

"This town has been plagued by some weird shit," said Amara. "I don't think you went as far back as a hundred years when you did your research at the library."

Nell shook her head.

"If you did, you would have seen that scores of people were found with the blood drained from their bodies and puncture wounds on their flesh. Back then, it was assumed that the victims were snatched by kidnappers looking to make a buck. There was an underground trade in blood at the time. Unlicensed doctors and some less-than-scrupulous hospitals needed it for transfusions, and didn't ask questions. They didn't have the tracking or screening we do now."

"The Red Claws," said Nell, as if it was beyond doubt.

"I think we might be getting ahead of ourselves," said Amara. "Let's start with the library, that's the one thing that I can get a handle on."

Nell led her inside, skipping over the atrium with the drained body hanging from its ankles. Too much, too soon, she reasoned. They reached the end of the stone passageway and Nell threw open the wooden doors.

"Oh...My...God," said Amara, visibly stunned. "I think I'm in heaven."

Amara walked along the shelves, running her fingers across the spines of the books. She climbed some of the ladders and studied the volumes on the higher shelves. Then she ascended even higher, taking a bird's-eye view of the whole cavernous room. Nell sat and watched from the ornate table in the center.

She had no idea where to even begin looking for the prophecy section. There were no handy signs hanging over the various areas, no computer terminal and no card catalog. She was pretty sure vampires didn't use the Dewey Decimal system.

But Amara seemed to be listening to an inner voice. She would look at a shelf and within a few seconds be climbing up or down to move on to a different section. She kicked off her shoes and began traversing the wooden ladders in her yellow socks. Some sections she skipped altogether, some she crawled along slowly as if each title needed to be examined in detail. There seemed to be no consistency to her method.

"Any progress?" called out Nell. "Let me know if I can help. I feel like a bit of lemon just sitting here."

Amara shimmied down a ladder and came over to Nell.

"This is incredible," she said, breathless and wide-eyed.

"That it is," said Nell, with a smile, feeding off Amara's enthusiasm.

"These books...they're hundreds of years old," said the librarian. "No one's ever had access to these. I'm sure they don't exist in any other library or collection. In fact, I think each one might be completely unique. They're also in mint condition because most of them have never been touched."

"Most of the Red Claws aren't the bookish type, from what I've heard," said Nell. "They're more into bleeding than reading."

Amara smiled.

"What about the prophecy of the chosen son who would emancipate the world," said Nell. "Are we any closer to learning more about that?"

"Not yet, but I'll get there," said Amara, determinedly. "The library uses an archaic filing system. For my postgraduate degree in librarianship I wrote a paper on esoteric classifications used at the world's oldest libraries — The House of Wisdom in Baghdad, The Imperial Library of Constantinople, The Villa of the Papyri and The Library of Ashurbanipal."

"That's kinda inside baseball," said Nell, laughing.

"Sorry, this is my passion. Once you get me started..."

"You don't have to apologize," said Nell. "I'm glad this is not complete drudgery for you."

"A lot of the books are in an older form of Romanian," continued Amara. "Some of them are in English. There's also German and other earlier languages, such as Aramaic, Hebrew, Sanskrit and Egyptian. But I think I have the lay of the land when it comes to the various areas of the library."

Nell felt relieved. She let Amara continue scaling ladders and studying the vast array of books. Nell felt she couldn't just sit there being useless, so she started thumbing through the titles on the shelves just behind her. After another hour had passed, she began to get a little concerned. She stood at the bottom of a ladder and looked up as Amara rifled through a selection of titles above her.

"Have you found anything?"

"You know," Amara said. "It's strange. The books are all filed so fastidiously, but there seem to be some titles missing, which is odd when everything else is so precise." She looked down at Nell. "See this section at about the height of my hips?"

Nell nodded from below.

"These are the books on prophecies and predictions, but nothing matches what you described to me earlier — the chosen vampire who would revert back to human form. Also, there are titles absent from the sequence of books."

Nell scaled up the ladder and stood beside Amara, who

began pulling books off the shelf. Nell read some of the titles: *Sanguisuge Ephemeris, Ex-lamia Hemerologies, Dascalu Prognosticate Vampiri.* Amara suddenly narrowed her eyes and began to push books aside. She dug into the back of the shelf with an arm and slowly dragged something out. It was a small book. Amara held it up to look at the title, but there were no words on the outside, just a completely black cover. Amara flicked through the pages.

"It's in old English," she said. "It has to be a few hundred years old, judging by the typography and paper stock."

"Why was it stuffed behind the other books?" asked Nell.

"No idea. But there's a note in here," Amara said.

She had stopped in the middle of the book. Between the open pages was a folded piece of parchment. Amara put down the book and unfolded it carefully. She frowned.

"It's hand-written in a baroque script, but I think this is old Romanian."

"Is there any way to read it?" Nell asked.

"Maybe," Amara said.

She took out her phone and tapped on an app. She hovered the camera lens over the first few words and then began scanning across the text. After she was done she began tapping icons on the app.

"The translation algorithm can only recognize some of the words," said Amara. "Probably because it's an outdated language and the script is too ornate. I think it's got the gist of it, though. It talks about a son speaking to his father – he calls him Lucianu. It says something about tracking down every copy except this one, and destroying them, and also destroying the owners. Kinda grisly."

"I read the name Lucianu," said Nell, eagerly. "Downstairs,

when I was going through some books." She pointed down to the area behind the table.

"That's the genealogy section," Amara said.

Nell led Amara down to where she had been, then ran her finger over the spines of the books.

"Yes, here it is," she said, hastily retracting a book. She thumbed it open, scanning the pages. She got to the page she was looking for then handed the book to Amara, who read intently.

"It says that Lucianu was the *Progentrius* of the Red Claws," said Amara. "I think that's an antiquated form of 'progenitor' in modern language, which means original one. The source. Whoever destroyed all the other copies of the book, they must've done it because there was something in it that threatened the Family."

Amara looked down at the plain black book in Nell's hands.

"We need to have a closer look at that," she said. "I think it might just hold the key."

Chapter 15

Loris Valkari, ancient vampire and Warden of the South, along with the Council of Elders had almost arrived at the grand estate. They had traveled via private plane to Atlanta and then taken two blacked-out people carriers into Angel Falls. Loris had given the address to the Council drivers and they were now traveling along a narrow dirt track. Loris looked around at the Elders, who were all sitting silently with their hands in their laps.

"Have you made your decision yet?" he asked.

They were silent and impassive. Just when Loris concluded they were not going to answer him, the Speaker leaned forward.

"We have decided. The High Chancellor has spoken," said Dragos Vacarescu.

Loris waited. He wasn't going to push it. The Council would either tell him or not.

"The Family shall have another chance to exist under our laws," said Dragos.

Loris nodded, respectfully.

"I take that to mean you are planning on waking them today," he said.

"We are allowing them to awaken," the Speaker replied.

"There is a difference."

Loris sat back against the luxurious leather seat of the car. If the Council allowed the Red Claws back into this world, his territory could be in chaos very soon. Yet he could not question the Council's wisdom which, in truth, he saw very little evidence of.

They finally arrived at the mansion. Loris got out of the car and stretched, looking around. There were two cars parked ahead of them in the driveway. What was the caretaker up to? Why buy two dismal cars when you could buy one decent one. He was paid a small fortune every month and these pathetic vehicles were all he saw fit to purchase? On the back of the smaller vehicle were two bumper stickers, he noticed. One showed a pile of books with the words 'Check Me Out' next to them, the other read 'Support Your Local library'. Loris was unnerved.

The six members of the Council of Elders got out behind him. From the other vehicle emerged four bodyguards. The group moved towards the mansion door. But as they approached it, they knew something was wrong. It was in the very air.

"There are humans here," spat the Speaker. "At least two scents."

The bodyguards hurried ahead, sniffing at the door. One of them kicked it open.

"They came through here," he said, then inhaled deeply. "They are still in the house."

"Find them," the Speaker commanded. "Immediately."

Chapter 16

Nell and Amara stared open-mouthed at Christopher, who had just burst into the library. He looked at them with wild eyes, panic etched on his face.

"They know you are here," he screamed. "Come on, you have to run. NOW."

Both women remained rooted to the spot, seemingly unable to process what was going on.

"It's the Council of Elders, along with the one who turned me," explained Christopher, breathlessly. "They have body-guards. They know you are here. We don't have time to waste."

Nell quickly folded up the parchment and placed it back inside the small black book. Amara raced to collect her shoes. They met Christopher at the door.

Quietly as possible, he led them back along the stone passageway and up the stairs to the lavish hallway. He then ushered them through another door close by.

They found themselves in a large kitchen with dark wooden work surfaces and stainless steel utility areas. It looked disused. They followed Christopher to the very back, where a large hearth stood. Christopher ducked down and entered the granite enclosure. He struggled with what appeared to be one of the large stones at the back. As the boulder slowly rolled away, a gap appeared behind.

"Through here," Christopher guided, urgently.

Nell and Amara pushed past him into the dark passage beyond, before Christopher joined them. He grabbed the stone from the other side and laboriously rolled it back in place. The tunnel was pitch black and smelled like damp and decay.

Amara turned on her phone's torch light, illuminating the three of them in ghostly shadows.

Nell looked anxious, her eyes furtively scanning the surroundings, while Christopher had a determined look on his face.

"I don't think they know about this route," he whispered. "I only discovered it by accident. Hopefully, it will weaken your scent. But we must get some distance between us. Let's go."

They had to walk in single file while ducking low to avoid bumping their heads. At one point when the tunnel narrowed Christopher placed a protective hand on Nell's head to shield her from the hard stone above. Amara slapped at her face a few times as cobwebs brushed her skin. They moved as fast as they could down the tunnel. Every once in a while, Christopher would cock his head and listen. Nell knew he had enhanced hearing.

"Do you sense anything?" she asked, concern etched on her face.

"No," he replied, looking relieved. "They haven't found the tunnel…yet. Did you find anything back there?"

"We think so," said Nell, holding up the book.

"We found a note in this book. It might be significant."

She glanced at Amara and couldn't help but smile, despite their grim predicament.

"This is my friend, Amara. It was thanks to her. I told you she was the best."

The abashed librarian gave a nod to Christopher.

"Hello Amara," said Christopher. "I'm truly grateful for your assistance, and sorry we had to meet in such circumstances."

"It's okay," said Amara, appearing surprisingly calm. "I usually get my adventures through books, so it makes a change to live one for real."

Nell saw Amara give Christopher a sidelong glance in the harsh glow of the phone light.

"So, you're like really…erm…"

"Yes," said Christopher, resigned. "Really."

"What is this Council and why are they here?" asked Nell.

"They're the governing body of our kind," Christopher explained. "As to why they are here, I have no idea. I didn't receive any warn…"

He stopped suddenly, his expression looked pained.

"Shit," he exclaimed.

He padded the pockets of his black jeans then retrieved the envelope. He ripped it open and hastily took out the note, which he began reading intently. Amara moved the light closer to him to better illuminate the writing.

Christopher read silently for a moment and then turned back to Nell and Amara. His mouth hung open and his eyes were wide. Nell thought his face seemed even paler than usual.

"This is bad. Very bad," he said, staring back at the letter. "The Red Claws are going to be awakened. I was meant to prepare for the Council's arrival today. But I forgot I even had this letter."

"Hold on a minute," Nell said, her brow furrowing. "You implied that would be bad, right? Like epically bad? The

Family couldn't control their bloodlust, I think were your exact words."

Christopher nodded, grimly.

"From what I have been led to believe, if the Red Claw Family is allowed to awaken they will most likely destroy this town, and probably the entire region," he said. "They will feed on humans without care or caution and likely attract every Hunter within a three-hundred-mile radius. Both vampires and humans will pay a heavy price for their freedom."

"My aunt," said Nell, stricken.

Her face seemed to collapse and her eyes were moist.

Christopher instinctively reached out and scooped her into a protective hug. A long silence ensued, before Christopher broke it.

"Let's deal with the immediate problem for now," he urged. "From what you've told me, your aunt is quite isolated, removed from other people. That works in her favor. We are right at the epicenter. We need to get away from here."

He led them down the tunnel until they reached an iron gate. Sunlight filtered in through the lattice pattern. Christopher stepped forward and pulled the latch. The gate swung inward with a groan of protest.

One by one, they exited the tunnel and entered the thick canopy of trees beyond. They were in the lush forest behind the mansion. Nell had seen it off in the distance when she arrived at the house, but she hadn't paid much attention at the time.

"Now what's the plan?" asked Amara, blinking in the bright sunlight after the darkness of the tunnel.

"I say we creep around to the front of the house and make off in our cars," suggested Nell. "It's the quickest way to put some distance between us and the Council."

"Not wise," said Christopher, his face set. "They'll have your scent by now, so creeping around out of sight isn't going to hide you. Besides, double-backing is the obvious ploy. They will have a guard patrolling the front."

"So let's stay hidden here in the forest and wait them out," suggested Amara, looking behind her at the dense mass of tall trees and thick foliage that stretched further than the eye could see. "They're here for a purpose, right. When their work is done and they leave, we can jump in the cars."

"I don't think you understand the magnitude of the situation, Amara," Christopher said. "They are awakening the Red Claw Family, possibly right now as we speak. There are over one hundred of them. They will be hungry and eager for the hunt. It's likely they will spread out in every direction, leaving destruction in their wake. I doubt the Council will show you much mercy. But with the Red Claws, there's no doubt at all."

A flock of birds suddenly cawed and fluttered away from nearby trees, making them all jump.

"So what do we do then?" Nell asked, panic rising in her voice.

"Hopefully, it will take them some time to rouse the Family," Christopher said. "The rest of the night at least, I'd anticipate. We have to ideally make it outside of town by then, or at the very least find a good place to hide, away from the general populace."

"So we head east through the forest back onto the high road?" asked Nell.

"It's either that or we risk getting lost in the woods," Amara said. "The forest stretches pretty far." She looked at her phone. "I have no signal here. How about you?"

Nell took out her handset. The signal strength bars were all light gray. She shook her head.

"Christopher, this is your home, sort of. What's the best route away from here?" asked Nell.

"I have to admit," Christopher said, a little embarrassed. "My job as caretaker has made me rather spoiled. I no longer have to hunt. I haven't explored the area surrounding the mansion."

"Well," Amara said, drumming her fingers on her thigh. "Running or hiding both involve putting distance between us and the mansion. So let's get go..."

Before she could finish her sentence, a giant shape burst out of the woods. It hurtled straight towards Christopher and knocked him off his feet. He was now just a rolling shape, like his attacker. As they finally came to a stop, Nell saw with horror that Christopher's assailant was at least 10-feet tall and covered in thick brown fur. It had long limbs and stooped forwards as it circled Christopher, who shot to his feet, looking stunned.

Nell instantly knew that it was the thing she had seen in the shadows near the diner. The shape was identical. So she hadn't been seeing things, after all. Now that it was out in the light, Nell could see that the giant hulking creature had the head of a wolf, with sharp yellow eyes. The arms were so long that they nearly dragged on the ground, with razor-sharp claws on the ends of the fingers. The muscles on its thick haunches flexed as it stalked Christopher. They began circling each other.

"Get out of here, Nell," Christopher shouted, desperately, glancing between her and the beast. "Take Amara and go."

"Don't trust him," the enormous creature said, in a deep sonorous voice, which Nell found that she almost recognized.

"Don't listen to a word of it. He's a vampire," it added.

Nell stood rooted to the spot in shock. Amara looked on, wide-eyed.

Realizing the two women weren't moving, Christopher launched himself at the creature. He was lightning quick and flew high through the air, defying gravity. He grabbed the giant beast's throat and began to squeeze.

The beast jerked its long arms around and slashed with its sharp claws at Christopher's back. Jagged lines appeared in Christopher's shirt, showing pale flesh underneath that was split into ugly dark red gashes.

"Christopher!" Nell called out, fear lacing her voice.

The creature turned to Nell. It seemed momentarily confused as it registered her alarm and concern for Christopher. It then pulled away from the injured vampire and began to transform. The thick fur started to recede. The head grew smaller and the wolf-like features softened. It shrank in stature and the long limbs began to retract to more human proportions. The claws that had been razor-sharp became fingers. The haunches and large paws planted on the ground became legs and feet. It was now completely human in flesh, with olive colored skin and dark straight hair.

Nell was dumbfounded as she stared at a naked Devan.

"Oh...My...God," Amara said, for the second time that day. "Sorry for doubting you before, Nell. You can safely say I'm a believer now."

Nell stared at Devan, standing in his birthday suit before her. She had allowed vampires into her worldview just recently, but she never imagined other creatures existed. As a result, she was having a hard time convincing herself that what she was seeing was real.

"What's going on?" Nell asked, quietly, almost to herself. "I don't understand what's happening."

"Well," Amara said. "Your boyfriend appears to be an authentic, card-carrying vampire and your other…erm friend… or whoever he is, appears to be a lycanthrope, to give it the correct name."

Trust Amara to sum up the facts so bluntly. But Nell's attention was distracted by the fact that Devan and Christopher were squaring up to each other again.

"What are you doing here, Devan?" Nell asked. "And why are you stark naked?"

Devan looked down at his bare body as if he'd just realized it was there. He instinctively tried to cover his modesty with a spread hand.

"When I transform, my clothes don't change with me," he said, embarrassed. "This isn't the movies. I have to take them off first or else they get ripped to shreds. That's how things work in the real world."

He glared daggers at Christopher, then pointed at him with his free hand.

"You knew he was a vampire?"

"Yes," Nell said. "I didn't know you were a werewolf, though. That was a pretty big surprise, to say the absolute least."

"Actually," interjected Amara. "Werewolf is the modern, you could say corrupted, term for a lycan. The original term is werwulf."

"Oh, that's so you, Amara," said Nell, exasperated. "Perhaps now's not the time."

"She's correct, in fact," said Devan, tentatively.

"Reading takes you in one direction…" said Amara, brightly.

"I don't care about etymology right now," fumed Nell. "I

just want to know why you've been following me, Mr Lycan, Lycanthrope, Werwulf, Big fur-ball horror show. Now and at the diner before."

"Why do you think?!" said Devan, petulantly. "He's a goddamn vampire, Nell. He doesn't have your best interests at heart. I was trying to look out for you, as a friend, or maybe..." He paused, considering his words, then shook his head. "I can't believe you knew what he was this whole time."

"Not the whole time," Nell said. "We've been... sort of seeing each other... but he only just told me."

The words 'seeing each other' stopped Devan in his tracks. It appeared to wound him.

"I know vampires," Devan said, venomously. "They don't 'see people' because they don't feel."

"As opposed to werewolves, or werwulfs, or weird-woofs," spat Christopher. "Who hunt down humans and rip their throats out."

The two began to circle each other again.

"I have not attacked a human once in my life," Devan said, pointing once again at the vampire. "Can you say the same, fang?"

"ENOUGH!" Nell cried.

She rushed forward and placed her body between the two, facing Devan.

"Look, Devan. What you did in looking out for me was sweet in a terror-inducing, demented sort of way, but I don't ne..."

She stopped mid-sentence as she suddenly recalled his sharp yellow eyes only moments ago as a werwulf. Then it hit her, where she had seen those eyes before. Her stomach dropped to the floor in sheer mortification. She could feel her cheeks burning red. She stepped close up to Devan, so she couldn't be overheard.

"It was you, wasn't it," she hissed, jabbing at his chest with a finger. "That night behind the trees in my aunt's garden. When I was…" She couldn't even begin to describe it. "When I was acting way out of character. Did that have something to do with you?"

Nell knew this wasn't the right time, but she couldn't help herself.

Now it was Devan's turn to blush red.

"As I said, I was only looking out for you, for your safety," he ventured.

"Did that have something to do with you?" Nell repeated, more sternly.

"Look," said Devan, beseechingly. "Werwulfs are primal creatures. When we have…um…certain types of feelings for others, it can sometimes project out. If there's a full moon, it just amplifies everything. Humans aren't used to being on the receiving end of that, and it can make them a little… erm…lascivious. I think that's the correct term. Shall we ask Amara?"

"Don't you goddamn dare!" said Nell, feeling her enmity burning hot.

"Here's what's going to happen," she said. "You're going to live out your life never breathing a single word of this to a living soul," she instructed.

Devan nodded his head, compliantly.

"Or an undead one!" Nell added, glancing at Christopher.

Nell hoped that would be the end of the matter, for eternity. But in her anger at Devan, she had overlooked the fact that Christopher had extra-sensitive hearing.

The vampire pounced on Devan and slammed him backwards into the nearest tree. Birds took off into the sky as the vibration reverberated up the trunk and shook the branches. Christopher wrapped his hands around Devan's neck. In human form, Devan didn't have the strength to resist. He could only stare in shock at the vampire.

"Just *what* have you been doing?" said Christopher, his voice edged with menace.

Devan couldn't answer. The wind had been knocked out of him and Christopher's hands were restricting his breathing.

Nell ran forwards and grabbed Christopher's arms. She pushed down but they didn't budge.

"Stop it, Christopher," she pleaded. "He didn't know."

Christopher turned his head slowly to look at Nell's frightened face and then glanced at Devan again, before looking at his own arms, as if seeing what he was doing for the first time. He released his grip.

Devan took a long, gasping breath and clutched at his neck. Christopher was quiet. Nell still held his arm.

"These feelings," Christopher said, almost in a whisper. "Sometimes I can't..."

"It's okay," said Nell. "It will take some getting used to. It's not wrong to feel what you feel. But you need to stop it from overwhelming you."

Christopher looked at Devan, who was still trying to catch his breath, then walked away with his head hanging down.

Nell approached Devan.

"Are you okay?"

"I'll live, just about," he said between ragged breaths. "But your bloodsucker there needs to learn to play nicer. I didn't know about you and him."

"It's okay, Devan," she replied. "It's not really your fault. He's going through a lot right now. This is all so messed up."

"I knew he was a vampire," Devan said, sullenly. "I wasn't there that night for a peep show. I had no control over that. I was looking out for you. It's not safe to be out after dark in Angel Falls."

"WILL EVERYONE PLEASE STOP SAYING THAT TO ME!!" Nell virtually screamed, releasing all the pent up tension of the day. "Especially the very ones I should have been afraid of all along."

"You don't know the half of it," said Devan, cryptically.

"Shhhhh," said Christopher, approaching Nell and placing his hands on her shoulders. He seemed back to his controlled self. Christopher then turned to Devan.

"My actions were perhaps a little too harsh, wolfman," he conceded.

Nell raised her eyebrows at the sorry attempt at an apology.

"I got the message," said Devan, not particularly politely.

"Well that was fun," said Amara, clapping her hands together and stepping forwards. "Nothing like a macho test-fest to fire up the old spirits. But perhaps we should get back to the matter at hand, namely staying alive."

"We must find a place to hide," said Christopher. "The Council could discover us at any moment."

"What's this Council?" Devan asked, still sounding sullen. "And why do *you* need a place to hide, fang?"

"Suffice to say that I have turned against my own kind," Christopher said. "They know I have allowed humans into the nest. They will hunt me down as surely as any mortal."

There was a long moment of silence. Devan looked at Nell.

"I have a cabin," he said, finally. "It's about an eight-hour hike from here. It's in the wilderness, secluded. I can lead you there."

The other three looked at each other.

"It might be our least worst option," conceded Christopher.

"Let me go get my clothes," said Devan. "They're not far."

"All right," Nell said, exhaling. "We'll stay here and wait for you."

Devan nodded. He took one last look at the other three and then took off through the trees. His dusky body disappeared in the thick foliage.

Nell looked at the other two.

"Do we trust him?" she asked.

Amara and Christopher found a spot on the forest floor to lower themselves onto.

"It seems we have little choice at the moment," Christopher said. "Hiding might be our best option. Time is not on our side and we wouldn't make it very far on foot, at least you two wouldn't."

"Sorry for being human," said Nell. "I didn't realize it was such a crime."

"Not a crime," Christopher huffed. "But it does have its drawbacks."

"Speaking of that," said Amara. "If the Council searches these woods, won't they be able to track our scent all the way to the cabin?"

"That's a very astute observation," said Christopher.

Amara smiled. Nell rolled her eyes.

"And it is why we must disguise your pungent odor," he continued.

"You know," said Nell. "I think I liked you a little better before."

Christopher began to search along the ground, moving branches and loose dirt aside.

"This will do the job," he said, with a slight smile.

Nell and Amara walked over and looked down.

On the ground was a fresh steaming heap of deer poop.

"You are kidding?" Nell said, incredulously.

"What do you want us to do with that?" added Amara, alarmed.

"You're smart, Amara. I thought it would be obvious," said Christopher.

"It is," replied the librarian. "But my brain is refusing to acknowledge it."

"Rub it all over your body from head to toe," said Christopher, matter-of-factly.

The two women looked horrified.

"Right now, your bodies are expelling a variety of scents, pheromones and chemical messengers that are unique to you. A signature, if you like," said Christopher. "To a vampire using its senses, you are effectively a walking radar beacon."

They both looked at the deer poop with even more trepidation.

"This is going to be the grossest thing ever," Nell said.

"You must hurry," urged Christopher. "They could begin searching the woods at any time."

Nell roughly handed Christopher the book of prophecy. She then held her breath, closed her eyes and reached down, scooping out a clump of the deer poop.

"Oh God," she said in disgust. "It's still wet."

"Better for spreading," said Christopher.

Nell began to smear it over her body, only just keeping control of her gag reflex. She worked it into her exposed skin before applying it under her clothes. Amara began, reluctantly, to do the same. They spread it over their arms, neck, face and torso. Christopher even made them put it in their hair. He turned around as they stripped down to apply it on their legs, before covering up again.

Once they were done, Christopher approached them and sampled the air.

"Not perfect but much better," he said. "Now let's hope it doesn't rain."

Devan came back, this time fully dressed in jeans, boots and a green pullover. His eyes widened when he saw Amara and Nell.

"Don't even," said Nell, as a pre-emptive warning.

Devan held up his hands in placation before turning around and leading the way.

Amara and Nell followed in single file with Christopher keeping watch at the rear. Nell wrapped the book in a piece of Christopher's ripped shirt and deposited it safely under her arm. It was going to be a long hike.

Chapter 17

The sun went down and the sky grew dark long before they reached the cabin. Luckily, the moon was bright and it helped to illuminate their route through the trees.

Devan evidently knew the terrain of the forest extremely well. He hadn't once wavered in his directions since they set out, even though to Nell everything looked the same. Even in the dark, as the tree branches overhead crowded in to form a canopy that blocked out the light, Devan knew exactly where he was going. It was instinctive. All they had to do was follow in his wake.

Nell had time to be with her thoughts, most of which reminded her how downright bizarre this all was. She had lived her entire life (up until now) believing that werwulfs and vampires only existed in books and movies. This was no book. This was no movie. She couldn't help feeling that there wasn't going to be a neat and tidy ending to this real-life drama.

But she had to keep going. She wanted to see her beloved aunt again. She wanted to ensure that the big-hearted and seemingly unflappable Amara made it to safety. She wanted to repay Devan for his harebrained and terrifying, yet touching, attempts at protecting her. She wanted to explore if anything was possible with the noble Christopher, who strived to do the right thing and obviously cared deeply for her.

The deer feces had dried and was now caked onto her skin. But at least it didn't smell as bad in its dry form. Nell was desperate for a warm shower and clean set of clothes, but didn't expect either one anytime soon. She apologized profusely to Amara at regular intervals throughout the journey. She felt awful for dragging her friend into this mess. However, the librarian assured her that it wasn't her fault. No one could have predicted how crazy this day would turn out to be. Seeing into the future eluded even vampires and werwulfs.

The fatigue that comes with an eight-hour trek was wearing on every nerve and muscle in Nell's body. The group had stopped four times to rest and Devan knew where the streams ran for fresh water, but she just wasn't used to traversing such distances. Her hamstrings and calves were burning and every step was painful. Her feet were killing her, even though they were used to punishment from busy waitressing shifts. She didn't have the benefit of gel insoles today.

Just as Nell was about to give up and sink down onto the forest floor for some much-needed recuperation, she caught sight of the cabin just up ahead. It was larger than she had anticipated and nestled into the trees. The sight of the angular wooden structure motivated everyone to pick up the pace. They quickly made it to the front door. Devan extracted a key hidden at the bottom of one of the posts holding up the porch roof. He unlocked the door and they shuffled inside.

There was no electricity, but Devan lit several oil lanterns using matches, which illuminated the interior. In front of them was a large living area with a fireplace, beige couch plus a storage cupboard in the corner. Another door led to a small kitchen with a primus stove and dark oak larder. There was also a bathroom with a tin tub, sink and actual running water from a pump mechanism. The cabin was rudimentary, but it felt like a palace after their arduous expedition.

"Nice digs," said Amara. The relief in her voice was palpable.

"Thanks, I sometimes come up here with... friends," Devan said. "For hunting."

Nell and Amara stared at him.

He quickly shook his head.

"Just animals," he clarified. "We don't eat people."

The two women must have looked unconvinced because he added: "No, seriously. Our ancestors did, I have to admit. But that came to an end a few decades ago. We just hunt animals."

Amara's eyes widened.

"The unexplained murders back in the day. Those were your ancestors?" she asked.

Devan nodded, reluctantly.

"You can't blame me for any of that. I wasn't even born then. I didn't even know them. Werwulfs are both animal and human. I'm trying to lead with my human side. It's just when we're transformed..." He looked away. "It's difficult to control ourselves." He looked back at Nell briefly.

"I'm sorry," said Amara. "I wasn't trying to accuse you of anything."

"This," Devan gestured around the cabin. "Is where I come when the hunt beckons. Far away from any humans. Werwulfs can also shift into full wolf form. So on the hunt I look just like an ordinary wolf hunting its prey."

Christopher looked at him almost sympathetically.

"Well," said the vampire. "That was all very interesting. But shall we focus on the here and now?"

Nell thought Christopher was actually trying to help Devan by taking the attention away from him. This day was throwing up surprises by the minute.

"We'll spend the night here, to rest," Christopher continued. "I'm fairly certain the Council was not able to track us. Also, no one knows that Devan is on our side."

He looked at Devan, who nodded briefly in affirmation.

"So no one should be able to connect us with this cabin," added Christopher.

Nell exhaled deeply then collapsed onto the soft couch. Amara followed suit.

"I am sure that the two of you wish to bathe," said Christopher. He looked at Devan. "Is that possible?"

"There's no running hot water," Devan explained. "But if you fill the bathtub halfway from the pump tap, I can heat up a few buckets on the primus and mix it in. It won't be like taking a bath at home, but you won't be freezing, either."

"We'll take whatever we can get," said Nell.

"Amen to that. Anything is greatly appreciated, Devan," added Amara, taking a whiff of her soiled clothes.

"I don't have anything for you to wear," Devan said. "But if you want to use the sink to scrub your clothes, I can get the fireplace going. You can hang them above to dry."

Nell was just about to speak, but Devan addressed the obvious question.

"I have towels," he said. "You can wrap yourselves in those while you are waiting for your clothes."

"What about sustenance?" Christopher asked Devan. "Nell and Amara must be hungry."

"You are not wrong there," chimed Amara.

"Do you have the DoorDash app on your phone?" Devan

asked the librarian.

She looked at him open-mouthed.

"Kidding, just kidding," he said. "I can fetch us something." He expanded his arms. "The forest is nothing if not bountiful." He looked at Christopher. "Do you eat... like human food?"

Now Devan appeared to be concerned for Christopher's welfare. Adversity was certainly making strange bedfellows.

Christopher shook his head.

"I will be fine. I fed this morning."

"How long can you go without feeding?" Nell asked.

"For a while. Do not concern yourself with me," Christopher said, resolutely.

"O-k-e-y d-o-k-e-y, then," said Devan. "I'll get that hot water going."

About twenty minutes later Nell went into the bathroom and closed the door. She tested the water in the tub with her fingers. Devan had poured in three pails from the stove to mix with the water Nell had filled earlier. It was surprisingly warm. Nell quickly took off her clothes and began scrubbing and rinsing them in the sink with a bar of soap. When she could smell no more deer poop on anything, she wrung them out and hung them up on hooks on the wall. Then she quickly lowered herself into the bath. The water felt heavenly. She relaxed for a minute or two with her eyes closed before washing her skin and hair with shampoo and more soap she had found. She knew Amara was waiting so she didn't dawdle, even though it would have been wonderful just to soak in the bath.

When Nell was done she stepped out of the tub, feeling almost human again. She wrapped herself tightly in a large towel before cleaning up as best as she could, so Amara wasn't faced with her grime. She then retrieved a comb from a drawer before gathering her things and heading out, allowing Amara her turn.

About half an hour later, both women sat in front of the fire, wrapped in towels. Their clothes hung from a line above the hearth.

The boys stole furtive glances at them before quickly averting their eyes.

"They should be dry by morning," said Devan, pointing to the hanging garments.

He retrieved a blanket from under the couch and draped it over their legs. His eyes lingered on Nell again.

"Something extra to keep out the chill," he said, before heading into the kitchen to prepare the ingredients he had foraged from the forest earlier.

Christopher sat on the couch, looking calm but alert.

After some time, delicious smells began wafting out of the kitchen and permeated the cabin. Of course, at this point anything edible would have seemed delicious, but Nell detected the scent of some kind of meat and root vegetables cooking. Her stomach growled and saliva flooded her mouth. She needed something to distract herself, or the anticipation would drive her crazy.

She carefully unwrapped the book of prophecy from Christopher's tattered shirt and began to flick through it in the amber glow of the fire. Amara stared at the dancing flames. Christopher kept his vigil on the couch. Devan continued cooking.

"It's strange they made such a monumental effort to destroy every copy but one," Amara said, turning to Nell.

"Scholars can't bear to eliminate information," said Christopher. "It's in their nature to preserve, not destroy."

"But they made sure there was only one copy of this, and in their exclusive possession," Nell mused. "There must be something in here that they wanted to ensure never saw the light of day."

She began to peruse the book more closely. There were several chapters about periods in history that had already come to pass. They had titles such as *Coven Decretum, Antecedent Dharma, The Viperous Fledgling, Lazarius Unconcealed* and *Oblian's Consequential Meridians.* Finally, Nell found a passage that seemed relevant in a chapter entitled *Cimmerian Prognostications*. She read it out loud:

"When the multitudes disperse across the hemispheres, the seeds of darkness will be relegated to the shadows. They will live by rules unwritten, designed only to keep them behind the veil. One brood will ascend into the new dawn. This Family is the obsidian, representing replete darkness. Its proliferation will herald the end of all things. For darkness must exist in shadow.

The obsidian faction will spread like a disease, growing vast enough to engulf all that is. The seeds of darkness will struggle but fail to tame the affliction. A war will rage and devastate the landscape. Creatures of the night will come together to fight as one. Unlikely allegiances will be forged. They will be tested. They will be sacrificed. They will be broken. Creation teeters on a perilous balance between light and dark.

Salvation lies in one soul. A death-walker turned young. One of tainted blood. He will endure a betrayal, a loss and an awakening. He will love, as no other of his kin has before. He will abandon those he serves. He will develop abilities unknown while reverting to the origin. These abilities can corrupt and besiege, for they stem from the transmutation of loss, the most powerful emotion. He must drain the one he loves, filling his essence and ending theirs. This act alone brings forth the genesis.

Yet the Eminence of abominations will rise again. Out of light comes darkness, out of darkness comes light. Out of love comes hate. The blood of destruction. The blood of creation. A new Family is born. Tainted blood will clash in the final apocalypse.

Blood connects all. Blood is the liberator. Blood is the destroyer. Blood is the answer."

After Nell finished reading the passage they all stared at each other, dumbstruck.

Finally, Amara broke the silence.

"It said '*develop abilities unknown while reverting to the origin*.'"

She looked at Christopher.

"If you're this death-walker turned young, then I think it's implying you are going to become human again. Wouldn't that explain a few things?"

"No," he said, emphatically, shaking his head. "That prophecy has nothing to do with me."

"Can we really dismiss it so easily?" suggested Amara, leaning forward. "This knowledge could be what the Red Claws were so desperate to protect. It appears to explain how they can be defeated."

"It says I must drain Nell's blood, to end her," said Christopher, almost in a whisper.

Nell was taken aback. Both by the idea of having her blood drained and by the fact that Christopher had identified her as '*the one he loves*'. It was a lot to take in. Her emotions were all over the place.

Christopher's eyes darted to Nell's face and then slowly traveled down to the pulse point on her neck. The same spot on the human body where she'd seen him bite the pimp only a few nights ago.

Nell's heart thundered in her chest as she tracked Christopher's eyes. Surely he wouldn't save her just to kill her? She doubted it, not after everything they had gone through. But what was he thinking? Why was he fixated on her neck?

Christopher closed his eyes tightly and a shudder ran through his entire body.

"I will not do that. Never," he declared.

Nell let out the breath that she hadn't even realized she was holding.

Amara looked pained.

"You can't dismiss the prophecy on the basis that it's unpalatable to you," she said. "You objecting to the contents doesn't make it any less valid." She glanced at Nell. "Which I'm not saying it is, not at all," she added, hurriedly. "But Christopher's logic isn't, well, logical."

Nell sat frozen. She still had the book open in her lap and hadn't moved an inch from the time she stopped reading. She was breathing quickly and shallowly, but that was the only movement her body was making. Her thoughts were racing around her head so fast that she couldn't pin down any one of them. Amara grabbed her arm.

"Nell, are you okay? Nell?"

She slowly turned and looked at Amara and then at Christopher.

"It could be about us," she said, slowly, running the idea out loud. "You were turned young, Christopher. You say you're experiencing rekindled emotions, love even. The prophecy states that if you don't drain me then the Red Claws will destroy the entire human race. Plus vampires, plus werwulfs, plus everything else that exists out there."

"I don't care," Christopher said, banging a fist down on the couch. "I'm not doing that. I could never hurt you, much less..." He couldn't even finish the sentence.

Nell closed the book and they all sat in silence. She stared into the fire, as if transfixed. Amara wrapped her arms around Nell's shoulders and stroked the top of her arm. Christopher buried his fist deeper into the sofa, twisting it until his skin burned.

After a few minutes, Devan came in from the kitchen carrying a wooden tray with three steaming bowls resting on it. The bowls contained a hearty stew with chunky pieces of rabbit meat and a variety of chopped vegetables. He'd even managed to pick a few herbs to add flavor. He looked at the pensive faces around him.

"Well that's just great," he exclaimed. "I spend all evening slaving away over a hot stove and *this* is the appreciation I get."

"Sorry," said Amara, distractedly. "It's not you."

Devan handed bowls to Amara and Nell along with spoons and then planted himself on the couch next to Christopher. He looked around again at the sullen faces.

"Well, screw you all. I'm chowing down," he said, before digging in with gusto. Soup dribbled from the side of his mouth as he took big slurping spoonfuls.

"Do you have to *wolf* down your food?" said Amara.

"Bite me," came the answer.

Amara also began eating, slowly at first and then ravenously.

Nell looked tentatively at Christopher, who didn't meet her gaze. He was still staring down at his first as he continued to twist it into the fabric.

Nell stared back into the orange glow of the crackling

fire. She didn't even touch her spoon. Suddenly, she had no appetite.

Chapter 18

Eventually, and on Amara's insistence, Nell ate some of the stew before turning in for the night. She and Amara slept close to each other in front of the fire using cushions from the couch.

Nell had wanted to spend the night next to Christopher, but he turned away from her when she had gone over and touched his shoulder. He looked deeply troubled. Nell went back to Amara and crawled under the blanket, then gently wept.

"Sssh, it's okay," comforted Amara, as she stroked Nell's hair. "Everyone is out of their depth here. No one's thinking straight."

This was all so messed up. A week ago, Nell had no idea that creatures of the night existed or that there was potentially a huge war looming that could wipe out *'all that is'*, as the prophecy so bluntly put it. She almost wanted to be back inside that comforting bubble of ignorance. She was chilled to her core at the thought that it might be her very existence that was standing in the way of the man she cared so deeply for defending Earth against the Red Claws. It was all too big and scary to contemplate.

She lay awake for a long time, her thoughts churning, but was finally able to drift off to sleep thanks to sheer exhaustion.

The warmth of the fire – which was slowly dying down now – also helped.

Just as Nell finally entered a state of deep sleep she was jolted awake by the sound of pounding on the door. At first Nell thought she was dreaming. But, as the final layers of sleep peeled away, she realized with horror that the sound was real.

Christopher was already at the door. He had probably sensed the intrusion before the dreadful sound began echoing through the cabin. Devan was next to him, looking apprehensive. Amara was also up, her eyes hazy from sleep. Nell gripped her arm.

The pounding sounded again. They all jumped and Nell gripped Amara more tightly.

Devan and Christopher exchanged a glance. Christopher nodded slightly. Nell watched as Devan transformed, growing in height and bulking out with thick sinewy muscle. His boxer shorts ripped and fell to the floor. Thick hair sprouted from his skin, turning into dark fur that covered his body. Fingers became claws, feet became paws. His head elongated out, forming a pointed muzzle with razor-sharp teeth in his mouth. Finally, his dark eyes took on the primal yellow hue.

The vampire and werwulf both moved towards the door, which Christopher opened quickly. They both stared out. Nell and Amara weren't able to see outside from their angle, but if it was a pack of ravenous vampires, they had so far resisted attacking. Finally, a voice came from outside.

"Angajamentul de neintervenție," shouted the male voice.

The four of them looked at each other, baffled. After a few moments the voice called out again.

"Angajamentul de neintervenție."

Once again the strange words were met with silence from

inside the cabin.

“In the name of the Omni-Father, do you youngsters not know anything of the old ways,” said the exasperated voice. “I despair for the vampire race. I really do.”

“Who are you and what do you want?” shouted Christopher into the night.

“Well, if you knew a damned thing about your own kind, boy, you would have known that I just recited the pledge of neutrality.”

“Pledge of neutrality?” questioned Christopher. Then it dawned on him. “Oh, that means you are…”

“Yes, it bloody well does,” came the rude interruption. “We are here to help you. Though right now strangling you seems the far more enticing option.”

Christopher stepped through the door to take in the visitors, before returning inside a few moments later.

“It's okay,” he said to his three companions. “They won't harm us. They're like me, except more evolved or something. I can't remember what else I was told about them. Oh, yes, they can be temperamental, something about living such a long time expanding the emotional range. Not always in a positive way, it seems.”

He turned back to the opened door.

“Come in, then,” he called out.

“Are you a complete heathen ignoramus, or are you just testing our patience, lad?” said the voice.

“I don't know what you mean,” replied Christopher, confused.

“Death, decay and damnation!” said the voice. “You need to invite us past the threshold or we cannot enter.”

“Oh, right,” said Christopher. “I knew that…probably.”

He cleared his throat then spoke aloud. "Please kindly enter within and…traverse our door's threshold…from the outside…into our dwelling abode so…"

"'You may enter' would have sufficed," came the irked reply.

After a long moment, Devan and Christopher moved back and five individuals came into the cabin. There were four men and a woman. They were all wearing black robes and ranged in age from late thirties to early sixties. They glanced over to where Amara and Nell were sitting then looked back at Christopher and Devan, completely unphased by the presence of a werwulf in the room.

"What do you want? Who are you?" Nell asked, alarmed.

"Vamps, old ones," Devan said, derisively, in his gravelly lycan voice. "I can smell them from here."

"Thank you, wolf," said the oldest robbed figure.

Nell could tell from his voice that he was the one who had been speaking earlier. He had a bald head with delicate creases covering his alabaster face. Nell remained sitting next to Amara in her towel, worried that standing might reveal a lot more of her than she was comfortable with.

"He's a Magister," said Christopher. "That's not quite the same thing."

"It appears you are not an unmitigated imbecile, after all," said the bald Magister. "My name is Fabian Bamford and I am indeed a Magister," he informed Nell. "I presume that term means nothing to you?"

"No, sir," she said.

She had no idea why she had just addressed him as sir, but something about having five robed figures standing over her made her a little nervous.

"Magister is Latin for teacher," said Amara.

Everyone turned to look at her.

"Indeed," said Fabian, eyebrows raised. "Indeed."

"Nerd," said Devan, before shifting back to human form. He stood completely naked, and didn't seem to care a hoot at this point. He walked over to the cupboard in the corner of the room and pulled out a fresh pair of boxer shorts. He slipped them on and, in one fluid motion, vaulted the back of the sofa and sat down, crossing his right leg over his left before yawning.

"The five of us are named such that we are the keepers of lore and heritage, we are among the oldest of our kind," said the Magister.

"That's just what we need," said Devan, leaning back. "Five more librarians to join the word-nerd over there."

Amara gave him a withering look.

"It is part of our duties to give guidance to those newly turned and share knowledge with the Council," said Fabian. "However, we are strictly nonpartisan. Our function transcends petty politics."

Nell and Amara nodded, Devan looked thoroughly bored, while Christopher was hanging off the Magister's every word, like a struggling student trying to swat up before an exam.

Devan leaned forward.

"So what does Count Dorkula here and his bathrobe brigade have to do with us?" he said.

"You would be wise to moderate your tongue, beast," said Fabian, sharply.

"It's a fair, if rudely asked, question," said Nell, shooting a stern glance at Devan. "Why are you here? I didn't think Christopher was a new vampire."

"We are not here for his instruction," the Magister responded. "Though he sorely needs it."

Fabian looked back at his companions and then continued. "Red Claws. I am sure *that* term is familiar to you."

This time he didn't wait for an answer.

"The Council has made the decision that the Family will be awakened, so we are here to warn you."

"Warn us of what?" Christopher asked.

The female Magister stepped forward.

"Child, surely you realize what you've done?" she said.

She had sharp oriental features but was far more soft-spoken than Nell had anticipated.

"No, can't say I do," Christopher ventured, but his tone of voice betrayed his words.

"Told you he might have bats in the belfry, Jiangshina," said Fabian.

"You have something of theirs," the Magister named Jiangshina said, patiently. She brushed her sleek black hair out of her face, tucking it back into her robe.

Nell picked up the plain black book. There was no point in trying to pretend.

"I think this is what she's referring to," Nell said, resigned.

"You left in a hurry, leaving a mess," said Jiangshina. "They will know it's gone. It is only a matter of time before they trace the theft back to you. They are good hunters."

"Good hunters," scoffed Devan. "I'll go toe-to-toe with you fangbangers any time."

The Magisters didn't even look at Devan.

"The Red Claw Family are of a different breed, I'm afraid," said Jiangshina in her sublime voice. "Even now, as they are awakening, they are scheming. Blood will out. It always does." Her eyes looked somber.

Christopher nodded his head, then turned to Nell.

"No matter what you hear about the Red Claws, they don't represent all of us," he implored. "We are not all the same, please remember that."

"Christopher here does seem to be one of a kind," Jiangshina said, knowingly.

"Yes," the older Magister affirmed. "Which brings us to our next point. The Red Claws will know that you took the book. Which means they will assume you possess knowledge about the prophecy."

Silence descended on the room.

"Really, are we going to do this?" said Fabian. "Do you think we have the time to play games?"

"Go on," said Christopher.

"We have one advantage," said Jiangshina. "They don't know the prophecy is about you two." She looked from Christopher to Nell. "As long as that remains the case, you are not a mortal threat to them."

Nell's heart sank into the floor. Christopher looked stricken. It seemed their worst fear had been realized.

"Hang on a minute," Amara exclaimed. "How do you know that the prophecy is about Christopher and Nell? For that matter, how did you know we took the book? How did you even know we were here?"

"It is our job to know," Jiangshina said, calmly. "We are Magisters."

"That didn't answer my question," Amara contested.

"That is all the answer you are going to receive, young lady," Fabian said, in a measured yet final tone. "As long as the Red Claws do not know that you two are the subject of the prophecy, we will be able to keep you safe. However, be aware that you are still at risk simply for taking their property."

"The Red Claws have never actually met Christopher, despite him taking care of them," mused Jiangshina. "They won't know that he breaks the mold. We need to keep it that way."

"Agreed," said Fabian.

"I don't understand," said Nell. "If you Magisters are non-partisan, why are you here helping us?" Nell directed her question to the even-tempered Jiangshina.

Fabian answered, instead.

"Because it has begun. Our hand is forced. The wheels are in motion. Now the fate of all hangs in the balance. Did you not understand the words of the foretelling?"

"Contrary to what you might believe," said Jiangshina in her placating tone. "It is not the desire of our kind to wipe out humans. As the prophecy states, we are meant to live in the shadows. It is a symbiotic relationship. A balance. Without the life-force that runs through your veins, vampires would be no more. It would be mutually assured destruction, as self-serving as that no doubt sounds to you."

Nell wasn't super thrilled that the Magister had just openly admitted that people were a food source, but at least they had an imperative to keep humans alive. However, if the prophecy really concerned her and Christopher, then she herself wouldn't be enjoying that particular privilege for long. But when you compared one life to that of all the people on the planet, there simply wasn't room for much argument. She felt strangely serene, given the circumstances.

She noticed Christopher staring at her. She could tell he was unnerved by the way she was reacting. It was clear that Nell was at the forefront of his mind, which was reassuring, but also heartbreaking, if it meant he'd have to kill her. None of that was important right now. What was critical was keeping the Red Claw Family ignorant of Christopher's true nature.

"So what do we do?" asked Nell.

"The only thing there is to do. Run," said Jiangshina.

"Why doesn't that surprise me," Nell said, looking at her tired feet. She looked up at the Magisters with resolve in her eyes. "I'm taking my Aunt Laura," she added in a stern voice. "There's no way I'm leaving her behind."

It wasn't up for debate. No one argued. Nell thought about all the other people she knew in Angel Falls. Rowdy Peck, Hattie Lee, Charlie Miller, Dwayne Redmond. She wished she could place them all out of harm's way, but that simply wasn't possible.

"And where do we go, exactly?" asked Devan.

"Vhik'h-Tal-Eskemon," said Fabian. "It's where the High Chancellor resides. It is the most protected dwelling among our kind. It's the safest place for you to be right now."

"Hang on," said Amara. "Isn't the High Chancellor the commander, so to speak, of the Council of Elders? And aren't they the very reason we trekked for eight hours to hide out here?"

"That was before they knew about the prophecy," Jiangshina said, glancing at the Magisters for approval. "Things are moving apace."

"You only just told them about the prophecy?" said Devan, incredulous. "Did it ever occur to you to mention it beforehand, so the murderous brood would never be allowed to wake? The Council could have left them sleeping or, better yet, exterminated them, so none of this would be an issue right now."

"Things aren't that simple," said Jiangshina. "Destiny must unfold in a pre-ordained order. Diverging off the path will risk chaos in all realms. There are wheels within wheels."

"What's more, wolf," added Fabian. "The Council entered into a blood oath one hundred years ago with the Red Claws. Breaking that sacred pact risks unleashing forces unknown. Old Magick is unforgiving."

"So we just sit back and watch the Red Claws go on a murderous rampage?" said Nell.

"The Council will see the deaths in Angel Falls and realize something needs to be done," said Jiangshina. "They'll also know about the prophecy. Which means that for the exact same reason the Red Claws would want to kill you, the Council will want to protect you at all costs. Because you represent the potential downfall of the Red Claws. In you and Christopher, they have a get out of jail free card."

"So we have to blindly trust the cryptic writings in an old book?" said Devan. "Why don't we just take out the Red Claws? Kill every last one of the bastards so there's no threat to worry about?"

"These prophecies have an uncanny way of making their way into the world, despite any efforts to the contrary," said Jiangshina. "The book states how the Red Claws can be defeated. You will find that other courses of action will not be effectual."

"Wait, what other prophecies are there?" Nell asked, looking around the room.

Christopher shrugged, clearly not privy to that information.

"That's on a strictly need to know basis," said Fabian. "As long as you and Christopher play your allotted roles in your own, the rest of them will take care of themselves without your prying, thank you very much."

"My role in the prophecy seems to be certain death," said Nell.

She thought about her parents. Perhaps she'd be joining them soon. The prospect both comforted and terrified her.

Jiangshina looked away.

"We all have a part to play for the greater good," said Fabian, somberly. "Unfortunately, this is yours…and you will be expected to fulfill it."

"Nell is going to play *no* part in this," snapped Christopher. "It's not your place to tell her she must die. The prophecy won't be fulfilled, not by us at least. You'll have to find somebody else to do it. I can't be the only one in existence it could apply to."

"It's true," said Amara. "Haven't you read Harmony Constance? What about Seamus Sedgwick? A prophecy can always apply to somebody else."

"Remember to whom you are speaking," said Fabian, sternly. "Questioning a Magister can be considered sacrilege. We have no time for children's fables. Seamus Sedgwick, indeed."

"Children's fable?" grumbled Amara. "Now *that* is sacrilege."

"Let's all calm down," suggested Jiangshina.

"I'm not going to calm down when you tell the woman I love she needs to die," spat Christopher.

Nell felt a small current of energy travel up her chest and into her face, where it both warmed and reddened her cheeks. This was the first time Christopher had spoken of love for her, even if the declaration was inadvertent. It seemed to literally electrify her on the inside. She took it as a good sign.

Jiangshina sighed as she addressed Christopher. Sympathy reflected in her eyes.

"I understand that this is difficult to accept," she said. "But as far as we are concerned, there's only one Christopher Deverell. This means that, unfortunately, there's also only one Petronella Cartwright."

Devan burst out laughing. He couldn't help himself. Amara fought hard to maintain a straight face. She had to look at the floor and hold her breath.

"Shut up, Devan," said Nell. "I was named after my grandmother, not that it's any of *your* business."

The sudden change in tone seemed to serve as a release valve for the building tension in the room. However, Christopher was still tense and defensive. Nell went over to him and grasped his hand tightly, towel slippage be damned. He seemed to relax a little at her touch.

"You're wrong, and you will have to find somebody else," he said, more evenly. "We are going to have to agree to disagree on that point."

"Let's deal with the matter at hand," said Fabian. "You are in immediate danger and we need to make sure that you are both safe so that you can fulfill the prophecy...should the need arise," he added, by way of placation. "You will head to Vhik'h-Tal-Eskemon where you will stay until we can thoroughly assess the situation. In an ideal world, the Red Claws will calm down and become decent citizens, perhaps get jobs in the civil service and join the bridge club, but I find that highly unlikely." He laughed at his own joke, but no one else was amused.

"All that is left for you to do is sit tight," he continued. "You never know, the prophecy might not play out until Nell is an old woman. Prophecies don't come with timelines, you know."

"The timeline of this particular prophecy is never," said Devan. "You will have to come through me to get to her, and I don't rate your chances. Nell is part of my pack. Among my kind, we protect the pack at all costs. No one gets left behind."

Everyone stared at him, but he didn't flinch.

It was a lot to take in. Best case scenario, Nell would live a long and happy life under the protection of the Council. Worst case, Christopher would have to dispatch her imminently to take on the rampaging Red Claws. Or even worse still, the Red Claws might get to them first and eliminate the possibility of the prophecy playing out altogether. If Christopher managed to keep his cool, there was little chance they would discover he was the one the prophecy spoke of. From what she knew of the boy in the black jacket, he could hide his feelings pretty well.

Amara was quiet. Christopher stared at the Magisters with not much else to say. Devan looked sullen.

"We have procured a vehicle for you," said Jiangshina. "Head directly east for two miles where the forest thins. There's a derelict stone structure, it's just behind that."

"The old seminary ruins," said Devan. "I can take us there."

"These are the coordinates for Vhik'h-Tal-Eskemon."

Jiangshina took a piece of paper out of her robe and handed it to Devan.

"Pick up any belongings you need and quickly head out of town," she continued. "If our calculations are correct, which they usually are, the Red Claws will concentrate on feeding close to their old home. You have a window of time, but do not take it for granted. I wish you all the very best. We won't be far away. Somebody will be watching you." She bowed before saying: "Angajamentul de neintervenție."

"Angajamentul de neintervenție," said the other four Magisters in unison.

"Angina mental-day nine-intervention," said Christopher, rather hopelessly.

Fabian rolled his eyes, then the Magisters swept out of the room.

"Shit," was all Devan said, running a hand through his hair.

"Shit, indeed," Christopher concurred.

Chapter 19

It was the middle of the night and Nell was fed up with the silence. Barely any words had been exchanged since the Magisters left abruptly and the four of them had made their way to the forest clearing, where a nondescript Subaru Impreza was waiting for them.

Nell sat beside Christopher in the back. They held hands but he was distracted, his brain seemingly turning over at double speed. Amara was staring straight ahead in the passenger seat, while Devan drove. Nell felt terrible that the both of them had been caught up in this. She knew that Christopher felt the same way, which was part of the reason they were in this mess. Because he could feel.

"Damn it," Devan said as he swerved around an oncoming car that was hogging both lanes on a blind turn.

His senses clearly benefited him when it came to driving. Nell was sure that his reactions weren't those of an ordinary person, even though he was now in human form.

Nell gave directions and Devan eventually pulled up outside Aunt Laura's home. Christopher and Nell climbed out of the car and walked to the house hand in hand.

"Hello," Nell called tentatively, after opening the door with her key.

It was late and Aunt Laura usually went to bed early. But she might be up, as Nell hadn't returned home yet.

"Nell, thank goodness," came the urgent reply from the kitchen. "I was worried. I tried your cell, but it kept going straight to voicemail."

"Sorry, Aunt Laura," said Nell. "I can explain."

Nell led Christopher into the small living room.

"There's honey cake on the table here," Aunt Laura called out. "Do you want me to fix you a cocoa? I'm having one myself."

Nell took a sharp intake of breath. For her aunt, today was no doubt a fairly normal day. She probably did a bunch of 'Aunt Laura things', like baking, gardening and reading about ceramics. Her worldview didn't include vampires, werwulfs, Magisters, the Council of Elders, prophecies, Red Claws, the High Chancellor (whoever he was), blood oaths, Old Magick and all the other astonishing things that had entered Nell's reality. She also wasn't yet aware that both Nell and her boyfriend were completely and irrevocably screwed.

"Oh," Aunt Laura said as she walked into the living room carrying a mug. "You have company."

"Hello ma'am, it's nice to meet you properly. I'm Christopher," he said.

They had briefly seen each other when Nell had performed at the open mic, but hadn't spoken.

"A pleasure to meet you, Christopher. Do you want cocoa and honey cake?" Aunt Laura said, smiling warmly.

"Thank you, ma'am, but we're in a bit of a hurry. Actually, I think Nell might have some things to share with you."

Christopher smiled sweetly. You would never guess that the weight of the world was on his shoulders.

"Thank you, Christopher," said Nell, eyebrows raised, lips tight.

He patted her hand, earnestly.

"May I?" he said, standing up and pointing at the kitchen.

"Of course," replied Aunt Laura. "Help yourself to cocoa and honey cake, there's plenty."

Nell guided Aunt Laura fully into the living room and sat her down on the plush couch, before taking a seat next to her.

"So," Nell exhaled, "I'm not sure where to start."

"You're pregnant," Aunt Laura exclaimed.

Nell could have sworn she heard Christopher snort in the kitchen.

"No, of course not," said Nell, taken aback. "But I think it's actually worse than that."

She took Aunt Laura's hands in her own, then proceeded to tell the whole story. From start to finish. Wolves, vampires, prophecies, the whole nine yards.

To Nell's surprise, Aunt Laura sat placidly throughout the telling. There was no interrupting, no smirking, no laughing out loud, no defiance — even when Nell explained that Aunt Laura had to leave with them for her own safety. Was she actually taking what Nell was saying seriously?

Once the tall tale was told, Aunt Laura contemplated for a few moments, then said: "You love him? He loves you?"

Nell couldn't help but chuckle. This was the one thing Aunt Laura was concerned about? Not the supernatural shenanigans, not the state of Nell's mental health. No, it appeared she was interested to know whether Nell had fallen in love.

"Yes," Nell said, simply.

Christopher walked back into the room, his enhanced

hearing having no doubt picked up every nuance of the conversation.

"And there's nothing in the world that I wouldn't do for you niece," he stated.

Aunt Laura looked between the two of them.

"Okay, that's good enough for me," she said, clapping her hands together. "What are we waiting for then? We have to get to the mountains. We have to keep the two of you safe."

Christopher and Nell exchanged bewildered glances.

"Oh my dear," said Aunt Laura. "You don't grow up in Angel Falls without knowing about strange creatures of the night."

Nell was taken aback by the statement, but then she thought about all the warnings she received from townsfolk about being wary after dark. She recalled Amara informing her of the grisly slayings and drained bodies. Nell also remembered that odd comment from her aunt about it being safer for the stores to close early, as well as her caution about 'ghosts and ghouls, and all manner of things that go bump in the night'. At the time Nell had simply dismissed it as light-hearted banter, but now she realized there was a deeper meaning behind it.

"I must admit, I didn't think vampires fell in love with humans," continued Aunt Laura. "But Christopher here clearly has. So let's do what must be done."

"So you're ready to join us?" Nell asked, her head tilted like a confused puppy.

"Of course, young lady," came the unwavering reply. "While I'm not one to be scared out of my own home, I can't have you gallivanting off with werwulfs and vampires on your own now, can I? My sister is no longer here to look out for her baby. So that responsibility falls on me. Let's both grab our things and meet back here in five minutes."

Nell couldn't help but tear up a little. They met back in the living room in less than five minutes.

"Ready, happy campers?" said Aunt Laura, as if this was the most fun she'd had in ages. "Tell your friends outside that I'm driving. My truck has more space and is designed for rough terrain. Just because she's getting on in years doesn't mean there's no life left in her."

Nell wasn't sure if her aunt was referring to her old pickup or herself.

They left the house and Aunt Laura marched over to her faded yellow Mazda truck, where she placed her bags in the back. Christopher and Nell went to the Subaru to inform Devan and Amara of the change in plan.

After a few minutes and with the introductions made, Aunt Laura took the wheel with Nell beside her, holding tight to the book of prophecy. The rest of the motley crew crammed into the back seats, with Amara wedged between Devan and Christopher.

The truck started with a prolonged rattle but eventually roared into life. They headed off towards their destination – a set of coordinates provided by the Magisters that would take them close to the small community of Micaville. It was nestled in the Blue Ridge Mountains, part of the sparse Appalachian range in North Carolina. There, apparently, they would find Vhik'h-Tal-Eskemon.

Once they reached the end of Marsh Valley Road a decision had to be made. While the quaint little town of Angel Falls had its charms, its small size also came with drawbacks. There was only one main road into and away from it.

"The most direct route would take us close to the Red Claw mansion," said Christopher. "Circumventing it will cost us time and add a fair few miles to the journey as we'd need to go in the opposite direction initially and then circle back."

"The Magister said we had a window of time," said Nell. "The Red Claws might not be awake yet. I think we need to leave the area as soon as possible."

"Direct route it is, then," said Aunt Laura, taking a left turn and then pressing down on the gas pedal. The old truck protested as it was asked to gain speed.

The pickup eventually settled into a low growl as it trundled along the straight road out of Angel Falls towards the main highway. The sky lightened as a new day dawned. Luckily, there was no other traffic this early in the morning. Aunt Laura drove at a steady 55 miles per hour as she reached the outskirts of town.

Things were going well until Christopher and Devan sat up straight in their seats. They both tilted their heads and then went stone still.

"Shit," Devan whispered.

"Shit indeed," Christopher said. "Aunt Laura, floor it. NOW!"

Chapter 20

Eyes blinking.

Once.

Twice.

And finally opened fully.

His mind was thick and foggy.

He didn't know where he was or how he'd got there.

He lay on his back on a hard surface. It was cold. Like a tomb.

Darkness.

But his eyes were slowly getting used to the low light.

With great effort he reached up an arm. It looked hazy in front of him, but his vision slowly sharpened. Something alien was dangling from it. A tube of some kind. It didn't belong there. It sullied his flesh. He lifted his other arm and ripped away the foreign object.

Better now. He was regaining his strength. And his mind.

Klaus.

He was Klaus Romanov.

He had been turned when he was…23. The gift had been bestowed on him by…Klaus couldn't remember his name.

Zachariah. That was it. Zachariah… Red Claw.

Klaus Red Claw. Not Klaus Romanov. Not anymore. Red

Claw.

He was part of a Family.

A new Family.

The Red Claws had taken him in. Taught him how to be a vampire. Taught him how to take what was his by right. The strong survive. The weak are mere prey.

But that glorious ethos had been their undoing in the end. They were punished for killing too many humans.

Klaus scoffed aloud.

Killing humans was what vampires were *supposed* to do. The meek, worthless Council didn't share that opinion, however. Klaus, along with his beloved Family, had been put to sleep. For one hundred years. The unjustness of the sentence filled him with renewed bitterness.

Time must be up. Had the moment really come at last? What else could this be?

He used all his strength to sit up.

Eyes blinking again.

He stretched his aching limbs as a fierce hunger overcame him.

In the name of the Omni-Father, he was starving.

He was weak. Maybe after he'd had something to consume he'd feel more himself again.

Female, young. They always had the sweetest blood. That was what he craved. He'd go out and find it. After he'd spoken to Zachariah, of course. You didn't do anything until you spoke to Zachariah.

He surveyed the cavernous room.

Cables snaked out from a bizarre machine in the center.

He looked down at the floor, where he discarded the tube going into his arm. The tube ran all the way into the heart of the machine. He looked around and saw the same thin pipes going into each of the stone boxes that littered the room.

What kind of sacrilege was this?

He tried to lift himself up, to leave his accursed tomb.

"If it was a tomb you would be dead. They're hibernation pods."

One of the Council members emerged from behind him. This vampire could read thoughts, so he had to be powerful.

Klaus focused his eyes on the face before him.

Recognition hit him.

Loris Valkari, Warden of the South. They'd had run-ins in the past.

"We're not yours to store, traitor," Klaus spat.

"Now now, Klaus," another voice behind Loris reprimanded.

This time Klaus recognized it instantly.

Zachariah.

"Treat our brethren with some respect," said Zachariah. "They have honored the blood oath. For that our Family is obliged."

Klaus snorted, but kept his mouth shut. You didn't argue with Zachariah.

"Listen well, Zachariah," said Loris. "I have made no secret of the fact that if it was up to me, you'd still be accruing your beauty sleep. But the High Chancellor and the Council, in their infinite wisdom, have chosen to rouse you. I am here as a warning of vengeance incarnate. You will moderate your actions. Killing humans indiscriminately will not be tolerated. Learn something from your long exile. Humans might be feeble, but they are not stupid. Anything that threatens the vampire race will be seen as an act of treachery, and be punished accordingly."

"What, by prescribing more nap-time?" The words escaped Klaus's mouth before he could stop himself.

Zachariah was on top of him in an instant, slapping him across the face with the flat of his hand.

"I will not tolerate disrespect towards the Council," he admonished. "You have been warned."

Klaus turned away, sulking, trying to hide the blush that came to his pale white cheeks.

As a human, he'd been susceptible to blushing, something to do with his red hair, he surmised. It annoyed Klaus to no end that even as a vampire, he still blushed. Not as much as when he was human, of course, but none of the other vampires blushed. It wasn't fair.

Klaus looked around again.

More vampires emerged from the pods, like children being birthed from stone wombs. Klaus's brothers and sisters. His Family.

Other members of the Council of Elders looked on. He noticed with revulsion that one had a withered stump for an arm. It disgusted him. There was no such weakness among the Red Claws.

"We shall heed your warning, Warden Loris," said Zachariah. "Thank you. I think we can take it from here. I'm sure you won't be far away to check on our progress," he added in a sickly-sweet voice. Klaus knew Zachariah hated the Council and everything it stood for.

"I'm warning you, Zachariah," replied Loris. "At the first hint of defiance I will do everything in my power to see you turned to ash."

"Always a pleasure," Zachariah said, as Loris walked away.

A few hours later, all 102 Red Claws were assembled in the

grand dining room of the mansion. A large oval table sat in the center, with about 30 plush leather-backed chairs surrounding it. The oldest vampires sat. The rest of them stood around the room. Zachariah was seated at the head of the table with Klaus standing in his customary position, by the side of his master.

"Hello, my children. It is wonderful to see you all again," began Zachariah. "I trust you slept well."

Laughter rippled through the room.

"I called you all here to welcome you back, and also to reassure you. Now that the prying Council has left, we are free to speak our minds. I am here to tell you that the future is as bright and bloody as it has always been."

Cheers rang out. The seated Red Claws began banging the table with their fists.

"We will not alter the ways of our creed in order to subscribe to craven principles dictated by a governing body that does not represent us," continued Zachariah. "The Council is archaic. We are the future. After our…little set-back…we are ready to reclaim our rights. We are vampires, are we not? We are the pinnacle of creation. We are the apex predator."

More cheers rang out.

"We drink blood. We kill people. It's what we do," said the Red Claw leader over the raucous applause. "Why in the name of the Omni-Father should we not take what is ours? Just because a cabal of jaded old fools think they know how to keep us safe? Humans should tremble in fear. That is the natural order of things. Why else do we exist? We are no accident. We are the next stage of the true God's unholy plan. We shall spread. We shall evolve. We shall conquer. Rise of the Red Claws — Ridicarea ghearelor roșii!"

"Ridicarea ghearelor roșii," chanted the assembled brood in old Romanian. "Ridicarea ghearelor roșii, Ridicarea ghearelor roșii, Ridicarea ghearelor roșii..."

Klaus threw back his head and screamed in joy and anticipation of what was to come.

After seeing Zachariah bow down to the warden, he thought the worst, that his brood would have to submit to the ruling order. Now it was clear that it was just an act. They would turn the world red and evade capture this time. The Council couldn't punish what it couldn't catch.

"Excuse me, Zachariah," a young female vampire said.

Klaus thought her name was Elliyahh. She was one of the newer Family members. Low-key and inconspicuous. She was a keeper of the knowledge, Klaus recalled. Her voice was low, almost a whisper. Klaus nearly didn't catch her words.

"Yes Elliyahh," Zachariah said kindly, eyebrows raised.

"I'm very sorry to interrupt you, master, but I noticed something. After I awoke, I went to check on the library. We have been defiled. It seems the Council broke their promise. On the first level, there were books moved from a shelf and discarded on the floor. I just thought that..."

Zachariah shot to his feet and ran out of the room before Elliyahh could finish her sentence.

The rest of the Family attempted to follow, which resulted in a bottleneck at the dining room door. Klaus got stuck at the back. He panicked, having no idea why Zachariah fled.

He pushed his way through into the hallway, thankful that even though he was tall, he was slight and stealthy. When he finally reached the library he looked up and saw Zachariah knelt in front of a bookshelf. His head in his hands.

Zachariah began rocking slightly, repeating the word 'no'

over and over again.

Klaus looked around at the other vampires to see if anyone understood what was happening. They all appeared equally confused.

However, Elliyahh looked perturbed. She seemed to realize the gravity of the situation.

"This can't be. This just can't be," said Zachariah. "Those profane bastards. This was part of the dark consecration, our sacred ground. Liars!"

Nobody spoke. Nobody breathed, not that vampires did in the normal sense, of course. The room was silent.

"It's gone. It's gone."

"Zachariah?" One of the elder vampires named Lizetta said, tentatively. "What is gone?"

"There was only one left. One left in the world," said Zachariah, seeming to ignore her.

Klaus was dismayed. Zachariah, who had always seemed so powerful, now looked like a frightened child.

"The *Adumbrate Invictus*, Lizetta," Zachariah finally said to the old vampire. "It chronicles our beginning...and our end."

"And you kept it in the library?" said Lizetta.

She opened her mouth to say more. But, very wisely, decided against it.

"We had their solemn undertaking," is all Zachariah said. Anger suddenly clouded his features. He stood up abruptly and looked out.

"Klaus! Klaus! I need you," he called out.

Klaus stood to attention at the sound of his name. He was needed!

"Here, Zachariah," Klaus shouted up. "I'm here. How may I serve?"

"Find the baseborn vermin who took the book and kill them all. Bring me back the *Invictus*."

Klaus was known for his tracking skills. As far as the Family went, he was the most proficient hunter among them. It was likely thanks to his former life as a human. He'd spent most of his spare time hunting large mammals in the forests near his home in Pennsylvania. The bigger the better, as far as he was concerned. These skills were amplified many times over after he was turned.

The throng of vampires parted so that Klaus could reach the front. He climbed the ladder and stood next to Zachariah, giving him a respectful nod. He then bent down and used his hyper-sensitive nose to scan the area. He picked up a few books that were on the floor. The smells were mixed. More than one human, but also a vampire, a different signature to the Red Claw emanations. That was a good thing. It likely meant that the vampire had the humans captive, or had killed them already. All Klaus had to do was track the vampire and retrieve the book. Easy.

"Got it," Klaus said. His senses tingling, ready to track.

"Take Ramone and Corbyn with you," Zachariah instructed.

"I don't think I'll need..."

"Take them." Zachariah left no room for argument.

Ramone and Corbyn stepped forward, following Klaus out of the library. As the group exited the house, Klaus tipped his head backward, sampling the air.

West.

Without a word to his comrades, he leaped into action, setting off after the scent. The trail took them to the outskirts of Angel Falls. Klaus's stomach rumbled, but now wasn't the time for snacks. He had a job to do. After half an hour of traversing fields at speed they were able to intersect the path of the yellow vehicle.

Klaus had to do a double-take when he saw it. He hadn't seen anything like it before. The cars he remembered were lumbering things with large, thin wheels and square bodies. They only came in black and made an incessant clicking sound as they ambled down the road. This yellow vehicle with its smooth shape and small, metal wheels seemed almost alien to Klaus. He would need to get used to this new world, and all its wonders. All of the Red Claws would need to. He put those thoughts aside and focused back on the hunt.

The smells were different now. Three distinct humans, a vampire, and something else. An earthy, primeval odor. It turned Klaus's stomach. Even though he recoiled at the stench, Klaus kept running towards it. Eventually, the Red Claws left the field and met the road. Klaus could hear the truck rattling towards them.

He instructed Ramone and Corbyn to remain at the edge of the field and then calmly walked out into the middle of the road.

Chapter 21

Aunt Laura pressed down hard on the gas pedal, accelerating at the fastest speed her aging truck was capable of. But it wasn't fast enough.

A figure emerged from the fields just up ahead. Slowly, gracefully, it walked out into the middle of the road.

Aunt Laura barely had time to react, instinctively slamming her foot on the brake and yanking the steering wheel to the right as far as it would go.

To Nell's amazement, the truck didn't flip. Instead, it wound up doing a 180, pointing the way it had come from.

They all twisted around in their seats.

The figure in the road stood in place, unmoving against the back of the truck. It was now clearly visible.

Vampire.

It had to be a Red Claw.

Nell's first thought was that he was strangely pale compared to Christopher. But of course he would be. Not only had he lain immobile in a stone tomb for a century, he also hadn't had a bite to eat in all that time, surviving only on the meager trickle of sustenance provided.

"Klaus," Christopher breathed, looking stunned.

He must have recognized the flame-haired vampire from

the hibernation pod.

However, for two decades Christopher had only ever seen the Red Claw asleep in that familiar serine repose. Christopher's eyes were wide as he took in Klaus now, very much awake and standing only feet from the truck.

As the group was momentarily overcome by shock and disorientation, the driver's side door was flung open and Aunt Laura was dragged from the vehicle, her arms flailing. Her scream was bone-chilling.

Christopher leapt into action, opening his own door and swiftly running around the side of the vehicle to cut Klaus off. Devan followed behind.

"The trunk..." Aunt Laura choked out, her body buffeted like a rag doll in the vampire's hold.

Nell didn't know what Aunt Laura was referring to, but didn't have time to question it.

Both she and Amara jumped out of the truck and ran around to the back.

Nell rolled back the covering on the cargo bed, trying to block from her mind the fact that Aunt Laura was being attacked.

Devan and Christopher had jumped to her defense and Nell knew that there was little she could do to help. Or at least that was what she thought, until she looked at the back of the truck. In front of her was an open duffle bag full of guns. Nell gaped in astonishment.

She had only ever shot a gun a few times with her dad when he'd reluctantly taken her hunting for a season, but she still remembered how to lock and load.

Grabbing a pistol, she ran towards the fray without thinking.

To her horror, there were three Red Claws now. One

battling Christopher for Aunt Laura and the other two entangled with Devan, who was tearing at them in his werwulf form.

Even though it was two against one, Devan towered over the vampires and was able to hurl them to the ground before taking chunks out of them with his teeth and claws. It was a sight to behold. It appeared werwulfs were much stronger than vampires when it came to pure brute strength.

The red-haired vampire holding Aunt Laura had her in a fireman's lift. She was thrown over his shoulder haphazardly. Her flailing had ceased, which Nell took as a bad sign.

Nell's breath caught in her chest and her blood ran cold.

She had only just lost her parents and now her aunt was in mortal danger, or worse. Her mind screamed for her poor aunt, who was one of the kindest and most selfless souls she had ever encountered.

One of the attacker's arms was wrapped around Aunt Laura's legs, holding her in place. His other arm was fending off Christopher's advances. The fight was too quick for Nell to follow.

While werwulfs were strong, vampires were fast. Lightning fast, in fact. The attacks and counter-attacks were a blur. It was too quick for the human eye to follow.

Nell tentatively lifted and pointed the gun, as her dad had shown her. Dominant hand on the backstrap, fingers wrapped firmly around the grip, index finger hovering over the trigger. Her left hand enclosed her right as she tried to aim.

But the vampires were moving too fast. There was too big a risk that she would hit Christopher or, God forbid, Aunt Laura. It was a no-go.

Nell desperately looked around her.

She saw that Devan had pinned down one of his attackers to the ground. The other was clinging to his thick back with his arms wrapped around Devan's neck. To the werwulf's credit, both vampires looked pretty beat up.

This was her chance.

Nell quickly lowered the gun and fired.

The gun flashed and roared.

She hit her target.

Dark, almost black, blood shot from the vampire's shoulder.

For a moment he looked confused. Then he saw the gun in her hand.

He grimaced with pain and fury then lunged towards her with an arm outstretched.

Nell shot again. Then again.

She hit his shoulder once more and then got him squarely between the eyes. The final shot knocked him down, temporarily at least.

The next few minutes happened in what felt like seconds.

Devan made a violent bowing motion, which sent the vampire on his back flying over his head. It landed on the ground with a heavy crunch.

Devan reached down and snapped his neck. The werwulf then picked up a thick branch from the side of the road and jammed it into the base of the vampire's skull, before grabbing its head with his claws and wrenching it clean off.

The body went slack, then turned to ash in front of Nell's eyes, cascading away in the breeze. The severed head cradled in Devan's hands also crumbled away to nothing, leaving him clutching thin air.

The other Red Claw was still on the ground. To Nell's disgust, it was squirming and thrashing, trying to dig the bullet out of its own head.

Devan closed in on him.

Nell focused back on her aunt, who was now laying on the road at the feet of her attacker. The red-haired vampire shouted something before Christopher barreled into him, shoving him away from Aunt Laura's body.

The other vampire fled while Christopher was rooted to the spot, seemingly frozen in place with a glazed expression on his face.

Nell couldn't fathom what was going on.

Chapter 22

Christopher felt like he was suspended in time. He felt disorientated. This had never happened before.

As he grabbed Klaus and pushed him away from Aunt Laura's body, Christopher saw something. A multitude of things, actually. Visions poured into his mind. Klaus's memories after being awakened. Sounds, images, thoughts, feelings, smell, touch.

He could see and sense it all: opening his eyes on the cold stone slab as Klaus; disgust at the plastic tube in his arm; conversations with the other Red Claws; the discovery that the book of prophesy — the *Adumbrate Invictus* they had called it — was gone; the moment they set off to find it. It all flooded into Christopher's consciousness as if he had lived it himself.

As a vampire, he could sense the odd human thought and, more often than not, tune into their feelings. As he was particularly close to Nell, he was sure he could read her thoughts if he really tried, though it would exhaust him. He also felt it was unethical, so he had never attempted it.

But nothing like this. This was new. This was terrifying. He looked down at Aunt Laura's prone body. His breath caught as he thought back to the attack, but now through the eyes of Klaus...

***

He had just told Ramone and Corbyn to stay back and then casually stepped out into the road. The battered yellow truck trundled towards him. He could see the driver was an old woman. Good for her, Klaus thought, in a rare magnanimous moment. At least she'd had a decent run at life before meeting her end.

The tires screeched as the truck slowed dramatically, then it spun all the way around, ending up only feet away from the impassive Klaus.

He needed to get to the driver so the vehicle couldn't make off.

He sprang into action, wrenching open the door and yanking out the woman. She was light as a feather, but managed to shout something. He was about to sink his teeth into her for a quick little pick-me-up (she wouldn't be fresh, but beggars can't be choosers) when the other vampire came flying out of the truck after her, quickly followed by a human male, who was no doubt seizing his opportunity to escape the vampire's captivity.

To Klaus's amazement, the vampire, a youngster with a mess of dark hair, began attacking him. He had to put the old woman on his shoulder to free up a hand so he could defend himself. The moronic vampire thought Klaus was stealing his prey. Klaus didn't have the opportunity to explain he had no interest in the humans, he was too busy fending off the blows.

Ramone and Corbyn joined the fray. They piled on top of the fleeing man. Idiots. This was no time to feed, however great the hunger. They had a job to do. Klaus watched on in amazement as Ramone and Corbyn were thrown off by the hum…not human….but wolf. It was a werwulf. The foul scent suddenly made sense. The two Red Claws regrouped and launched themselves at the feral beast.

The old woman was flailing on his shoulder, distracting him as he fought the young vampire. Klaus dragged his long fingernails across her throat before making a sharp jerking motion, which stilled her.

He looked around. The foul beast was getting the better of Ramone and Corbyn. It was a tall feral mass of rage, snapping and tearing at his hapless companions.

Now a human female stood close to them, pointing a gun of all things. Shots were fired. Ramone slumped to the ground.

Klaus couldn't process what was going on. It was too chaotic.

The book. He was here for the book. That was all that mattered.

"Have her," Klaus spat, before dumping the old woman's body on the road.

He was pushed away by the dark-haired vampire, who was reclaiming his prey.

***

The alien thoughts and images suddenly cut off in Christopher's consciousness. His new gift of insight went dark and he was cast out of Klaus's mind and body.

It made sense. He wouldn't have been able to see beyond the point of physical contact between them.

So what Christopher didn't see was that Klaus hadn't simply made his escape into the fields. He instead darted to the truck. Christopher's focus at this point was on Aunt Laura's body lying unceremoniously on the road.

When Klaus briefly looked back he saw the other vampire leaning over the body, no doubt finally able to enjoy his feast.

Klaus scanned the interior of the truck, but didn't have to look far. The book was right there on the passenger seat. He grabbed it and looked back around. Just in time to see the wolf-beast jam a wooden spike into Corbyn's skull before tearing his head clean off with his bare hands. The Red Claw stilled before disintegrating.

Ramone was flailing on the ground, in obvious distress. Klaus considered whether he should come to the aid of his Family member.

The decision wasn't difficult. He fled into the fields.

Chapter 23

Nell watched as Christopher snapped out of his trance and came back to the here and now. He went down on his knees and held Aunt Laura's limp body.

A huge, ugly gash ran across her throat. Her neck was bent at a grotesque angle.

Nell screamed in anguish as she ran over and knelt beside Christopher. She felt like her heart was being torn from her chest. Another person she loved dearly had been ripped from her. Her breath came in long, ragged heaves as she touched her beloved aunt's face.

"I'm so sorry, Nell," she heard Christopher say.

The words sounded fuzzy, like they were coming from inside a bubble. His voice was thick, husky.

"Where is he?" Nell asked, not looking away from her aunt.

Grief was making way for rage inside her.

"He ran. When he killed her, he ran. I didn't know what to do, so I stayed with her. I should have gone after him. I should have..."

Christopher looked like he was mulling something, but then simply hung his head down.

"Oh, Nell. I'm so sorry," he said. "This is my fault. All of this is my fault."

Nell didn't really register much after the two words *'he ran'.* The bastard got away. He killed her aunt, the woman who had so selflessly taken her in, then fled.

Nell gritted her teeth and then the floodgates opened. Tears cascaded down her face as she cradled her aunt's delicate head in her hands.

"I will kill him, Nell," said Christopher. "I promise you that. The next time we cross paths, he's mine. But right now I'm not leaving your side."

A low crack came from behind them.

Devan had snapped the neck of the other vampire.

Nell turned just in time to see him ramming a thick branch into his skull and then tearing the head away. The vampire transformed to dust, then drifted away in the wind.

Devan looked at her, apologetically. Even in his wolf form, she could register the remorse in his eyes.

"I'm sorry," he said, his voice raspy and hoarse. "I wasn't quick enough."

"It's not your fault, Devan," she said, fighting the tears and watching the ash cascade away into nothingness. "You did more than enough."

She looked down at her lifeless aunt again.

"What do we do now?" she asked, weakly.

Amara walked over and put a hand on her back. In the maelstrom of events, Nell had forgotten she was even there.

"We have to bury her," Christopher said, gently.

Nell looked horrified.

"Now? Here?" she choked out.

Christopher nodded, grimly.

Amara rubbed her back in a gentle circular motion.

"No way," said Nell. "Are you out of your mind? We have to

take her to a hospital. Things have to be done properly."

Christopher looked pained.

"It's not what any of us want to do, but we need to get away quickly," he explained. "Going to hospital will place us all in danger. Knowing Aunt Laura, I don't think that's what she would have wanted."

Nell stared at him in disbelief.

"But we can't leave her here, in the middle of nowhere," she implored, through tears. "She comes with us, then."

Christopher sighed.

"If we take her with us, the blood will attract the Red Claws," he explained. "The Council can't do anything for her at this point."

"I hate to say it, Nell," said Amara, softly. "But I think he's right."

Nell stared despondently at the librarian before bending down and burying her head in her aunt's shoulder. She began sobbing.

Amara continued rubbing her back. Christopher and Devan maintained a respectful silence.

After a long moment Nell raised her head.

"Okay..." she whispered. "Okay...she'll stay here. For now."

She gently placed her aunt's head back on the ground and moved back.

Christopher leaned over and picked the body up gently, as if he was carrying a newborn baby.

He exchanged a look with Devan and they walked off together into the field.

Amara remained at Nell's side, placing a supportive arm around her shoulder and squeezing tight.

Eventually, Nell's tears dried and she looked up. Christopher and Devan were back. Soft earth was matted to Devan's lush fur.

"It's done," Christopher said, gently, kneeling down. "Do you want to say goodbye?"

"No, not like this. Not here," Nell said, resolute. "I'll be back to do it properly. I owe her that much."

After another long moment Christopher stood.

"I'm sorry, Nell, but we have to go now," he said, more urgently. "It will be full morning soon and there will be other cars. Plus the Red Claws won't be far behind. They'll be furious we killed two of their own."

"Two down," Devan said, as they walked the short way back to the pickup.

Nell caught the wary glance Amara gave Devan. But truth be told, she agreed with him completely. Two Red Claws down.

At the truck, Nell scanned the front passenger seat for the book of prophecy. Then the back seats. Then the area all around the truck.

"Shit," she said. "The book's missing."

"That might explain the attack," said Amara. "Remember what the Magisters said."

"There's not much we can do about that now," said Christopher. "Let's get moving."

Devan transformed then pulled a pair of jeans and a T-shirt from the truck, which he put on. He hopped into the driver's seat. Amara took the front passenger seat and Nell and Christopher climbed into the back.

Devan started the engine and did a three-point turn, heading in the direction of the I-95 highway, which would take them to North Carolina.

After an hour on the road, Amara's eyes drew shut. Devan

kept his sharp senses on the road. Nell snuggled into the side of Christopher, her head resting on his chest.

Thoughts raced around her head. She couldn't find the right words to say to him. How did you tell the love of your life that you wanted to die?

Seeing Aunt Laura's frail body broken on the road had convinced her of what she needed to do. She had to fulfill her role in the prophecy. The Red Claws needed to be wiped from the face of the Earth before they inflicted any more carnage. If the only way to do that was to allow Christopher to drain her blood, then she would do it. Gladly. But how to tell him?

Recalling Christopher's reaction when the Magisters had essentially signed her death warrant made Nell wary about the difficult conversation ahead of her. She was still raw from Aunt Laura's death, but there was no point putting off talking about what needed to be done. Without lifting her head she spoke softly.

"Christopher?"

"Yes, Nell," he replied, stroking her arm.

"About the prophecy..."

She waited for his response, but he stayed silent beside her. However, his body tensed, betraying his thoughts.

She breathed in, ready to speak again.

"Don't say it," said Christopher.

His voice was quiet, pleading.

"You have to do it. If it means that you end the Red Claws for good, you have to," she said. "I can't let them...do to other people...what they did to Aunt Laura. I can't live with that on my conscience. If it's my life against countless other people, I choose the others every time. I'm just one person."

"You're not just one person," he replied. "You are the person I love more than anything in the world. Which is crazy because I've only just met you, but it's true nonetheless. You are my one true love. The prophecy at least got that much right. If I have to kill you to save the world, then let the world burn."

Nell looked up into his eyes.

"I won't do it," he said, resolutely. "Don't ask me, Nell."

His last words were broken, fragmented. It was hard to listen to. Almost like a child who didn't quite understand the harsh ways of the world.

"Christopher, people are dying. Probably right now as we speak," Nell begged. "If you drain me, then you'll be able to kill the bastards who murdered Aunt Laura. It's what the prophecy says."

"I know," was all he said for the rest of the journey.

Chapter 24

Zachariah was seated back at the head of the large oval table when Klaus arrived.

"So?" Zachariah said.

Klaus placed the *Adumbrate Invictus* on the table in front of him.

"I got it," Klaus said, his held head high.

"And Ramone and Corbyn?" asked Zachariah, carefully picking up the book and turning it over in his hands, as if it were a rare antique.

Klaus lowered his head.

"Corbyn is dead," he confided. "Ramone was dying when I left. I tried my best to save them but..."

"How so?" Zachariah interrupted.

He looked calm but it was hard to know what was bubbling under the surface.

"There was a werwulf."

"Werwulf?" said Zachariah, looking perturbed. "That's odd, don't you think? What about the vampire that was holding them all captive?"

"It was a strange situation, I must admit," confided Klaus. "The vampire was preoccupied with reclaiming the driver — an old woman who I snatched at the outset. I had stolen his meal and he wasn't happy. I didn't have time to explain. When the younger woman fired the gun at Ramone I..."

"Gun!" exclaimed Zachariah. "What was the woman doing with a gun if the vampire was holding her captive? And why did the werwulf attack Corbyn and Ramone instead of fleeing?"

Oh God, thought Klaus. *This is way over my head.*

"Tell me you killed them all, Klaus!" Zachariah shouted. "Tell me that much, at least!"

Klaus backed away towards the corner of the room. Although putting physical distance between them wouldn't save Klaus from Zachariah's wrath, it made him feel a little calmer.

"I got you the book," mumbled Klaus. "That was the objective."

"Excuse me?" Zachariah was seething now. His eyes narrowed. "Didn't I expressly tell you to kill them all?"

"The werwulf, he was too strong," pleaded Klaus. "We would have *all* ended up dead...with nothing to show for it."

Zachariah raised his hands to his head.

"This is not right, not right at all," he said, massaging his temples. "Why would the girl be in possession of a weapon if the vampire had captured her for feeding? Moreover, why would she fire at Ramone, thus aiding the werwulf?"

He suddenly looked up at Klaus.

"Did you see the vampire feeding on the dead woman?" asked Zachariah, urgently. "Think carefully, Klaus."

"Yes," he replied, without hesitation. "After I went for the book I saw him hunched over her."

"Did you see the vampire feeding on her?" Zachariah asked again, more sternly.

"Not exactly, no, but I was certain he..."

"You useless bloodsucker!" Zachariah screamed. "Are you still too feeble-minded to see what was actually occurring?"

Klaus stared blankly.

"They were in league with each other," cried Zachariah. "The vampire was trying to protect the driver, not feed on her, you cretin."

As a Red Claw, Klaus couldn't fathom the possibility of vampires being on the side of humans. Surely all vampires only saw them as food.

"I'm…I'm sorry, Zachariah," he pleaded. "I didn't know what…it was all happening so quickly…"

Zachariah suddenly looked stricken.

"If the vampire was allied with the human girl," he said. "That could possibly mean…"

Zachariah grabbed the *Invictus* and began flipping through the pages urgently. He stopped near the end and began reading aloud.

"Salvation lies in one soul. A death-walker turned young...He will love, as no other of his kin has before. He will abandon those he serves. He will develop abilities unknown..."

"In the name of the Omni-Father, what have you done, Klaus?" he scolded. "We need to fix this, or we're possibly all dead. Call the Family together, NOW!"

Klaus ran out of the room. He didn't fully understand what was going on. But if Zachariah was right, and the vampire was conspiring with humans and also a vile wolf-beast, then the world as he knew it was truly broken.

Chapter 25

The drive to the Blue Ridge Mountains was tense. Quiet. Christopher held tightly to Nell's hand, as if she might simply float away if he dared let go. He drew circles on her palm with his index finger and occasionally tapped out the rhythm to one of his songs.

Nell was subdued. Her rational mind told her that there was a good chance she was dreaming right now. There was no way she was actually driving to vampire central with her undead boyfriend, a werwulf and a librarian. There was also no way her Aunt Laura was dead, hastily buried in a field. No. Stuff like that just didn't happen.

She closed her eyes then reached down to her thigh and pinched herself hard. She was hoping to wake up in her warm bed with the alluring smell of bacon wafting into her room and the faint sounds of Aunt Laura puttering away in the kitchen downstairs.

Nell opened her eyes. She was still in the pickup. She took a deep breath and attempted to find some composure. It was impossible. So she leaned her head against Christopher's firm shoulder and closed her eyes once more.

Christopher was on high alert, constantly turning his head this way and that in between comforting Nell. He would smell the air and stare out at the surrounding fields, on the lookout for any fast-moving shapes. Four hours ticked by like this.

"We're here, Nell," Christopher whispered into her hair.

His lips softly brushed her forehead. She didn't remember falling asleep. The last thing she recalled was leaning her head against him. Nell groaned and moved, her neck aching from resting in an awkward position. She could sense that the truck was now stationary. Blinking against the light of day, she looked out of the window. The building she saw could not have been more conspicuous. It screamed *'Vampires live here! Bring garlic, lots of it'.*

It looked medieval. A sprawling gothic structure, complete with turrets and steeples. When it came to real estate, it seemed that vampires weren't familiar with the terms 'understated' or 'subtle'.

After stretching her stiff limbs, Nell climbed out of the truck, flanked by Devan and Christopher. Amara was the last out. She stood behind the other three, taking in the grandeur of the residence. She let out a low whistle of amazement. Who could blame her.

Christopher approached the tall wooden doors first, tapping the black iron knocker, which was in the shape of two serpents intertwined. They waited for a moment and then the heavy doors were hefted open, revealing an old man in a black suit.

"Master Christopher, you are expected. As are your friends."

His weathered face and ruddy complexion showed that he was human, which took Nell by surprise.

"Follow me, please," he said.

They walked down a long, dark hall that led to a sweeping staircase. Mahogany surfaces and rich, red carpets filled the house. Opulent was the word. Ostentatious, even. Some might even say garish. But Nell was too polite. Behind the staircase was a set of doors that opened onto a grand drawing room. Next to it was an old-fashioned metal cage elevator.

They were led into the drawing room. Leather-backed chaise lounges were scattered about while the back wall was filled with bookshelves. Six individuals with the palest skin Nell had ever seen sat in a circle in the center of the room. They looked up as Nell and her companions entered.

"Master Christopher and his associates," said their guide, before blowing curtly and leaving the room.

"Christopher, it is good to meet you at last," said a man with a very serious face.

He looked to be about fifty-five, but Nell knew appearances meant very little when trying to assess the age of a vampire. His face was criss-crossed with scars, but the most striking thing about him was his shrunken left arm. Nell tried not to stare.

"My name is Dragos Vacarescu," he continued. "I am the Speaker of the Council of Elders. I extend to you the protection and sanctuary of Vhik'h-Tal-Eskemon."

Christopher bowed. The others followed suit, feeling self-conscious but not wanting to offend their host.

"Thank you...sir," said Christopher. He gestured to his friends. "Allow me to introduce Devan, Amara and Petronella."

Devan snorted. Amara surreptitiously kicked his foot.

"A pleasure indeed," said Dragos. "Seated with me are my fellow Council members: Gustav Nielsen, Loshua Dascălu, Amos Smythe, Zulima Vargas and Shing-Lei Zan."

The five Council members nodded.

"We look after the Americas," explained Dragos. "There are other Councils all over the world."

"Fascinating," marveled Amara, who was no doubt keen to learn more about their inner workings.

Just then the butler reappeared at the door.

"The High Chancellor will be with you imminently," he said.

"Thank you, Sanford," replied Dragos.

Nell, Amara, Devan and Christopher all stiffened in anticipation. Nell's imagination ran away with her for a moment. She pictured the High Chancellor swooping down the stairs in bat form and then transforming into a Dracula-type figure in front of them, all swooping cloak and menacing eyes.

It was then that she noticed a faint buzzing noise. The sound grew steadily louder. It was actually a hum of sorts, a mechanical sound, now that she concentrated on it. Nell stared at the entrance of the drawing room. She wasn't sure what to expect, but what she saw left her speechless.

In came a small woman sitting on an electric wheelchair, which she was controlling with a tiny joystick on the arm rest. She had dark brown skin and wore an ornate Indian sari of red and green. Her black hair was parted in the middle and swept back into a neat plaited ponytail. A gold chain went from her left ear to her nose while her wrists were adorned with colorful bangles, which jangled when she moved the joystick. She had deep brown eyes and startlingly white teeth, which stood out against her dusky skin.

She looked at the four surprised newcomers, then smiled broadly.

"I know, I know," she said in a soft, musical voice with a hint of an eastern accent. "I often disappoint myself. I hope you weren't expecting Christopher Lee or Gary Oldman, I really don't have the gravitas. Nor the offbeat charm of Robert Pattinson, who rather fittingly played a vampire and a bat. But

I can say that I'm probably the same height as Tom Cruise, in heels at least. Pity I can't stand, though." She looked down at her own body: "Fate can be cruel, but also somewhat ironic, don't you think?"

The four of them just stood there, not having the first clue how to respond.

"High Chancellor," said Dragos. "Please let me introduce Christopher, Amara, Devan and Petronella."

"It's Nell, just Nell," said Nell, finding her voice.

"How lovely to meet you, Nell," said the High Chancellor. "My name is Kavisha Devi, but please call me Kavi, as nobody does, despite my efforts."

Kavisha looked intensely at Nell.

"Come here, child," she said, gently.

Nell approached.

Kavisha held out her hands, which Nell instinctively gripped.

"So you're the one," said the High Chancellor, gently squeezing Nell's hands. "That's something we have in common…fate being unkind."

Kavisha pointed at the empty seats around them.

"Sit, please. We have much to discuss."

The four of them sat down on a long green chaise lounge.

Christopher began to talk. He described escaping the mansion, meeting the Magisters and the journey to Vhik'h-Tal-Eskemon. He recounted the ambush on the road as quickly as he could, not wanting Nell to have to dwell on her aunt's cruel death.

Kavisha looked stricken.

"I'm so terribly sorry," she said to Nell. "It must have been awful."

Nell stifled a sob and looked down at her hands.

"We have to make her death mean something," added Christopher, emphatically. "So she didn't die in vain."

As he spoke he recalled seeing the version of events from Klaus's perspective, that bizarre leap into his mind. He didn't know whether to mention it to the Council now that he was here. Something made him keep his cards close to his chest. It didn't feel right to share this information just yet. They had to focus on keeping Nell safe above all else.

Nell fidgeted on the chaise lounge, leaning away from the hard leather back and then drumming her fingers on the shiny wooden armrest. She reached out and held Christopher's hand.

"I see that the Magisters were correct about the inception of the prophecy," Kavisha said, looking between Nell and Christopher. "You have feelings for each other." It wasn't a question, but a statement.

"Yes," both Nell and Christopher said at the same time.

Kavisha smiled.

"The Magisters have been tracking the Red Claws since our Warden of the South and Council went to rouse them," she said. "Things haven't turned out as we'd hoped. Pretty much as we expected, but not as we'd hoped."

Kavisha looked gravely at the seated Council members.

"Blood will out, as they say, and the Red Claws went right back to their old ways," she explained. "We now have a number of human corpses spread around the small town of Angel Falls, which will once again bring scrutiny down on us all."

The Council members lowered their heads, seemingly in unison.

Devan looked up, incandescent with rage. He opened his

mouth to speak.

Kavisha raised a placating hand.

"You might wonder why we chose to wake them if we suspected this would be the outcome," she continued. "Part of it is that we find killing our own detestable. Part of it is the unpredictable ramifications of breaking a blood oath sealed with Old Magick."

"We were told that," said Devan, indignantly. "It sounds pretty weak, if you ask me. There's no way we're going to sacrifice Nell because you and your Council don't have the balls to make tough decisions."

"Heed those words," added Christopher, pointing a finger. "Nell's not here to act as your scapegoat."

The High Chancellor sighed then looked at Dragos, who nodded.

"The prophecy that you read wasn't the only one related to the Red Claws," said the High Chancellor. "The Magisters have their own copy of the *Adumbrate Invictus.* Its existence is a tightly-guarded secret."

The visitors, apart from Christopher, looked confused.

"*Adumbrate Invictus is* the title of the book of prophecy that was taken from you," explained Kavisha.

"Or reclaimed, as the Red Claws no doubt view it," added Dragos.

"What's this other prophecy about?" asked Amara, ever the knowledge seeker.

"If you would be so kind, Speaker," said the High Chancellor.

"Of course," said Dragos. "The later prophecy goes as follows: *A millennia-long slumber ensures the obsidian spreads its immutable shadow across the world. Enmity unabated engulfs all that is for eternity. A century-long slumber will test the seeds of darkness. A millennia-long slumber will end them."*

"So we choose to face the consequences now, when we have a chance," said Kavisha. "Or we wait. Wait until the Red Claws awake from a one-thousand-year sleep, when the destruction of everything appears assured."

Nell didn't know what to say. The explanation didn't make her feel any better. It was selfish, but she couldn't help thinking that if the Council had put off their decision far into the future, she wouldn't be in this situation. It would be affecting somebody else, not her.

"I know what you're thinking, young lady," said Amos Smythe, one of the Council members.

He was portly with tufts of graying hair on either side of his head. He wore a brown tweed suit and tie, making him look like a deathly pale classics professor.

"What am I thinking?" Nell ventured.

"That if we would have waited, you wouldn't be involved," replied Amos, rather loftily. "You would have had a normal life. Your Aunt would be alive. Everything would have been sunshine and rainbows for you."

Nell took an instant dislike to him, but couldn't fault his reasoning.

"You don't get off that easy," he continued. "A foretelling is..."

"Please, Amos," Kavisha interrupted. "This is not called for." She turned back to Nell.

Amos looked irked.

"Prophecies have a strange way of working, I'm afraid," said the High Chancellor, in a sympathetic tone. "If you are supposed to be the one, then it always would have been you. Maybe you would have been born far into the future. But it always would have been you. Your unique soul. It always would have been Christopher, also. That's the nature of fate."

This didn't make Nell feel any better. In fact, it made her feel worse. She and Christopher were always doomed, it seemed.

"So what are we going to do?" Christopher said, facing the Elders.

"We hide the girl. We hide you," said Zulima Vargas, a tall, thin woman with long black hair that cascaded down her back. "We make sure you are ready for battle and, when the time comes, we might have to ask for the ultimate sacrifice from Nell. But we will ensure that it will not be in vain."

Nell nodded, having already accepted her fate.

Christopher was a long way from doing anything of the sort. The veins in his neck bulged. He roped a protective arm around Nell.

"And what are our other options?" he asked, staring at each of the Elders in turn.

"That is no concern of yours, boy," said Amos. "The decision is ours to take, and ours alone." He pointed a finger at Nell. "She has to exit the stage in this story."

He almost seemed to enjoy imparting bad news.

"That's not good enough," Christopher fired back. "There must be another way."

"Are you a simpleton, boy?" said Amos. "It has to be done, preferably now!"

All eyes were on the stout Elder.

"Waiting is madness," he continued. "This Council is short-sighted and someone needs to act for the greater good."

"Once again, Amos..." began Kavisha.

But Amos suddenly stood up and retracted something from the inside pocket of his blazer. It was moving. It curled itself around his pale wrist.

Nell was startled to see that it was a small green snake.

Amos reached into another pocket and swiftly pulled out a small ornate dagger.

Everyone was frozen in shock.

Kavisha held up her hand and shouted: "What do you th..."

Amos quickly slashed at the snake with the dagger, taking its head off in one stroke. He then uttered strange words: "Fă toți acești oameni nemișcați".

Kavisha's hand remained in the air, but she was now silent, and perfectly still.

Nell looked around her. She saw bodies frozen in motion, expressions fixed in place.

Christopher was leaning forward with his arms outstretched, ready to dive in front of Nell to protect her. But he was suspended in time. He looked like he was pushing an invisible car uphill.

"What have you done?" Nell breathed.

Amara turned her head towards Nell, looking panicked. Whatever had occurred, it hadn't affected either of them.

"Some kind of spell," said Amara.

"They told us you were the smart one," said Amos, derisively. "Hex is actually the correct term. Keeping company with spell-casters has its perks."

"What do you want?" asked Nell, taking in the surreal scene.

"Is it not obvious? Your immediate death, young lady," he replied, matter-of-factly. "Unlike you, I've been around for centuries. I've seen first-hand what the Red Claws are capable of. A battle with them would be folly of the highest order."

"But what's the alternative?" asked Amara.

"Not so clever after all, are we, Miss Uppity," he mocked.

"But then there's not much call for an education in 'da ghetto' is there, sista?" He chuckled to himself.

Amara stiffened.

Nell looked disgusted.

"You are truly despicable," she said.

Amos turned back to Amara.

"Your friend's death means the prophecy cannot be fulfilled, she cannot be drained by young lover-boy here." He wagged the dagger in the direction of Christopher. "After she's taken out of the equation, I escape and throw myself on the mercy of the Red Claws. As the one who ensured their survival, I'm sure I'll get a fitting position in the new order."

Both women looked horrified.

"Time to meet your maker," said Amos.

Nell's eyes immediately flew to the static Christopher.

"Not much hope there, I'm afraid," said Amos. "The Benumbing Hex is particularly effective on vampires."

The Elder pointed the blade at Nell and started walking towards her.

A brown blur flashed in front of Nell's eyes.

Amos's throat was ripped open and then his head separated from the rest of his body. It landed on the floor with a wide-eyed look of shock etched on his face. The headless body crumpled to the ground a few moments later.

Devan towered over the bloody scene, his sharp werwulf claws smeared with dark blood.

"Particularly effective on vampires, is it?" he said, mocking Amos's haughty tone. "Well, my claws are particularly effective on traitorous racist fucktards."

The hex was broken and gasps filled the room.

Christopher grabbed Nell and held her close.

Everything was silent for a while.

Nell had expected the other Elders to spring into action, to attack the werwulf in their midst, but they did no such thing. Instead, they tilted their heads, surveying the scene before them with curiosity.

"Well," Dragos said. "I think I speak for all of us when I say thank goodness for that."

Nell looked at him in shock.

Kavisha's face contorted into a thin smile, as did those of the other Elders.

"We've been waiting for someone to take him out for centuries," said Dragos. "Unhinged old fool that he was."

The body on the floor was already a pile of ash.

"Sanford," shouted Gustav Nielsen, speaking for the first time. "Clean up in aisle six."

The rest of the Elders chuckled.

The butler entered soon after.

"Please show our friends to their rooms first, Sanford," said the High Chancellor. "I'm sure they are in need of rest. And Devan here looks like he might need some new clothes."

"As you wish," replied Sanford.

He surveyed the bizarre scene but maintained his impassive demeanor.

Chapter 26

Nell and Christopher were assigned a room on the top floor. As they marched up the grand winding staircase Christopher wrapped an arm around Nell's shoulder and pulled her in for a sideways hug. Nell tilted her head towards him and buried it into the crook of his neck. They paused on their journey upwards. Christopher reached up his other hand and gently cradled her chin. He slowly turned her face towards him before planting a light kiss on her lips.

Nell was feeling a sea of different emotions. Grief, apprehension, remorse and uncertainty were high up in the mix. But Christopher's touch brought her a moment of respite. The physical contact soothed her. It seemed her body needed to feel right now.

Nell tentatively parted her lips a little. Christopher accepted the invitation and touched his tongue against hers. Nell turned her body to face him before wrapping her hands behind his neck and pulling him closer. When they finally released, both of them were breathing more quickly.

Christopher placed a hand on the small of Nell's back and guided her up the stairs. Nell was momentarily accosted by guilt. Was now really the time? But she decided to listen to her body. To go with her inner guide.

They had been given a huge bedroom, complete with en-suite bathroom and super-king size bed. The second they entered the room, Nell pushed Christopher against the wall, pressing her body into his. Facing your own death did strange things to a person. Suddenly propriety and moderation went out of the window. She needed comfort. She needed Christopher.

She brushed her lips against his, standing on her tiptoes. He kissed her back with vigor, reaching around to hold the back of her shoulders. Nell gently pulled away and looked into Christopher's face, searching for his feelings. Any anger seemed to have abated, making way for tenderness.

"I love you," Christopher breathed against Nell's neck as he trailed gentle kisses down to her shoulder.

"Ditto," she said, playfully, as she locked lips with him again and ran her hands up and down his firm torso.

With their lips still locked and tongues intertwined, Christopher grasped the hem of her top and pulled it up over her head. Nell lifted her arms, obligingly. She led him towards the bed. Clothes were soon strewn across the floor as the two of them gave physical expression to their emotions.

Nell pulled Christopher on top of her. He trailed kisses down the length of her upper body before stopping at her midsection. He took his time exploring her. Nell arched her back and lost herself to the currents of energy cascading through her center. Just before she came to the point of no return she reached down and grabbed Christopher's shoulders and guided him upwards. Their mouths locked. At the same time she parted her thighs slightly.

Christopher was gentle. He slipped inside her slowly, studying her face for any signs of discomfort. He needn't have worried. Nell snaked her legs around his waist and dug her heels into his back, while pulling him tighter to her. Christopher began to rock his hips, gently at first and then with more urgency. Nell squeezed his shoulder blades as sweet release flooded her body, sending out ripples of joy. Christopher moaned, stiffened then collapsed into Nell's arms, where they remained entwined in a tight embrace.

Eventually they lay on their backs, Nell resting her head on Christopher's chest as he lightly caressed her hair. Exhaustion had caught up with her body, but her thoughts were spinning.

It seemed she was safe, for now. Her death was certain, but not imminent. The plan was to keep her protected until the Magisters could assess the situation and advise on the best course forward. Nell was also a kind of bargaining chip – 'Hey bloodthirsty vamps, behave yourselves or we'll kill this human, which then gives her lover the ability to wipe you out'. If this wasn't her actual life, Nell would have found it farcical.

Nell's existence would revolve around these headquarters. She and Christopher wouldn't be allowed to leave, that was a given. But Amara and Devan would be permitted to remain here, too. A good-will gesture? Nell suspected it was more likely due to the fact that they would be hunted down the instant they left the refuge of Vhik'h-Tal-Eskemon. The Red Claws would be after information, or more likely use them as pawns to get to Nell. Not only was her own life utterly screwed, but she'd managed to ruin the lives of her friends.

Good one, Nell.

She needed sleep badly now. Both to restore her body and give her mind a break from her roiling thoughts. She closed her eyes and slowly succumbed to merciful slumber.

Christopher waited until Nell's eyes fluttered close and

her breathing evened out before zoning into his restorative trance. While his body was relaxed, he again thought about his connection with Klaus. It felt like a dirty little secret. He didn't like keeping things from Nell, but he didn't want to alarm her further. She had more than enough on her plate.

***

Loud banging awoke the both of them.

Christopher instinctively launched himself out of bed and stood in front of the door, ready to protect Nell and face down any threat.

"Guys! Come on, wake-up! The Magisters are here. Shit just got real," Devan shouted through the door before opening it and immediately covering his eyes with his hands after catching sight of a naked Christopher.

"Buddy, please," said Devan. "That's way too much information for my retinas."

"Dude, we've seen your junk like a dozen times over the past few days," replied an exasperated Christopher, reaching for his jeans.

"Yeah, but that was after saving your pasty ass which, unfortunately, I just seem to have confirmed is all-too real," said Devan.

Nell snickered. She wondered what Devan's response would have been if she'd been caught nude instead. A blush came to her cheeks.

Nell and Christopher threw on their clothes and hurried down to the drawing room.

Devan and Amara were already there on the other side of the room, along with Kavisha and the Council members. The

Magisters were stationed around the room in their dark robes, looking like harbingers of doom.

"The Magisters have news," Kavisha said, addressing the group. "But first let me introduce our new Elder, Loris Valkari, previously the Warden of the South. In the wake of Amos's demise, Loris is next in line. We welcome him."

Loris nodded at the assembled group. He was handsome, in a fatherly way, Nell thought.

The bald elder Magister stepped forward without being asked.

"The floor is yours, Fabian," said Kavisha.

"Thank you, High Chancellor," he replied. "Apologies for getting straight down to business. Time is of the essence now. We have been made aware that the Red Claws are making their way here, to Vhik'h-Tal-Eskemon."

Gasps sounded around the room.

"Apparently the trail was pretty easy to follow, thanks to the beastman," he continued, looking at Devan. "They have skilled hunters who tracked his sten...scent."

Devan bowed, theatrically.

"If you could bottle it, perhaps you might get laid for once in your excruciatingly long and miserable existence," he said.

Fabian wrinkled his nose. His fellow Magister Jiangshina might have smirked.

"Be assured, our headquarters are safe from attack," said Kavisha, moving the conversation on and trying to diffuse the animosity. "The Old Magick imbued in the walls of Vhik'h-Tal-Eskemon is unbreakable. However, we cannot guarantee the safety of anyone who leaves its perimeter. The Red Claws are not to be underestimated. They will kill their own if it ensures their ultimate survival. They will not hesitate to turn any of us to dust."

"You asked for our counsel, High Chancellor," said Fabian. "And we are here to deliver it. It is not our desire or custom to intervene in your affairs but we must ask that, in this instance, you allow us to lead."

"Your guidance is always highly regarded," said Kavisha.

"We agreed that now was not the right time to enact the prophecy and claim the life essence of the human women," said Fabian. "But that was before they killed two Red Claws. The enemy is now driven by rage as well as fear, a truly incendiary mix. I see no alternative at this juncture." He turned to Christopher. "It is time for you to do your duty, lad. That way, when the Red Claws arrive, you are prepared."

"No," said Kavisha and Christopher together.

Fabian flinched.

"This is not the way," the High Chancellor said. "We value your opinion, Magister, but the prophecy was quite clear on the order of events. Speaker, can you please recall for us the exact words."

"Of course," said Dragos, bowing slightly.

"A war will rage and devastate the landscape. Creatures of the night will come together to fight as one. Unlikely allegiances will be forged. They will be tested. They will be sacrificed."

"We are well aware of the text," said Fabian, testily. "We are Magisters. We don't need lectures from anyone."

"Thank you, Dragos," said Kavisha, turning to the Speaker and ignoring Fabian. "And does this passage come *before* any mention of the vampire-turned-young having to drain his one true love."

"It does indeed, High Chancellor," he replied.

"It would seem clear then," said Kavisha, finally addressing

Fabian. "The alliances have not been forged as yet. We are not allied with other creatures of the night. Taking this irrevocable action at this time does not appear to be in the correct sequence."

"And *you* have the wisdom and sagacity to deduce this?" Fabian scoffed.

"Zachariah will know by now that a vampire has sided with a human," said Kavisha. "He is many things, but not stupid. What explanation could there be other than the prophecy playing out? Killing the girl now will only make things worse for us. The Red Claws will see it as an act of war if they find out. They will feel their time is limited unless they act right away. We will have put the cogs in motion before we are ready. Apart from young Devan here, we have no outside allies. We also don't know if Christopher has developed any other abilities, besides being able to fall in love."

Nell blushed. She couldn't help but like Kavisha, despite the fact that the High Chancellor fully intended to sanction her death at some point in the future. But one day at a time.

What Nell couldn't quite understand, though, was the U-turn by the Magisters. Back at the cabin they made it a priority to protect her. Something had changed in the time since. Nell's head spun with all the ups and downs of the situation.

"I'm afraid you are wrong, High Chancellor," said Fabian, bluntly.

Kavisha looked surprised.

"The war must start now," he continued. "We know things you do not, which we are not at liberty to share with you." The Magister addressed Christopher. "Now be a dear young man and kill the girl."

Christopher turned to face Nell and placed his hands on the

sides of her neck.

Nell stared at him wide-eyed. Her heart began hammering. What the hell was he doing? She saw his eyes were rimmed red. Something was wrong here. Very wrong.

Christopher tilted her head slightly to better expose her neck and then bared his sharp teeth.

Nell screamed into his face and tried to wrench herself away, but his grip was like iron. Her head was locked in place. Was it all really going to end like this? She broke out in a cold sweat.

Christopher drew closer to her.

Nell kept struggling and screaming, beating at this body with her fists, but it was futile. Devan began sprinting towards them, transforming as he ran.

Loris slammed into Fabian, knocking the Magister to the floor. His robe fell away, revealing a bony, misshapen body covered in a cloth undergarment.

Christopher froze. His eyes returned to their usual color. He blinked as though waking from a trance and looked quizzically at Nell, then at Kavisha, Loris and the Magister.

Devan came to a halt by his side, in full werwulf form.

"Wh...what's happening?" Christopher asked, confused and bewildered.

"You were going to kill her!" said Amara.

She was visibly shaking.

"You were going to try, at least," said Devan, in his husky lycan voice.

"No. I wasn't. I wouldn't..."

But Christopher didn't look convinced. He looked horrified, in fact. He held up his hands and just stared at them, as if they were alien to him.

"It wasn't you, young man," said Loris, still pinning Fabian to the floor. "It was our distinguished friend here."

"I…I…don't understand…" Christopher stuttered. "Nell…"

His eyes pleaded with her.

She moved closer to hold him.

Instead of reciprocating, he backed away, unsure of himself. He didn't trust his own body.

"You're safe, Christopher," assured Loris. "Now that this one isn't inside your head. You are no longer a danger to her."

Christopher tentatively stepped into Nell's waiting arms.

"I'm sorry," he whispered into her hair. "I'm so sorry. I don't know what happened."

"Our esteemed Magister here tried to kill Nell, using Christopher's body, of course," explained Loris. "He couldn't do it himself or the prophecy wouldn't be fulfilled. You see, what Magisters often tend to miss out from their pious descriptions of themselves is that they have special little abilities. Controlling the minds of other vampires is one of them."

Loris gave the Magister a quick nudge in the ribs with his knee.

"Ooof," complained Fabian, riled and humiliated.

"But he can't control you?" Amara asked.

"I'm far too long in the tooth for his parlor tricks," said Loris. "You learn to block that nonsense out. But Christopher here doesn't have the experience."

Loris turned his attention back to the Magister, who was trying in vain to squirm free.

"I'll let you go if you swear a blood oath not to do that again," he admonished. "Just because you are a Magister, it doesn't mean you can act with impunity."

"Fools," Fabian spat, his voice labored. "If you'd just had the backbone to do it, I wouldn't have to intervene."

He shot a belligerent glance at Christopher, who returned an equally hostile look.

"Now is not the time to act, Fabian," said Kavisha. "Is there something about that you cannot understand?"

She pushed the joystick on her wheelchair and moved it closer to Loris and the struggling Fabian.

"We are not ready to declare war."

The High Chancellor spoke as if she were reprimanding an unruly child. She twisted her body in her chair to face the other Magisters. None of them moved or spoke.

"You are making a grave mistake," said Fabian. "The deed must be done."

"It won't come to that," Christopher reassured Nell. "There *has* to be another way."

Nell smiled sadly. She loved Christopher for trying to find a get-out clause. But she suspected there wasn't one. Her own fate was sealed. What upset Nell more than anything else was that the people she had come to love, Christopher, Devan and Amara, were now in the firing line. Poor Amara was an innocent soul. Nell cursed the day she had asked for the librarian's help to find the book of prophecy.

Kavisha pushed on the joystick again and swiveled her chair around to face Nell and her friends.

"You are all to remain here, within the boundary lines of Vhik'h-Tal-Eskemon," she instructed. "The Red Claws cannot penetrate the Old Magick without the most horrific consequences. They won't attempt it. Remain within the grounds and you are safe."

"How long do we need to stay here? I have a job!" Amara protested.

"Indefinitely," Loris responded, not without sympathy.

Amara looked defeated.

"Let me show you our library downstairs," Kavisha said, by way of apology. "You could be most useful in helping us with our store of knowledge."

"Ooh, a library!" said Amara, perhaps a little acerbically.

But then she smiled at the benevolent gesture from the High Chancellor, seemingly resigned to her situation.

While vampires weren't (usually) able to develop romantic feelings, it was evident that they could be friendly and even compassionate, from what Nell had seen so far. What a strange curse, she thought, that they lived such long lives but without the intimacy of a loving partner. To Nell, it seemed like life would be a bleak affair if you couldn't find love.

Loris hefted Fabian to his feet and then, rather charitably, picked up the Magister's robe from the floor and handed it to him.

Fabian grabbed at it contemptuously, before swiftly putting it on, covering his gnarled body.

Loris escorted him out of the room. On his way, the newly appointed Elder looked intently between Nell and Christopher.

Nell thought she could detect a hint of sadness in Loris's face. The way his brow furrowed and he bit his lip slightly. Nell wondered if vampires wished they could love too.

Chapter 27

The Red Claws arrived the next evening, as the blazing sun began to sink into the ochre sky. They were visible from Nell and Christopher's bedroom window.

Statuesque. Unmoving.

They lined the hilly range just outside the headquarters. They were spaced evenly, as though placed there by a giant hand in the sky. They reminded Nell of chess pieces, silhouetted against the dusky twilight.

Devan and Amara joined Nell and Christopher to stare out of their window. This vantage point provided the clearest view from Vhik'h-Tal-Eskemon. Standing there looking out, knowing that they were being watched by vampires intent on killing them, life felt stranger and more precarious than ever before.

Nell mentally tallied up her options.

Option 1: Stay hidden and do nothing. Wait to be killed by the only boy she's ever loved.
Option 2: Flee the house. Probably get murdered instantly.
Option 3: Kill herself and be done with it all. Thus likely also dooming the entire human race by preventing the prophecy from coming to fruition.

Option 4: Kill Christopher. It was thanks to him that they were all here. His stupid feelings had landed them in this mess.

Nell knew the last one was unfair, but the paucity of her options made her a little snarky. She smiled at Christopher, mentally apologizing for her cynicism.

"Option 5," whispered Christopher. "Stay put for now while we figure out how to kill the Red Claws and save you."

Bastard!

He was tracking her thoughts. Option 4 suddenly seemed more enticing.

Christopher squeezed her hand.

"Sorry, this is the first time I've done that, promise," he said. "I was just worried about how you were doing with..." He looked out of the window. "...the new development."

"It's not me that I'm worried about." Nell spoke softly, stroking Christopher's hand. She instinctively looked at Amara and Devan.

"Don't worry about me," said Devan. "The Drak-pack doesn't scare me one bit, and I'm sure Amara could bore them to death with her wide-ranging knowledge of etymology."

Amara chuckled, despite herself.

"Acquiescence," said the librarian. "Derived from the French *acquiescer*. Meaning 'the reluctant acceptance of something'. Seems like a fitting word right now."

Nell smiled wanly then turned her attention back to Christopher.

"Have no concern for me," he advised. "It would break me to kill you. I know that's what worries you. If I was ever forced to do that, I wouldn't want to live anyway."

His face was serene, as though killing himself was supposed

to make Nell feel better.

"You will do no such thing!" she reprimanded.

It was bad enough that her life would be cut short. She wasn't going to let Christopher be taken out of the equation, too. The prophecy didn't mention what happened to him if and when the army of darkness was defeated. Nell retained the hope that he would have an extraordinarily long and meaningful life, perhaps even love again, eventually. Though it pained her to think about it.

"Oh, believe me, I would," said Christopher, dramatically running a finger across his neck. "I've only just learnt what it means to love and if, by a cruel twist of fate, I have to kill you to save humanity, I couldn't live with myself no matter what good it did in the world. I am not going to go on without you."

Devan mimicked being sick in the background. Amara nudged him in the ribs.

In an attempt to lighten the mood, Devan proceeded to play charades with the watching Red Claws. They would be able to see him silhouetted through the glass. Devan made sure his answers were as insulting and downright filthy as possible to act out. His film choices included *Willy the Whale, Hard Impact* and *Snatch*. His friends, including Christopher, broke down in fits of laughter. The Red Claws observed impassively.

Nell laughed so much that she developed a cramp in her side. But it was worth it. In this perilous world she'd been thrown into, she was grateful for any moments of lightness.

Chapter 28

The next few days dragged by, as if time itself were mired in quicksand. The Red Claws didn't move. Or if they did it was so quick that nobody noticed. By Nell's own calculation, they must have needed to feed at least once in that period. Christopher did. He snuck off to the basement, where a large communal blood supply was kept in case of emergencies. Nell didn't ask about the details. It was one image she'd rather keep out of her mind.

What did concern her, however, was how long the blood supply would last. The Elders, High Chancellor and Christopher were the only vampires currently in residence at Vhik'h-Tal-Eskemon, but at some point the stores would run dry.

For the humans and Devan, food wasn't an issue, ironically. There was a large garden in the center of the property with plenty of vegetables and even some livestock. According to Kavisha, these headquarters were normally a hive of activity, with wardens, Council members, emissaries, functionaries and staff bustling about in the halls. Now it was virtually abandoned. Its sole function seemed to be keeping Nell alive, until such a time when that was no longer the optimal strategy.

Kavisha bemoaned how hard it was to muster an army of the night when nobody could come or go. Face-to-face diplomacy was out of the question with the Red Claws stationed just outside. But Vhik'h-Tal-Eskemon had a satellite line installed, which allowed for phone and internet access. The only issue was that supernatural beings weren't really hot on contact with the outside world. There were no hotlines for the fae, lamia, changelings, warlocks, daayans, werwulfs or spell-casters, to name but a few. The fact that these preternatural creatures couldn't respond was what was keeping Nell alive for the time being, so she couldn't really complain. Her demise was meant to come after the army was assembled.

Amara used the satellite phone to call her mother and sister in St. Louis. She told them she was embarking on a hiking expedition and would be out of touch for a while. When they asked the obvious questions, such as when did a chronic bookworm suddenly discover a love for the great outdoors, Amara had to claim the line was breaking up before (guiltily) hanging up.

Devan had no such family to call on. Nell felt a little sorry for him. A part of her wondered if that was why he had thrown himself so whole-heartedly into this risky escapade. Perhaps Amara, Christopher and her had become the family he didn't have.

Chapter 29

One evening, after Amara had gone to the library and Christopher had slipped away to feed, Devan found himself alone with Nell. Despite Nell effectively having turned him down, there was still some tension between them whenever they were alone. It was absent when they were in a group, but the second they were alone, that frisson of edginess would reappear. Nell often excused herself at this stage. But on this particular evening she stayed.

They sat in the only room of the sprawling complex with a television. 'The Den' as they had come to refer to it. There was a plush oversized couch with far too many cushions and no other furniture, meaning that Nell and Devan had to sit relatively close to each other.

After a few minutes of flicking through the limited channels available, Nell turned to Devan to ask what he'd like to watch. He had been studying her face all this time so she was a little taken aback when she noticed his intense gaze. Devan wondered whether she could detect the melancholy in his eyes, or in his soul.

"Nell," Devan said. His voice was unusually subdued. "Have you ever wondered if the prophecy isn't about you?"

"What do you mean? Who else could it be about?" she

replied.

"Maybe you're not the one. Not his true love, that is."

Devan gently placed a hand on top of Nell's.

She didn't move it.

"I am," she said, sounding sympathetic.

"I don't think you are," he replied, a touch too firmly.

She raised her eyebrows.

"How could you be?" he said. "When I have feelings for you, too. Strong feelings."

"Devan…I…."

"Nell, I love you," he blurted out, putting everything on the line. "I mean it. I'd do anything for you. I'm so into you that it rips me apart every day to see you with…him. From what I sense when we're around each other, I think you feel the same about me, deep down, if you're really true to your feelings."

Before Nell could react, Devan leaned forward and pressed his lips to hers. Delicately at first, light as a feather. When Nell didn't immediately pull away, Devan leaned in. Her lips were warm and inviting. Nell was responding, pulling Devan towards her.

He gently laid her down on the couch and kissed her passionately, their tongues dancing together. Nell reached for his T-shirt and scooped it over his head, revealing his muscled body. She quickly reached down and unbuckled his belt before swiftly relieving herself of her own clothes.

"Oh Devan, you're the one," Nell whispered into his ear as she pulled his head down to her. "You always have been."

Devan sprang back as though he'd been stung. It was too easy. This couldn't be right. Nell wouldn't just profess her love for him. She wouldn't sleep with him when she was with Christopher. This wasn't the woman he knew. Not by a country mile. But God, he wanted her so badly right now.

What was going on here? What was he even doing? He closed his eyes tightly, pushing his fists into his eye sockets. When he opened them the room was empty, apart from him. No Nell. Devan was alone. Naked and alone. Always alone. The constant theme of his life.

What had just happened here? Had he hallucinated? Was he going nuts? He had to know.

Devan threw on his clothes and ran to Nell and Christopher's room. He opened the door without knocking, or even thinking.

Nell was wrapped in Christopher's arms under the bed sheets. Their bodies intertwined.

"What the fuck, man!" Christopher yelled, turning to ensure that Nell's modesty was preserved.

He patted down the sheet then turned back to face Devan.

"What the fuck's wrong with you? Have you heard of the concept of knocking, or were you after a free show, again? Is that how you get your kicks?"

"Nell..." Devan breathed. "It wasn't you. It wasn't you."

Devan fell to his knees in the doorway just outside the room and placed his hands over his eyes, taking in big gulps of air.

Nell put on her clothes then hurried across the room.

Christopher rolled his eyes.

"What's wrong?" she asked.

Nell placed her hands on Devan's shoulders.

"You were there. It was you. I was sure it was you." Devan said.

Before Nell could delve further, another figure arrived and stood over Devan.

"I think I can be of help here," said Loris, looking somber.

“There’s been a development, which might go some way to explain this. You need to come with me.”

Chapter 30

Nell reached down and helped Devan to his feet and the two of them took off after Loris. She looked back to see Christopher, now dressed, pacing after them. She registered a brief look of annoyance on his face. Was it a pang of jealousy? Perhaps that was one emotion he wasn't so thrilled to have back. Not only had the Devan walked in on them, but Nell had run to him like he was a broken bird, leaving Christopher trailing behind. But there was no time for those considerations now.

After arriving in the cavernous basement library, the four of them were greeted by Amara, who was seated behind a large oak desk. Before her was a stack of books piled high, next to a silver laptop computer, with more opened volumes littering the desk. Kavisha sat in her wheelchair just off to the side. She was dressed in a lavish gold sari with matching bangles and tikka jewels adorning her forehead. She smiled at the newcomers, but there was a wariness in her eyes.

"Right, we're all here," began Loris, clapping his hands together. "First, I must apologize to you, Devan, for taking a peek inside your mind."

Devan looked like he wanted the ground to open up and swallow him whole.

"We sensed something was amiss," continued Loris, glancing

at the High Chancellor. She gave a brief nod. "As you know by now, it wasn't Nell you were....with."

Nell and Christopher shot glares at Devan, who suddenly found his shoes extremely fascinating.

"It seems that the Magisters, or at least one of them, are no longer on our side," said Loris. "The humiliation of being castigated appears too much for Fabian, and we know his particular party trick is to infiltrate the minds of those who are susceptible. He evidently has the power to breach our walls, which are primarily enchanted to keep physical threats out."

Loris turned to Devan.

"Fabian sensed your...affinity...for your comrade and also your somewhat volatile nature. He attempted to use this to his advantage, and that of the Red Claws. The fantasy that played out in your mind, it was intended to sow discord among you."

Nell and Christopher stared open-mouthed at Devan, who found his shoes were becoming more fascinating by the second. The stitch work, lace color and pattern of scuffs demanded his undivided attention.

"Wait, what?" Christopher choked out. "You thought you were...*with* Nell?"

"I don't think that's the important part of these developments," Kavisha interrupted.

Christopher walked over to Devan and squared-up to him.

"I'm not sure what's been germinating inside that beastly brain if yours," he reprimanded. "But you keep your hands, and claws for that matter, away from her."

"Again, as the High Chancellor indicated, that's not the critical point," said Loris as he parted the two men by pushing his body between them. "What matters is that at least one of the Magisters has defected, or the Red Claws have somehow corrupted him. This potentially puts us in great peril. It means they can control your actions from outside of Vhik'h-Tal-Eskemon. We already know Christopher is susceptible. Let's not forget what he attempted to do just days earlier."

Now it was Christopher's turn to find his shoes quite captivating.

Nell looked between Christopher and Devan. She couldn't completely focus on what Loris was saying. She was heartbroken for Devan. He must have been suffering in silence for a while now.

"We have learnt something useful, though," said Kavisha. "And it's thanks to Amara who, I am ashamed to admit, I sent to the library merely as a distraction for her. But she's proven herself a very talented scholar, putting the Magisters to shame, I have no doubt."

Kavisha placed a hand on Amara's shoulder.

"Dweeb," said Devan, under his breath.

Amara cleared her throat.

"I was looking through some old texts on the history of this building," she said. "I came across a passage that I think is relevant."

Amara picked up the book directly in front of her and began reading in a clear voice. A librarian's voice, thought Nell.

"Vhik'h-Tal-Eskemon was built by Italian architect and vampire Domizio Bottecheli in 1673 as a safe haven for the undead. All vampires invited past its threshold would be given refuge and protected within its hallowed walls. Bottecheli sought the assistance of renowned Levantine spell-caster Alcazar Cher Wahid to imbue the protective enchantments.

What Bottecheli did not know, however, was that Wahid's spell-casting also ensured sanctuary for all preternatural beings who should be in need of refuge. Wahid's move was supported by the Magisters of the day, who saw the wisdom in finding common cause with fellow supernatural entities.

Bottecheli, being a blood purist, was outraged on discovering Wahid's inclusion of 'lesser' races. The spell-caster was banished, while the Magisters were reprimanded by the Council of Elders for their perceived heresy.

Before leaving, Wahid set a final enchantment. It was stipulated that if all of the Magisters were united, they could combine to override the defenses of Vhik'h-Tal-Eskemon and thus gain access to the sanctuary."

Everyone in the room continued to stare at Amara expectantly, waiting for more.

"That's it," Amara said, caving under the pressure of the pregnant gazes. "It doesn't say how they will gain entry, only it's possible. The original spell-caster, Alcazar Cher Wahid, was no doubt acting from noble intentions in providing for a counter-power to the authoritarian Council of Elders, but he's royally screwed us in the here and now."

Amara looked apologetically at Kavisha.

"You've done really well, Amara," Kavisha assured her. "I knew about Bottecheli but I wasn't aware of Wahid's involvement. Any information is useful and now we know that the Red Claws are potentially closing in on us, via the Magisters. It allows us to act before they get a step ahead of us."

"It sounds like they're already a step ahead of us," Devan said.

"That's why drastic action is called for," said a new voice.

Zulima Vargas, the tall, slender Elder with long flowing black hair, emerged from the shadows. Nell hadn't even realized she was there.

"What did you have in mind?" asked Nell.

"We've been trying to find recruits from within the supernatural world, without much success," said Zulima. "But remember the prophecy stated that '*Unlikely allegiances will be forged*'. Well, Amara here suggested forging the unlikeliest alliance of all."

The room was silent.

"The *nocturnae hostium*," said Amara, finally.

"Enemies of the Night?" said Christopher, looking completely dumbfounded. "You mean Vampire Hunters, our mortal enemies? The group whose sole purpose is to ensure our complete and utter annihilation?"

"Yeah, that's the one," said Amara, chirpily. "They were right under our noses the whole time. Think about it. They're experts in hunting down vampires and also they make use of the latest technology. So reaching out to them won't be as problematic."

"Erm, what about the fact that they want to wipe us all out," said Christopher. "Might that be a small fly in the ointment?"

"There is that," Amara conceded. "But we need to convince them of the greater threat to humanity posed by the Red Claws. The enemy of my enemy is my friend, and all that. If we show them the urgency of the situation, they might, just might, help us."

"The Hunters track down and decimate sleeping covens," said Christopher. "They haven't fought an enemy like the Red Claws before."

"They might be able to buy us a little time, perhaps disperse the brood that has trapped us here in Vhik'h-Tal-Eskemon," said Zulima. "That would give us a chance to recruit more powerful forces to our side."

"I'm going to reach out to the Hunters," said Amara. "It seems we don't have much to lose at this point. Kavisha and the Elders are going to see what they can do about upping the protection on these headquarters, and stopping the Magisters from getting inside our heads."

Nell was impressed by how Amara was stepping up to the plate. The librarian looked motivated and capable behind the large oak desk. It was gratifying to see that she wasn't letting the situation break her down. Instead, it seemed to be building her up. Nell wished she could say the same about herself.

"We might be able to lessen the telepathic infiltration, but I cannot guarantee anything," said Kavisha, looking on edge. "So you need to be aware of yourselves at all times. If something feels off to you or strange, then you could be being manipulated. Devan might have more of an insight based on his experience today."

Everyone turned to Devan.

"It feels pretty real, that's all I can say," he said, turning a shade of red that Nell had never seen on a person before.

"So the plan, for now, is to carry on as normal, trying to keep your minds clear from any outside influence," said the High Chancellor, bringing her wheelchair forward. "If you start seeing strange things, find another person and ask them if what you are experiencing is real. If you suspect your thoughts or emotions are being manipulated, take yourself away from others. Isolate yourself. This isn't a game. The Magisters could easily make you hurt somebody you care for. They want us to turn on each other."

Loris turned to Christopher and Nell.

"I'm sorry, but you two cannot be alone at night," he said. "You are both too important to the cause and also susceptible to psychic manipulation."

Christopher opened his mouth to speak, but seemed to have nothing to say. It appeared he had no good argument.

The thought of being without Christopher when she needed him the most hurt Nell deeply. However, she also knew that neither of them would forgive themselves if they hurt the other one, or anyone else.

"It's for the best," Christopher said to Nell, placing his hands on her shoulders. He looked weak in the moment. "I couldn't stand it if I hurt you."

"I know," conceded Nell.

She gently kissed him on the cheek.

Chapter 31

The words were crystal clear in Nell's mind.

Come to us. If you do not, we will kill your friends and everyone inside. There is no escape. Surrender and you will live. They will live.
Come to us. We will break the prophecy. We will rewrite the future. Humans need not fear us.
Come to us. If you do not, Christopher will be killed. Devan will be killed. Amara will be killed.
Come to us. Or we take what we want. Come to us.

The words were dripping with menace. Her eyes flew open on the bed. Now the words were dripping in red, etched on the wall in front of her, illuminated by the moonlight coming in from the window.

COME TO US

She thought she had dreamt the voice. But the words were right there, as clear as day. She was bathed in a cold sweat, trying to process her thoughts. Her heart raced.

Nell felt it was a matter of when, not if, there would be a

massacre inside these walls. Christopher wouldn't have time to drain her. There was no army of the night. They were all as good as dead. It would mean the end of everything.

But if she did what the voice instructed, what would that mean?

She wanted to save her friends. To save the one she loved.

The Red Claws had promised to keep them alive. They wanted to break the prophecy, or so they said. '*Humans need not fear us*' were the words she had heard.

Could they be trusted? Of course not.

But could Nell buy her friends and the Council some time? Perhaps. Christopher needed to be alive to play his part.

Nell lay deliberating. Nothing was clear. Her thoughts churned.

She suddenly got out of bed and pulled on her clothes.

One thing stood out. If the Red Claws entered the building now, it was all over. Her thoughts were still in turmoil as she picked up a pen and notepad from the dresser and began writing:

My Dearest Christopher,

I'm sorry. I love you more than words can say. Please don't try to come after me. Concentrate on recruiting the army. We can still end this, together. I have to do this, to keep you alive, to keep you all alive. I will be waiting for you. I promise. Don't give up on me. I will never give up on you.

All my love,
Nell x

She placed the paper on top of her pillow, then quietly walked out of her room and down the stairs. She didn't come across a single soul. All was still and silent. She thought about Christopher, alone in his room. She missed him already. But this was the right thing to do. It would buy much-needed time. It would provide a fighting chance.

Nell walked out of the front door into the moonlight, and then along the path. At the end she was met by two figures. One had sharp green eyes and a shock of red hair. The other was taller, more stately in his baring, with jet-black hair and cold dark eyes.

"Good evening, Nell, my name is Zachariah," said the taller one. "Rest assured, you've made a wise choice."

She was led away from the headquarters. Away from Christopher. Away from everything she knew.

She hoped to God she was doing the right thing.

Chapter 32

"Nooooooo!"

Christopher's long scream broke the silence of early morning.

It had been their first night apart in a while and he'd longed to be close to Nell.

Devan came racing into the room.

"Maybe she's in the bathroom," Devan shrugged, thinking Christopher might be over-reacting.

Christopher thrust the paper at Devan. He read it, and his hands began shaking. He looked up, then noticed the words on the wall.

"Oh fuck!"

He ran for the door. Devan leaned over the banister of the stairs and shouted down.

"Kavisha, Loris, get in here, NOW!"

His voice echoed into the void of the cavernous building.

A few minutes later the High Chancellor and the Elder were there, Kavisha having taken the elevator.

Devan passed the note to Loris, who knelt down and held it between himself and Kavisha.

"No," Kavisha said, quietly. "In the name of the Omni-Father, what has she done?"

"She's gone…she's gone…" Christopher was repeating, over and over.

Amara appeared at the door, blood-soaked. Her white nightclothes were stained red.

Everything was happening too fast.

"I don't know what happened to me…" she said, in a daze.

She held up her right hand. It was covered in blood. The tip of her index finger was missing.

Devan sensed it immediately. The change in Christopher, Loris and even Kavisha. There was a sudden alertness, a fixation, a hunger. The sight (and no-doubt scent) of Amara's blood had instinctively awakened something elementary within them. All that liquid nourishment must have proved almost irresistible to a vampire. Yet they didn't act. They maintained control.

Amara looked around the room, frantically. Her eyes fell on the dripping red letters on the wall.

"I…I did that?" she questioned, eyes wide with shock.

"It would appear so," said Loris.

He retrieved a handkerchief from his pocket and wrapped it around Amara's finger, applying gentle pressure. He had to look away from the blood, for the opposite reason to most humans.

Kavisha went to Amara in her wheelchair. She held her other hand.

"This is not your fault," she said, looking up. "There was nothing you could do. We evidently didn't do enough to block the psychic attacks."

"It seems the Red Claws have won this round," said Loris.

"This isn't a fucking game!" Devan yelled, trying to hold back his transformation. He was unsuccessful. His rush of emotions and primal instincts won out, despite the fact that a werwulf wasn't of much use right now.

"They took her," Christopher said.

He punched the wall, a huge chunk of which came away.

"Destroying our headquarters perhaps isn't the optimal strategy at this time," said Loris. "It's time to evaluate. We need a plan accord..."

"Fuck your plans!" shouted Christopher. "Where have they got us so far? I'm going to get her back."

He made to leave the room.

"That is stupid and reckless," said Kavisha. "You read the letter. Nell had some wits about her. You walking into the hands of the Red Claws is the worst thing that can happen right now. Think about the bigger picture, Christopher."

Devan grabbed Christopher's arm to stop him from going any further.

"I'll go find her," he said in his sonorous lycan voice. "I can track her better. I'll bring her back to you, man, and find help. Even if I have to go to the ends of the Earth."

Devan was gone before anybody could argue with him, leaving Christopher standing there, distraught.

Epilogue

Amara was hunched over the laptop in the basement library. Her right hand was bandaged up, so she was typing just with her left. It took some getting used to, but Nell's absence was weighing heavily on her. She needed to take action. While she couldn't transform into a wolf or leap tall walls, she could use the abilities she did have. So she was frantically researching, learning and communicating, trying to find some help.

She sent out more emails to the Vampire Hunters and, with Kavisha's help, even unearthed potential contacts among the fae, lamia, changelings and daayans. But her pleas for help went unanswered. Her inbox remained pristine in its emptiness.

The High Chancellor joined her at the large desk. Amara nodded to her, dispiritedly.

The librarian glanced down and noticed the book she read from yesterday, still open at the same page. But something looked slightly different about the pattern of text. She began reading.

"No. No. That can't be right."

Amara shook her head in confusion.

Kavisha looked up at her.

The passage Amara read yesterday, about the Magisters

being able to infiltrate Vhik'h-Tal-Eskemon, was no longer there. Instead, the text simply described the materials used to build the headquarters. The particular types of granite and where the timber and slate originated from. There was no mention of the spell-caster Alcazar Cher Wahid or any special enchantments placed on the building.

Amara placed her head in her hands.

"I was manipulated," she said, on the verge of tears. "It's my fault. It's all my fault. The passage about Vhik'h-Tal-Eskemon being vulnerable was never there."

Kavisha looked shocked.

"You are not to blame," said the High Chancellor, finally. "I never thought to check the book for myself. I even said yesterday that I knew that Bottecheli had built Vhik'h-Tal-Eskemon, but I was unaware of Wahid. That should have rung an alarm bell."

Amara's tears were flowing now.

"Nell," she said, in a broken voice. "She fled because she thought the Magisters could allow the Red Claws to storm the headquarters. She thought that we were all in danger. But it was a trick."

"At least we know now that the headquarters are safe from physically being breached," said Kavisha. "But they have Nell." She thumped a fist on the desk. "They played us expertly. Always one step ahead. We need to get back into the lead."

Thinking back on what she thought she read yesterday, something struck a chord in Amara's mind. She opened a fresh Notepad document on the computer and typed briefly. She then stared at the text for a long moment, her eyes growing wider.

"It seems they added insult to injury," she said, sounding

thoroughly defeated.

Kavisha was quiet.

"Alcazar Cher Wahid," said Amara, looking up at the High Chancellor. "The one who supposedly made it possible to breach our defenses. It's an anagram of Zachariah Redclaw."

Just then the computer made a loud 'ding' noise, making them both jump. It was the unmistakable sound of an email landing in the inbox.

***

Dear Reader,

Thank you so much for choosing to read my first book. I'd like to make a humble plea if I may.

As a part-time indie writer with a full-time job, I would be truly grateful if you could leave me a review on Amazon, as I have no other way of raising awareness. Even just one simple sentence would be perfect. Thank you so much in advance.

Join my readers' club!

Join my readers' club to receive special offers, previews of upcoming releases and other great stuff just for members. It's totally free.

Scan the QR to join:

Lastly, if you would like to contact me for any reason (such as to point out a mistake!) or simply to say hi, that would be great. My email address is:

anyakelner@gmail.com

The story continues

Book 2 is filled with shocks, surprises and thrilling action.

The prophesy appears to be playing out.

Strange creatures of the night come together to take on a barbarous common foe.

But trust and tolerance are hard to come by in this new world.

Christopher is bereft and broken, with a savage anger coursing through his veins.

A fierce battle rages but a stunning revelation turns everything on its head.

The thrilling second book from Anya Kelner raises the stakes, action and suspense.

Scan the QR code on the next page to read now!

Printed in Great Britain
by Amazon

56032992R00165